Redemption

LEGENDS OF LAIRHEIM

A NOVEL

Also By Tora Moon

Legends of Lairheim (Science-Fantasy)

Ancient Enemies (Book 1)
Ancient Allies (Book 2)
The Scourge Incursion (Book 3)
Exile's Vengeance (Book 4)
Redemption - A Novel

The Sentinel Witches (Urban Fantasy)

Crossroads to Destiny (Book 1)
Descent Into Darkness (Book 2)
Well of Sorrows (Book 3)

Indie Author Guides

Business & Accounting for Authors
Business Plans for Authors (forthcoming)

To get an up-to-date listing of all my books or to purchase visit
ToraMoon.com

LEGENDS OF LAIRHEIM

REDEMPTION

BONUS NOVEL

TORA MOON

Lunar Alchemy Publishing

ACKNOWLEDGMENTS

An author may sit alone at the computer, but no book is completed without help. To my beta readers, Angelique and Kathryn, my thanks for reading my story and giving me input to help me tell a better story.

Thank you to all the authors I've had the pleasure of reading their stories and making me want to tell my own. Without story, this world would be a much poorer place.

And especially to my daughter, Sasha, you have made me become a better person by being your parent. I couldn't have asked for a more amazing daughter.

Thank you to all my readers. Thank you for spending time with my stories and letting me be a part of your life. I hope you love them as much I loved writing them.

EXTRAS

The world of Lairheim isn't a re-imagining of Earth. It has its own culture, language, and landmasses. I've created several extras and resources to help you enjoy this fantasy world more. You can find these on my website at: ***ToraMoon.com/Legends-Extras***.

Extras you may like:

Pronunciation audio - While the appendix includes a cast and glossary, fantasy names and words can be difficult to figure out how to say. I've recorded audios for each name and Posair word.

Maps - There is a map at the beginning of the book to help you orient into the world of Lairheim. A black and white pdf map is available to download for free. Or if you love maps, I've created a beautiful, hand-drawn, color map you can purchase.

Merchandise - I've created some fun merchandise centered around the books and the world of Lairheim. Check them out in my shop!

MAP OF LAIRHEIM

Chapter 1

Activity filled the stable and courtyard as the platoon of fighters readied their horses. The early morning sunlight caught the temple's crystal dome, sending rainbow light across the plaza. Histrun led his big, black stallion, Telen, through the organized chaos.

A dark-blue roan mare, already saddled, stood dozing with her rear leg cocked at the hitching post in front of the keep-house. She had blue-gray stripes and a white mane, tail, and socks. Kylara opened her eyes when Histrun tied Telen next to her and nosed him.

Histrun scanned the courtyard, searching for Kylara's rider and his bond-mate, Zehala.

He climbed the steps to the keep-house. Naila, Zehala's eldest daughter, burst out the door, flinging her bright-red hair streaked with gold over her shoulder.

He stepped back quickly, moving out of her way. "Do you know where Zehala is? It's nearly time to leave."

Naila laughed. "Of course I do. Where else would she be? She's in the crèche. I'm heading there now." She skipped down the stairs. "Are you coming?"

Histrun envied her youth and energy. He sighed as he ran a hand through his red hair, the once bright color dulled with age. He still kept active and fought the Malvers' monsters with the younger fighters.

After their retirement as the Strunlair Clan Alphas, he and Zehala discovered a new method to fight the monsters. They, along with their team, spent the last few years traveling the length and breadth of Lairheim, teaching the new fighting method to the other clans. He rubbed his knee. The constant traveling was wearing him down. The team only had one more clan to teach.

Histrun trudged across the plaza, following in Naila's wake toward the center of the keep. He wasn't in a rush to leave for this last training mission.

Until recently, the Dehanlair clan alpha, Mendehan, had adamantly refused to learn the method, mostly because he and Histrun were bitter rivals—and he was a stubborn old fool. He'd finally relented due to the pressure from his people, but he'd insisted he'd only learn the new life-saving method from its creators, Histrun and Zehala. Histrun distrusted the request. His past dealings with Mendehan hadn't ended well, and it made him uneasy.

Shaking off the apprehension, Histrun hurried to catch up to Naila. They soon left the courtyard's bustle and noise behind and entered the quieter sections of the keep. In the well-protected center, amid a sea of grass, stood a large stone house, surrounded by a sheadash stone fence. Toys and playground equipment littered the yard. Their feet crunched on the crushed sheadash stone walkway. The ten-foot wide path and the fence ensured if any Malvers' monsters made it this far into the keep, the Posairs' children would be safe.

The constant threat of attack, and the fighter's need to always be ready to battle the monsters, meant caregivers raised their children, who lived together in the crèche. Histrun believed the tradition was a good practice to keep the fighters from being distracted by little ones. He grew up in a crèche and had never suffered a lack of attention or love. He didn't understand Zehala and Naila's need to stay in contact with their daughters after they turned them over to the nursery caregivers. Other women he knew hadn't done so—certainly not his last lover, Sujeen. As soon as she'd weaned the twins, she'd placed them in the crèche and returned to her training to become the next clan alpha of Strunlair. He'd rarely interacted with them afterwards, especially when he and Sujeen parted ways.

He and Naila quietly entered the house. A woman with dark-auburn hair sat in a chair, holding two little girls the same age on her lap, singing softly. One had red-brown hair, and the other had creamy-white hair with thin streaks of gray. The white-haired girl looked up, and her joyful smile lit her pale blue eyes.

"Mama!" she cried, wiggling off Zehala's lap and running to Naila.

Naila picked her up. "My, you're getting big, Wisah."

"I'm almost five," Wisah said solemnly. "Did you come to tell us a story?"

Naila shook her head. "No, I came to say goodbye. We have to go to Dehanlair Province and teach their fighters how to fight the Malvers' monsters better."

"So more people don't die." Wisah tucked her head into Naila's shoulder. "I don't like seeing them cross the veil. They are so sad until they see the Goddess."

Histrun's eyes widened. He hadn't realized Wisah's powers were opening already, or that they were so strong. She'd need to be sent to the Sanctuary soon to train her White and Gray Talents and become a White Priestess. A person's Talents determined the work they did to support the whole community. His gaze turned back to the auburn-haired girl, watching them with her big, brown eyes. Rizelya would follow in her mother's— and his—footsteps and be a warrior, fighting the Malvers' monsters for everyone's survival. He hoped she'd also become a clan leader like her parents.

Rizelya climbed off Zehala's lap and slowly approached Histrun. "Bright blessings, sir."

He crouched, so he didn't loom over the little girl. "Bright blessings, Rizelya. Have you learned anything new?"

She nodded, stared at her hand, her eyes crinkled in concentration. When she opened her hand, a tiny flame appeared on her palm for a few moments before fading away.

Histrun patted her on the back. "That's very good. Soon you'll be able to make it dance." He'd been worried she had too much Brown Talent to be a strong Red. They needed Reds to fight the monsters, not more Browns to till the earth or tend the flocks. "Practice hard and eat your food so you can grow up to be a strong fighter like your mother."

"Yes, sir." She continued to stand in front of him, hope gleaming in her eyes.

He relented and gave her an awkward hug. He gazed over her shoulder at Zehala. She beamed at him. If it made his bond-mate happy to show affection to the waif, he would. "It's time to go."

Zehala nodded and joined them. She picked up Rizelya and squeezed her. "Mama has to go teach people how to fight the monsters. I'll be gone a long time, a lunadar. When the largest moon, Kelar, grows big and fat, I will be back. When I return, I'll teach you more fire magic tricks. I love you, Rizelya baby."

"I don't want you to go," Rizelya cried, clinging tighter to Zehala's neck. "Take me with you. I'll be good."

"You know I can't. It's too dangerous. You stay here and watch over your niece, Wisah. She needs you to be strong. Can you do that for me?"

Rizelya nodded, tears streaming down her face. "Love you, Mama."

Both children cried and clung onto their mother's necks. Zehala and Naila's cheeks were also wet. Histrun cringed at all the emotion and itched to rush from the room. Give him a good, fierce battle any day over weepy women and children. Finally, caregivers came into the room and took the little girls away. Histrun couldn't help his huge sigh of relief. Zehala glared at him.

"Let's go," she said as she strode out of the room.

Histrun and Naila hurried to catch up with her.

"The faster we leave, the faster we can return. Histrun, this is the last time I'm leaving my baby. When we get back, I'm not going again."

"Do you really think you can be a simple fighter?"

Zehala laughed. "No. You know me too well. Next year at the Alpha Competitions, I plan to challenge Koriana for the Strunland Keep Alpha position. That way, I'll have to stay here. We've trained enough people that we shouldn't have to continue doing it."

Histrun grinned. "Good! I need to be more than a platoon alpha." If it hadn't been for all the training trips, he would have gone crazy. He'd been a keep or clan alpha for too many years to be happy with leading a small platoon. He thought he could when he retired with Zehala. But he needed more.

The earlier chaos had settled by the time they reached the courtyard. As soon as their fighting-pack saw them, they stopped chatting and mounted their horses. Several grabbed the lead-lines of the multas, heavily laden with the group's supplies.

Alpha Koriana leaned her hands on the porch railing. She'd pulled her vermilion hair into a tight bun. Kolstrun, her co-alpha, stood at the edge of the steps, his arms crossed over his chest and his green eyes narrowed in a scowl. He wore his russet-brown hair cut close. At barely fifty, both leaders were young for keep alphas. Histrun decided he'd challenge the unpleasant man when Zehala challenged Koriana. Strunland would prosper better under his and Zehala's leadership than it was doing under the current alphas.

"You're finally here," Kolstrun sneered. "You need to get your pack out of here so the fighting-pack can leave."

Histrun glanced up at the early morning sun, then glared at Kolstrun. "There's plenty of time. The nest won't be active for another octar or more. The fighters will arrive before the monsters stir."

Koriana rolled her eyes before smiling at Histrun and Zehala. "Don't worry about him. Everything is under control. Have a safe journey, and we'll see you in a lunadar or so."

Histrun gave a sarcastic salute to the pair and turned to mount his horse. It grated on him that he must now follow his juniors, not only in years but also in experience. *Yes, it's time to take back the leadership role from these youngsters.*

As he settled into his saddle, he noted Zehala and Naila were on their horses. As Histrun lifted his fist high in the air, quiet filled the courtyard. "Let's go!" He dropped his arm and nudged Telen forward. Thirty-four battle-hardened warriors and six teenagers followed him out the gates.

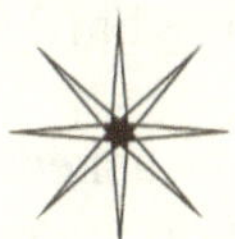

Histrun set the pace at a fast trot while they passed through the pastures and fields surrounding Strunland Keep. He scowled at the absence of a teenage Red and her counterpart wolf patrolling between the fields, ready to warn of approaching Malvers' monsters. He hated that the practice had fallen into disuse. Strunland Keep had been using the fighting method developed by him and Zehala, the Zehis method—he snorted at the name—for the last decade. Kolstrun didn't want to waste resources on an outmoded tradition. *One more reason for me to challenge Kolstrun next year.* Histrun remembered spending countless days loping beside his friend's horse as they patrolled the fields. It had taught him how to use his nose, how to shift quickly, and how to fight. He'd gained a sense of honor and duty, which the teenagers today lacked. When he became the keep alpha, he'd reinstate the practice.

Histrun picked up the pace as soon as they passed the fenced-in areas. They had a thousand measures to cross before they reached their destination, Dehanlair Province. He led his team in a walk, trot, gallop, trot, walk routine that ate up the measures while keeping the horses healthy. They didn't need a lame horse this early in their journey.

The land soon changed from cultivated fields to wild meadows. Tall pines lined the roadway, interspersed with birch and oak trees. The route avoided the known monster nest sites. But even so, beyond the crushed sheadash stone road, wide swaths of dead trees, killed by the monster's toxic slime, marked where they had passed several years ago. In those areas, new trees, only a few feet tall, reached for the sky, and grass and flowers covered the ground. Without the constant bombardment by rampaging monsters, the forest could regenerate.

As they rode, Histrun watched the horizon for any tentacles or bouncing spines that heralded a marauding janack or brecha. He pulled his attention back to the road. Since taking the fight to the nest sites, they'd eliminated the threat of roaming monsters. But old habits were hard to change, especially for an old wolf like himself.

"What's wrong?" Zehala asked, riding beside him a few octars later. "You're grumbling under your breath."

"This is so strange." Histrun shifted in his saddle. "We've already traveled thirty measures and haven't encountered any monsters. This may turn out to be a boring journey."

"I'll take boring and safe." Zehala smiled, then sighed. "I'm tired of fighting to survive. We developed the Zehis method so we could live better lives. I fervently hope it allows our people to thrive and prosper. We've fallen into a sort of stagnation from being in a never-ending war with the monsters. You've seen the ruins of our ancestors and what they had accomplished. There's much our people can't do anymore. For example, the crystal stemware we used in Strunlair Keep. We can't make it now. I want more for Rizelya than a life of fighting."

"It will take more than just one simple fighting method for that change to happen. We have to destroy the swamps where the monsters spawn, and no one has discovered how to do that."

"I know. I can hope, though." Zehala looked away.

Two more days of tedious riding made Histrun jittery. He'd never experienced so many quiet days on the road. Another few measures and they would pass out of Strunland Territory and the regularly patrolled nest sites.

They rode down the gentle slope and out of the trees, leaving the foothills behind them. On the horizon, the golden plains grass undulated like waves in the slight breeze. Out of habit, Histrun took a deep breath, sampling the scents in the air. His eyes flew open, and he let his breath go in a whoosh.

"Monsters!" he yelled.

Tension filled the air as the women reached for their helbraughts. The men reached for the magic to change into the fearsome warriors that were more than a match for the monsters. Histrun scanned the area, trying to locate where the monster stench originated. He twisted in his saddle toward the trees behind them. A flock of crows burst from cover and into the sky. A long tentacle snaked into the air, snatching a slow bird. Histrun threw his horse's reins at Zehala, and jumped from the saddle, shifting as he landed.

His bones lengthened, and his muscles bulked. Fur sprouted, covering his skin. In less than a milcron, he completed his change. He shook out the last tingles. He now stood nearly nine feet tall and weighed 150 pounds more than normal. The long claws on his hands could slash and rip through the tough monster hides. Sharp teeth filled his powerful jaws. His saliva was a deadly toxin to the monsters, and he had venom sacks under the pads of his front claws. The warrior form was built for one thing: to destroy and kill the Malvers' monsters.

A shiver of magic in the air announced the other men shifting into their warrior forms. The teenagers grabbed the horse's reins and pulled them into a tight group. If the monsters threatened the horses, the boys would shift to their warrior forms. Maheli and Andriel, the two girls, would use their helbraughts to drive any monsters toward the other fighters. He could smell the fear rolling off Maheli. At seventeen, this was her first real battle with the monsters. A moment later, he sensed Zehala's alpha magic reach out to soothe the youngsters and the horses.

Behind him, Zehala, Naila, and the other three women dismounted. Their helbraughts glowed from the fire magic they fed into them. Histrun glanced down at the ground and growled. Their method worked best in the wet swamp-lands where the fire-rings wouldn't cause a wildfire.

Ware, he said in mind-speech, *the ground is dry.*

"I noticed." Zehala caught Naila's and the other women's attention. "We do this carefully. Keep the fire controlled, and we'll be fine."

Naila's gold eyes widened and her breath came in fast pants as she gripped her helbraught tighter. Flames licked both her and Zehala's helbraught blades. Zehala stepped away, measuring twenty paces from Naila. Across from her, the other two Reds, Lorstriel and Kehali, moved into position. They tipped the blade of their helbraughts toward the ground, waiting for the Malvers' monsters to arrive.

The first brecha broke from the cover of the trees. It caught their scent and changed direction to barrel directly toward them. Behind it, three more brechas ran into the low-lying brush.

"Steady... steady," Zehala said. "Let them come. Kehali, add a bit more fire to your blade to draw out the janack."

Kehali's helbraught glowed brighter. Histrun paced, hating having to wait, but they needed all the monsters in one place to begin the battle. The janack rolled into view, its tentacles reaching forward, and slime marking its trail. Already the grass and brush behind it wilted and browned.

The first brecha reached them. Lestrun howled as he met it head on. Histrun waited for the janack to get closer.

"Now!" Zehala yelled.

A ring of fire blazed, surrounding the monsters. A brecha, disoriented, backed into, yowling as its rear haunches caught on fire. Dorstrun and Alixstrun pounced upon it, striking it with their long claws and quickly ending its misery. Histrun ran to the janack, tearing at its tentacles with his claws. Chestrun and Eidelstrun joined him in battling the janack.

A tentacle quested toward Histrun, wrapping around his ankle and jerking him off balance. He screamed, more in anger than in pain, as it dragged him toward the huge maw filled with sharp teeth. A moment later, the whoosh of a swinging helbraught blade sounded above him, and his forward momentum stopped. Zehala's blade dripped with green ichor from the severed tentacle.

"Well, are you just going to lie there, or are you going to fight?" She held out her hand to him and pulled him to his feet.

Together, they tore into the janack. Less than half an octar later, the janack toppled over, dead. Histrun surveyed the battlefield. All the other monsters had been killed. He said a prayer of gratitude when there weren't any Posairs lying on the ground. The new method allowed them to keep the monsters in one place and prevented strays from attacking from behind. It resulted in much fewer injuries and casualties.

The fire-ring dwindled and went out. The scorched ground marked where it had been, but no other fires had started because of it. He whistled in appreciation of the women's tight control. The Reds, joined by Maheli and Andriel, walked across the field, burning any monster debris to ash so the malignant magic wouldn't pollute the ground or endanger other animals.

Zehala passed him in her rounds and tossed him a canteen of water and a rag. He checked his pelt for monster ichor. The damned stuff was acidic and toxic. His fur protected him, but if any touched his human skin, he'd be in trouble. He smirked with satisfaction when he could find only a few, easily wiped off, drops. Alixstrun struggled to reach a large patch of ichor on his upper back, and Histrun hurried over to help the young man clean it off.

Once finished, Histrun shifted to his natural form and jogged to catch up to Zehala.

"I'm impressed with the control you and the other Reds showed." He slipped an arm around her shoulders and pulled her into a quick hug. Any more of a public display of affection made him uncomfortable.

"Me too. We've come a long way since those first attempts." Zehala laughed, her brown eyes crinkling with amusement. "You remember the time when instead of forming the fire-ring, I turned the practice sand into small globules of glass?"

Histrun rubbed his cheek and grimaced. "Yeah, I remember. The damned stuff rained down on me. That's where I got this." He pointed to the scar on his cheek.

Zehala kissed her fingertips, then gently pressed them to his scar. "You're still the handsome man I adore."

She turned away from him, walked to the blackened earth, and crouched to examine it. "It's still hot and could start a fire if the wind picked up. We need to experiment more. Perhaps a cold-fire at the ground level, and it growing hotter as it extends upward."

She stood and brushed the soot off her fingertips. "You know what this means, don't you? We've been worried the Haaslair aren't using the Zehis method in the plains for fear of setting the whole thing ablaze. But finding a different way to cast the fire-ring would allow them to fight the monsters better."

"You're smart. If anyone can figure it out, it will be you." Histrun brushed a quick kiss on the top of her head.

"We need to perfect the cold-fire portion first. I'll have to think about it. Hey! Kehali!"

"Yes, Alpha?" she called, trotting to them when Zehala waved her over.

"Use your cold-air trick to freeze the ground where we burned it. We need to leave if we're going to make it to the safe house before dark, and this is still too hot to be left safely."

"Sure thing." Kehali was almost more of a Yellow Talent with her dark strawberry-blond hair and yellow eyes. She had barely enough Red Talent to become a fighter. Only women with Red Talent were allowed to join the fighting-packs, as their fire magic was the only Talent effective against the Malvers' monsters.

Histrun made the rounds to check on his people and assure himself no one had been seriously injured. Ten milcrons later, they remounted, and rode the few measures to the last safe house in their territory.

Chapter 2

The next morning, Histrun directed his people to put their barding on their horses. They would be entering Haaslair Province a few measures from the safe house. The decorative reins, breast collars, and breeching proclaimed them to be from the Strunlair Clan. The rose-and-turquoise pattern, and the symbols embroidered on the saddle blankets, indicated they were from Strunland Keep. Fighting between clans happened occasionally, although the Supreme highly discouraged it. The barding helped keep any misunderstandings to a minimum.

Over the past thirty years, as the monster nests spewed out more beasts than ever, travel between Provinces had become almost non-existent. People only journeyed from one province to another to reach the Sanctuary and the biannual Alpha Competitions. The lack of travel and exchange of ideas spawned distrust and misunderstandings between the various clans. Histrun didn't remember it being the case when he was a young man. He hoped their method would help return the nests to some semblance of normal, and trade could resume.

Within measures, the landscape changed to the long, golden grass of the plains as they entered Haaslair Province. The terrain appeared flat, but in fact, it gently rolled from one hill to another. A few trees dotted the landscape. Swaths of dead grass marked where janacks had trundled across it, killing the vegetation with their slime.

Herds of wild horses roamed the grasslands. A stallion reared in the distance, and Telen answered the challenge with a loud whinny. Histrun's jerk on the reins and sharp command settled the horse, although he pranced and tugged on the bit until the wild stallion ran from view. The Haaslair clan had bred the majority of the horses Histrun's people rode, including Telen and Kylara.

A while later, a man astride a golden horse watched them pass from a hilltop. The man waved in salute, then rode off. The Haasper alphas would soon know they had visitors traveling through their territory.

At mid-morning, they stopped to rest at a cairn marking a spring. While they waited for the horses to be watered, Zehala experimented with creating a fire-ring safe for using on the plains. Blue flames licked her helbraught blade, and Histrun shivered from the cold radiating off it. She touched the tip to the ground, drawing a small circle. It instantly froze. The grass blades snapping like icicles. She knitted her brows in concentration. Suddenly, a fire raged within the circle, eating hungrily at the grass and threatening to escape.

Maheli, watering her horse at the spring, quickly pushed its nose away, scooped water out with her hands, and tossed it at the fire. It sizzled and steamed. Another scoop of water doused the flames.

"Damn! I hoped that would work." Zehala sank to knees, hunched her shoulders, and dropped her head.

"You did manage to create cold-fire." Awe tinged Naila's voice. "I haven't ever heard of anyone doing that before."

Zehala glared at the soggy, blackened ground. "Making cold-fire was the easy part. As soon as I added heat, which we need to keep the monsters in line, the spell fell apart. You saw the result. There has to be a way to do this!"

Histrun patted her shoulder. "You'll figure it out."

"Yes. Yes, I will." She surged to her feet, determination on her face as she paced. Her forehead crinkled in thought.

Later, when they stopped under the shade of a large tree, she tried again. This time, when her spell fell apart, the flame exploded and leaped high, reaching for the tree branches. People scrambled out of the way, cursing.

Kehali flung out a hand, surrounding the fire with cold air. She squeezed her hand closed. The air responded to her will, collapsing to suffocate the fire.

"Good job with your quick thinking, Kehali!" Histrun turned to glare at Zehala. "You need to be more careful. Your experiment could have set the entire plains ablaze."

"It wasn't what I intended to do," Zehala huffed, crossing her arms over her chest. "The cold and hot fires just don't mix. It's almost like trying to burn water. Argh! There has to be a way to make this work!" She tossed her hands into the air and stomped away.

Histrun watched her for a moment before turning to the other women. "She's on a quest now, and won't quit until she finds a solution. I want you to keep a watch on her, and someone who can put out the fires needs to be with her at all times."

They nodded solemnly.

"Maybe if we talk it out together, we'll find a way." Naila pushed to her feet and hurried after Zehala. Soon the other Reds joined them, forming a circle as they talked, and gesturing wildly.

Histrun smiled at the sight. It wouldn't be long before they found the key. Zehala's sharp intelligence and persistence in solving a problem had first attracted him to her. He'd fallen madly in love with her because of her passion and caring. A lust for power hadn't pushed her to be the youngest person ever to win the Clan Alpha position. Her desire to help and serve her people was always at the forefront of her actions. At seventy-seven, Histrun hadn't expected to fall in love and find a bond-mate. It had taken him quite by surprise when he realized he loved his co-alpha. Oh, he'd had multiple lovers over the years, but he hadn't ever been "in love." He continued to watch Zehala and the women a few more milcrons before he whistled and waved to call them back. They still had a dozen measures to ride before reaching the safe house for the night.

When they arrived, they discovered a Haaslair fighting-pack already there. A tall, lean man with pale green hair and amber eyes met them in the courtyard.

"Bright blessings," he said, holding up a hand in greeting. "I be Belhaas, Haasper Keep Alpha. Your barding tells me you be from Strunland Territory. Why be you traveling through my land?"

Histrun slid wearily from his saddle and gripped the other man's wrist. "I'm Histrun. This is my bond-mate, Zehala—"

"You be them!" Belhaas's eyes lit up with excitement as he pumped Histrun's arm and thumped him on the back. "I never thought I'd get to meet the famous Histrun and Zehala. It be my pleasure to meet you. You could have stopped at my keep for a proper meal and a good night's sleep instead of staying here."

"Our apologies, Belhaas, but we don't have the time. We're heading to Dehanlair Province—"

"You mean the old bastard, Mendehan, has finally given up and admitted your method be the best to fight the damned monsters?"

Histrun nodded.

"What, it be going on twelve years now since you developed it? He's always been a slow one to adopt change, if he ever does. We use your method near the keep, but it doesn't work out here on the plains."

"I'm working on the problem." Zehala dismounted and greeted Belhaas. "I'll find a way soon."

"That be good to hear, Alpha Zehala." He urged them toward the door.

Histrun absently handed his horse's reins to Maheli. Andriel took Zehala's reins from her with a nod. Belhaas led them inside and to a table at the rear of the room. As soon as they settled on the benches, someone brought them mugs of steaming taevo. Histrun sipped his, appreciating the spicy blend of the stimulating drink.

Belhaas set his mug down and crossed his arms over his chest. "We need a better way to fight the monsters and protect our horses. The horse herds be fast. They have to be to escape the monsters, but the herds can never grow to a proper size. If we could protect them better, we'd have more horses to send to the other clans."

"The plains-bred horses are the best," Histrun agreed. "They're the strongest and have amazing stamina. My Telen, as well as Zehala's mare, Kylara, are plains-bred. We see a big difference between them and the other horses. We're hoping to breed them soon."

"The foals from them would be fine animals." Belhaas wrapped his hands around his mug and leaned forward. "Be there anything I or my people can do to help you, Zehala?"

Zehala gazed at the ceiling while she thought. After a few moments, she turned back to Belhaas. "It would help if the grasses were more fire-resistant. I'd hate to cause a wildfire and destroy the plains and ruin your homes."

"Hmm... fire-resistant grass. That be a good idea, and one we hadn't considered before. We be always fighting wildfires. Good thing the grasses grow back quickly. I will talk to our Brown and Green Talents, who specialize in plant magic. They may be able to develop a strain the horses find palatable and will survive small fires." He beamed at Zehala. "Ah, dinner be ready."

Several young fighters carried bowls to their table and set them in front of the alphas. Histrun's stomach grumbled at the delicious aroma of rice and bean stew, with chunks of rabbit, wild onions, and carrots. Talk paused as crusty pan bread and fresh pots of taevo were passed around, and people dug into the food.

Histrun caught Zehala's eye and winked. He loved her innovative mind. He never would have thought of making the grass less susceptible to fire. If Rizelya had inherited her mother's inventiveness, there would be hope for the next generation of fighters.

When they left the safe house in the morning, much to Histrun's surprise, Belhaas and several of his fighters joined them. As they rode, Belhaas pointed out landmarks. Histrun mumbled a response, but to him, the endless sea of grass all appeared the same.

After the midday break, Belhaas pulled his horse to a stop at a tall cairn of rocks. "I be leaving you here. This be the boundary between Haasper and Haasneh Territories. Continue heading southeast and you'll reach the Storengher River in another forty measures. There be a small keep on the river with barges to take you downriver. Haasneh Keep be on your route. Alphas Maehaas and Armelya be good folk. They'd enjoy having you stay the night." Belhaas stuck out his hand and Histrun clasped it. "It be a pleasure to meet you two. More down-to-earth than I expected."

"Let me know if your earth Talents find something that will work on the grass," Zehala reminded him as she clasped his wrist.

"Will do. And when you develop your new fire-ring, teach it to us on your return north."

"It's a deal."

He wheeled his horse around, and galloped in the direction they'd come, his fighters in a tight formation behind him.

"I'm glad he has faith in me." Zehala urged Kylara forward. "I'm not so sure I can merge cold and hot fire."

Histrun reached across the distance and patted her knee. "I believe in you, too. You've done many amazing things."

She smiled at him and shrugged. "Are we going to stop at Haasneh Keep?"

He nodded. "The lure of a hot bath and a soft bed is too much to pass by. My old bones could use both."

He kicked his horse into a fast trot. They still had thirty more measures to cross before he could sink into a hot tub.

Late in the afternoon, a thundering noise made Histrun twist around in his saddle. A huge white stallion with wide black stripes led a herd of horses on a path directly toward them. A janack's tentacle waved as it chased after the herd. Histrun stood in his stirrups, scanning the area. Several brechas cut through the tall grass.

"Move it!" he yelled as he urged his horse into a gallop. A quick glance over his shoulder showed the monsters slowly gaining.

As the horses caught up to them, Histrun gaped at the golden centaur running alongside the herd, his silver tail streaming behind him. He held a long bow with a quiver full of arrows strapped to his back. Several other fighters came into view, their horses keeping pace with the herd.

"There!" the centaur yelled, gesturing to a tree. "Go there!"

Histrun nodded and turned his horse in the indicated direction. Before they reached the tree, the landscape dropped into a hidden ravine. Six Reds waited at the top, shooing the herd into the ravine. The horses raced down its sides and away. Histrun and his people rode into the ravine and pulled to a stop. He swung off his horse, trusting Maheli and the other teenagers to do their job of tending to the horses. He shifted and clambered up the hill.

By the time he reached the top, the battle with the monsters raged. The Haaslair fighters rode around the brechas and janack, shooting arrows to drive them into a large circle. As soon as they surrounded the monsters, the men jumped off their horses and shifted into their warrior forms. The women stayed on horseback, firing arrows at any brechas attempting to escape.

As Histrun watched, a brecha broke from the rest, and lumbered toward a woman. It arched its back and flung its spines at her. In a smooth move, the woman switched her bow for her helbraught and used it to knock away the flying spines, then formed a fire shield in front of her. Histrun blinked, dumbfounded that her horse didn't rear in fright at having fire so close to its nose.

He ran to the brecha, his powerful claws sinking into its hindquarters. It turned and snapped at him, baring its three rows of teeth at him. He leaped to the side, sucking in his belly, and felt a tug as the brecha caught a tuft of fur. Growling, he swung at the brecha's head, venom dripping from his claws. He ripped away a chunk of its flesh, and green ichor flowed from the wound. The grass hissed as the acidic ichor landed on it. With another swipe, he gouged a hole in the brecha's side. It shuddered and collapsed.

"Steady... steady," Zehala's voice intruded. "Control. Lorstriel, back off a bit."

Zehala, Naila, Lorstriel, and Kehali meticulously formed a fire-ring around the fighting. The fire flared as another brecha's spines flew toward them. The spines sizzled as they hit the barrier, flaring briefly before burning to ash. Histrun's eyes widened. The fire-ring floated a few inches above the ground. *I didn't think that was possible!* He sensed movement and the janack's tentacle whacked him, sending him flying. A sharp pang shot from his right knee as he landed on it. Snarling, he ignored the pain and ran at the janack. With a howl, he dug his claws into the offending tentacle, ripping a great chunk from it.

Nearly an octar later, the fighters finally killed the janack and brechas. Monster debris littered the battlefield. Histrun groaned at the sight of three blood-spattered men sprawled on the ground. His heart lifted when two of them moaned. The third one remained still. A Haaslair Red ran to him and knelt beside him, slowly shaking her head. Although he didn't know the man, Histrun hung his head in sorrow. Someday, he vowed, no more people would be killed by the damnable Malvers' monsters. He hoped he'd live to see such a day, even though he knew it was improbable. The Posairs had been fighting the monsters for a thousand years and hadn't stopped them yet.

He searched the area for Zehala. She sat crumpled on the ground. He ran over to her and crouched next to her. "You hurt?" he asked, his warrior jaws mangling the words.

She shook her head. "Forming the fire-ring above the earth drained me—us."

The other women also sprawled on the ground. Naila lay on her back, arms flung wide, taking deep breaths.

"I thought it would be a solution," Zehala continued. "But it takes too much energy to maintain."

The clopping of horse hooves interrupted them. A golden centaur loomed over them. A Red stood beside him, her apple-red hair escaping its braid with wisps curling around her face. She wiped away the smudge of blood on her cheek.

"I be Raelhaas," the centaur said, "and this be Vyolah. We be from Haasneh Keep. The barding I glimpsed as we ran past says you be Strunlair Clan. What be you doing in our territory?"

Zehala pushed to her feet. Histrun put out a paw to steady her. She straightened her shoulders and met the centaur's gaze. "We're from Strunland Keep, heading to Dehanlair Province to teach them the Zehis method. I'm Zehala. This is Histrun." She grinned at Vyolah. "That was pretty amazing. I haven't seen anyone fight the monsters from horseback before or use arrows."

"It'd be more effective if we could use fire arrows, but..." she shrugged. Her eyes narrowed as she looked back and forth at them. "Zehala... Histrun... Oh! Sweet Mother, you be them!"

Zehala nodded.

"The keep be not far," Raelhaas said. "As soon as the monster debris be disposed of, we can go there. Our keep alphas will want to speak with you and have you spend the night with us."

Histrun wished for a nearby stream to wash off the monster ichor. He wanted to shift back to his natural form and talk to Raelhaas. Mind-speech wasn't an option since they didn't know each other well enough. Besides, Histrun couldn't hold his warrior form for as long as he once had. He noticed several Haaslair men grab handfuls of grass and scrub the monster ichor from their fur before shifting. He followed their example and let out a gust of relief when he shifted.

Back in his natural form, he gripped Raelhaas's wrist in greeting. "I'll happily take your guidance. I'm not sure we are heading in the right direction. The grasslands lack the type of landmarks I'm used to." He shrugged. "One clump of grass looks the same as the next to me."

Raelhaas laughed. "I be sure if I went to your forest land, I'd think one tree or rock looked just like all the others."

Shortly after, Maheli and Andriel trotted up the ravine, leading the fighter's horses. Maheli handed Telen's reins to Histrun. "Here. Take the stupid beast."

Histrun raised an eyebrow at her.

"He kept trying to run after the herd, and when I wouldn't let him, he tried to bite me!"

Histrun rubbed Telen's nose. "Feeling a bit frisky, are we, old boy?"

"He be back on his home turf." Raelhaas grinned. He approached the big horse and ran a hand along Telen's withers, soothing him. "Telen be foaled not too far from here. The stallion he be wanting to chase be his sire. We be ready to leave."

Histrun swung into the saddle, grimacing at the sudden pain. A shallow cut scored his thigh where the brecha's claws had penetrated his fur. He was getting too old to fight the monsters. After this training trip, he'd think about retiring. Zehala could be the keep alpha, and he'd sit back and relax. He snorted at his fantasy.

As they rode, he kept glancing at the centaur. He wouldn't want to be stuck in such a shape for the rest of his life. He'd never wanted to stay in his warrior form longer than necessary, although he had known a few men who preferred to remain in it as long as possible. But even they had limits and needs. The one piece of anatomy that didn't work in warrior form was the one used to make love.

"So what's it like, being a centaur?" he finally asked.

"We be stronger, have more stamina for running, and be able to communicate better with the horses."

"How does one become a centaur? I understand your clan tends to shift more into horses than wolves, like the rest of us. Is that part of it?"

Raelhaas nodded. "To some extent. We come to love our horse brothers and sisters deeply, and this be a way to be part of the herds and still be part of the clan. It takes great discipline and long practice before being able to manage the difficult shift to split your form. Not many of us can accomplish it. You will not see any young centaurs. It also requires dedication, because it be an enormous change in lifestyle, too." Raelhaas glanced over at Vyolah and sighed. "The biggest downside be never making love to a woman again." He sighed again.

Histrun gazed at Zehala, fingering his bond-mate torque. He never removed the symbol of his bond with Zehala. He couldn't imagine never making love to her again. He rejoiced he hadn't ever had to make the choice.

A short while later, the walls of Haasneh Keep rose above the grasslands like a beacon of light. The setting sun shone from the temple's dome. A young chestnut horse sped from the gates and gamboled to their side. He had dark blue-gray stripes, and his tail and the feathering on his legs were the same chestnut color as his body.

"Jaehaas, settle down," Raelhaas admonished. "Be that the proper way to greet guests?"

The horse's head drooped. A shiver started at his tail and worked toward his head. When it finished, a young boy about twelve with rich chestnut-brown hair and slate-blue eyes stood where the horse had been.

"Sorry, sir," the boy said. His eyes widened as he stared at Telen. The big stallion, who at 17.2 hands towered over the boy, pawed the ground with a forefoot. "Be he from Jaelen's line? He has the look about him."

"You have a good eye," Raelhaas said.

"Did you see him? Did you see Jaelen? How many mares did he have this time?"

"Yes, we saw the old, wily stallion. He be running from a horde of monsters."

"But they didn't catch him, did they?"

"No, young scamp, they didn't." Raelhaas ruffled the boy's hair. "Jaehaas loves the old stallion. He keeps sneaking out of the keep to try to find him. One of these days, he's going to be caught by monsters."

"No, I won't!" Jaehaas grinned. "I run too fast." With a shiver, he returned to his horse form and galloped away, showing them how quickly he ran.

Raelhaas shook his head at the retreating boy. "If there be one destined to become a centaur, it be that boy. Even I didn't shift to my horse form as often as he does."

They rode into the courtyard and to the keep-house, where the alphas, Maehaas and Armelya, waited on the porch.

"Be welcome, Histrun and Zehala." Maehaas's voice boomed across the empty space. The big man leaned over the railing to grasp Histrun's wrist in greeting. "It be an honor to have you two stay with us."

"Yes, come in and be welcome." Armelya gave them a friendly smile. Her bright-red hair was coiled in a bun on top of her head, and she wore a daffodil-yellow gown. "Let the youngsters care for your horses."

She indicated the group of adolescents running to the porch. Histrun smiled when Jaehaas skidded to a stop in front of Telen's nose.

Ignoring the boy, Armelya continued. "I've cleared the bathing room for you and your people. Dinner will be ready by the time you finish."

"That is kind of you, Alpha Armelya," Zehala said.

"A hot bath is very welcome," Histrun said as he slid out of his saddle. "We've been on the road for days." He handed the reins to Jaehaas. "Take good care of him."

"Oh, I will, sir. He be gorgeous! Come on, Telen, let's get your saddle off, and then I'll give you some hot mash. How does that sound?"

The horse snorted and started toward the stables, with the boy stepping quickly to catch up. Histrun grinned and followed the others inside, looking forward to the hot bath and a dinner that wasn't camp stew.

Chapter 3

While Histrun and his people readied their horses to depart, Raelhaas and Vyolah met them in the courtyard.

"We be guiding you to Haasnelyn Keep." Raelhaas sidestepped, flicking his tail. "We'll also help arrange a barge for your travel down the Storengher River."

Histrun nodded. "We appreciate the help."

A short distance from the keep, a familiar chestnut horse raced across the grass to join the group.

"Jaehaas, you shouldn't be here," Vyolah admonished. "Don't you have duties to attend?"

The horse shook his head and pranced next to Telen.

"Oh, fine," Vyolah huffed. "But stay close. Don't go wandering off."

He nodded in agreement. Jaehaas walked with them for a while, then his youthful energy overtook him, and he raced ahead of them, kicking his rear hoofs into the air.

"Oh, to be that young again," Raelhaas sighed. Before the young horse could get too far ahead of them, Raelhaas gave a sharp whistle. Jaehaas reared, spun around, and galloped back.

"If we could use your fire-ring method," Vyolah said, sliding her reins through her hands, "it would be a big help in corralling the monsters while we fight them."

"I'm sure it would." Zehala pointed at the golden grass they rode through and wrinkled her nose. "It's a matter of not causing a wildfire. Belhaas is asking his earth Talents to research creating a fire-resistant strain of grass."

"Oh, that be a wonderful idea. If we had that, we could use fire arrows, too. You've given us much to think about, Zehala. Sometimes we don't see the solution to a problem because we be too close to it."

"The problem seems to be the hottest part of a flame is at the base." Zehala leaned her forearms on her pommel. "We've tried creating a cold fire, but when it combines with the hot, it explodes."

"Have you thought about turning your shield upside down? If you inverted your fire-shield, the cooler part of the flame would be at ground level. The hotter part would now cover the top, where it would be more effective against the monsters."

Zehala sat back in her saddle, causing her horse to skid to a stop. She slapped her forehead, then grinned at Vyolah. "That is genius! It could work. We're so used to building the fire-shield from the ground up, I didn't even think of doing it a different way." She turned in her saddle and shrugged at Histrun. "So much for me having all the great ideas. I can't wait to try this out!" She kicked her horse back into motion, urging it into a trot. Histrun and the others followed her lead.

After another octar of riding, the Storengher River came into view, cutting across the plains. A few boat sails dotted its wide expanse. The river traversed the length of Lairheim, with its headwaters in the northern Deep Mountains.

"It's so gentle," Histrun remarked to Raelhaas. "It's hard to believe it's the same tumultuous waters speeding down the mountains in my his home province. Few ships brave the river's rough and wild water."

"The river disappears at the edge of the Barrens." Raelhaas gazed to the south, as if he could see the demarcation where life stopped. "I've heard rumors that the river resurfaces beyond the Barrens to form the great southern swamp."

"Have you been there?"

Raelhaas shook his head vehemently. "Great Goddess, no! No one be alive who has traveled the swamp and returned to tell about it."

The spires and temple dome of a small keep on the river's edge glistened in the sunlight. Like all keeps, the walls were made from sheadash stone, most likely imported from Ledonlair or Strunlair provinces. Fields of grain and plots of vegetables surrounded the keep, giving the area a boost of green amid the prairie golds. Docks jutted into the placid river. Boats with bright sails and flat-bottomed barges floated on the wide expanse of water.

Raelhaas led them through the keep gates and directly to the docks, where several barges waited next to it. Thick ropes kept them from floating away. The men and women working on the vessels had various shades of blue or yellow hair. Their water and air Talents made them well suited for their work as sailors. Raelhaas stopped in front of a large, dark-green barge that had a tall mast with pale red sails wrapped tightly around it. A small cabin squatted in the center of the deck.

"Ho, Daelena!" Raelhaas lifted a hand in greeting.

A middle-aged woman with azure hair coiled a rope at her feet. She took in the platoon and grinned.

"Be these people here for my barge, Raelhaas?"

"Aye." Raelhaas nodded. "They be heading downriver to Dehanlair Keep. Taking the river down be much faster, and safer, than riding through the plains."

"So it be." She finished coiling her rope and laid it neatly at her feet, then put her hands on her hips. "Who might you be, then? And what do you have to barter for my services?"

"Daelena!" Raelhaas's eyes widened, and he stomped his front hoof. "These be the great Histrun and Zehala. Their gift of the Zehis method is payment enough. Maehaas authorized it."

Daelena bowed her head. "My apologies. How many be in your party, including the horses and multas?"

Histrun swung off his horse. "We have forty people, the same number of horses, and two multas. And we have items to trade." He gestured for Maheli to come forward and bring the bag of trade goods.

"No!" Raelhaas made a chopping gesture, frowning at Maheli. The girl stopped in her tracks. "No, those not be needed. Go put them back, girl. You have done enough for our world."

"But it doesn't work here," Zehala protested. She slid from her saddle and beckoned Maheli forward. "We can pay—"

Maheli held out the pack.

"Nonsense," Raelhaas scowled, flicking his tail in agitation, the tips hitting the bag, barely missing Maheli's fingers.

She quickly pulled it away and gave Histrun a what-do-I-do-now look. He motioned for her to return to her place within the group.

Raelhaas nodded and crossed his arms over his chest. "You be working on a way for it to work here, too. That be enough. Now, Daelena, be your barge big enough for this pack?"

Zehala nudged Histrun and said in mind speech, *When we leave the barge, we'll leave behind suitable trade items.*

He nodded in agreement.

"You know it be, Raelhaas." She turned to Histrun and Zehala. "Sleeping quarters might be a bit tight, but we can accommodate all your people and gear. Give my pack an octar to ready the boat and bring on supplies. You can leave the animals here while you go visit the keep." She turned her back to them and gave a loud whistle. "All right, mates, look lively! We have a fare."

The deck suddenly crawled with sailors. A wide plank clattered onto the stone pier, and four young people scampered across it, stopping in front of Raelhaas.

"Give them your horses," he said. "They'll take them over to the barge and get them settled. Come on and leave them to it. It be chaos until she be ready for you." He glanced up at the sun. "It be time for the mid-day meal, anyway."

Histrun and his group trailed Raelhaas and Vyolah into Haasnelyn Keep. The boy, Jaehaas, remained behind, helping load the horses. He had a way with them. They instantly calmed in his presence.

An octar later, they returned after having a pleasant lunch with the keep alphas. Boxes of supplies piled next to the railing filled the barge's bow end, while the stern held their saddle bags and packs. Histrun couldn't see a single horse or multa. Daelena met them on the dock.

"Where are our horses?" Zehala asked, shocked.

"They be in the hold." Daelena ran a hand through her hair. "It be safer and more pleasant for them if they can't see the river floating by. You'll have to sort out your belongings." She pointed to their packs. "That be where you'll stay and sleep. We be expecting fine weather the next chedan or so. The only sleeping quarters be in the crew cabin. We usually only haul cargo, not passengers."

"We'll be fine," Histrun said.

"Well, come aboard." Daelena made a wide, welcoming gesture. "Daylight's a-wasting."

Histrun walked carefully across the plank that bounced with each step, threatening to toss him into the water several feet below. Once aboard, he dug through the saddlebags, quickly finding his and Zehala's belongings. As the others joined him, he pulled Zehala to the side and let the younger ones stoop and bend as they sorted the pile.

"Let's find a place near the captain's cabin," Zehala said. "It will shelter us somewhat in case it storms or a wind comes up."

Histrun grunted in agreement. They found a spot facing the bow where they could watch the activity on the barge.

Sailors scurried on the deck and climbed up the mast. A loud pop sounded as the sails unfurled. As soon as the last person stepped off the plank, a sailor dragged it onto the deck. Several deckhands used long poles to push the barge away from the dock and into the deeper water.

A sigh of wind brushed Histrun's cheek, and the sails snapped as the breeze filled them. The barge shot down the river, throwing him off balance with the sudden, swift movement. He looked toward the stern. A woman with canary-yellow hair stood on a small platform, staring at the sails in concentration. The breeze picked up slightly, filling the sails even more.

Once the barge was underway, Daelena found Histrun and Zehala. "This be a good place for you to stay." She nodded in approval at their choice. "We will reach Dehanrolos Keep, Dehanlair Province's port Keep, in the afternoon two days from now, so you won't have to sleep on the hard deck for long."

Zehala's eyebrows rose. "This is much faster. It would take us over a chedan by land."

"The *Dawn Sister* be a fast barge." Daelena glanced at the rail, and shouted, "Hoy, tighten up those ropes!" She returned her attention to Histrun and Zehala. "I best get back to work. Enjoy your stay with us." She stomped toward a young man, struggling with a rope.

After checking on their people, Histrun and Zehala wandered to the rail, staying out of the deckhands' way, and watched the plains slide by. At one point, a ducorn herd bounded through the tall grass. Later, a herd of wild horses drank at the riverbank.

The next afternoon, a sailor caught a huge fish. Histrun gaped in disbelief at its five-foot length.

Daelena laughed. "This be a little one. Some of these grow to twelve, fifteen feet. We'll have a nice feast tonight."

That evening, Daelena guided the barge to shore, where the sailors built a bonfire. They roasted the fish along with tubers, carrots, and onions. Daelena broached a cask of ale, and the dinner turned into a party. When several sailors brought out small drums and pipes, Naila and Lestrun added their flutes to the impromptu ensemble. Zehala's clear, soprano floated across the gathering. Histrun leaned against the cabin, enjoying listening to her sing. He knew better than to try to join in. He was tone deaf and sang off key. Soon, people grabbed partners and danced to the music.

Chelar, the smallest moon, and Kelar, the largest moon, both nearly full, brightened the warm summer night. The moonlight made Zehala even more beautiful. As they danced, her hips swayed against his hands. He pulled her close, loving her softness against his chest.

"I want you, now. There has to be someplace where we can be alone," Zehala whispered, as she nibbled on his earlobe and pressed closer.

"Let's find a secluded spot on the riverbank," he agreed, his voice husky with lust. Holding hands, they walked along the river until they found a large tree. Its roots dangled into the river, forming a hidden oasis under its branches.

Histrun forgot his old age when Zehala's hot kisses trailed down his neck. They made love in the moonlight and under the stars, something they'd always wanted to do, but because of the dangers of predators, they never could indulge before. They fell asleep, wrapped in each other's arms, to the sound of the lapping water of the river and the distant music.

Shortly after midday, a bridge arched gracefully over the placid waters, high enough the ships' masts could pass underneath it. A stone keep guarded either end. Histrun and Zehala stood at the rail, watching boats jockey for position at the docks on both sides of the river.

Daelena sauntered to them. "We be docking on the Haaslair side at Haasneven Keep, shortly." She pointed to the keep on the river's east side, flying Haaslair brown and yellow pennons. On the opposite shore, blue and yellow flags in the Dehanlair colors flapped in the breeze. "It be a pleasure to ferry you downriver. If we be here when you be ready to return home, I'd be happy to have you again."

"We've enjoyed our time on board," Zehala said, turning to lean her back against the railing. "I don't think I've ever had a more scrumptious fish dinner."

"There are a few aboard who will be unhappy for us to leave." Histrun nodded toward the two couples locked in embraces.

Daelena's eyes crinkled as she snorted. "Oh, those lads always be finding someone to keep their beds warm. All right, mates, look alive! We be coming to the docks. Gaehaas, get your arse up the mainmast. Dorhaas, man your pole."

Lorstriel sadly stepped from Dorhaas, while Lestrun kissed Gaehaas deeply one last time. With a wave and grin, the crewmen scampered off to their duties.

"When we dock, please clear the deck quickly so we can bring up your horses." Daelena gripped their hands in farewell. As she strode to the barge's stern, she called out orders to her crew.

Lorstriel and Lestrun trudged to the railing, where they could watch their lovers. Lorstriel leaned next to Zehala. "Sweet Mother, these sailors are fit!"

"I do not want to hear about your sexual exploits," Histrun huffed and scowled at her. "Go away."

"Ah, Histrun, you're such a prude." Lorstriel dragged Zehala toward the prow.

Their giggles drifted to him on the breeze. He prayed his bondmate wasn't sharing anything about their moonlight adventure. Ignoring them, he called Naila to him and told her to ready their people to disembark. Ten milcrons later, the barge bumped into the pier, and the deckhands lowered the plank across the water. Histrun gingerly made his way over the plank and onto the stone pier. His people hustled across the gangway.

Within a few moments, sailors led his big stallion, Telen, then Zehala's mare, Kylara, from the hold and onto the dock. He quickly put on his horse's tack, including the barding. Mendehan was a stickler for tradition, which meant visiting clans announced themselves with their barding. An octar later, Daelena's crew had guided the horses off the barge and Histrun's people were ready to leave.

Histrun's stomach clenched as he contemplated the bridge. *This isn't going to be pleasant.* Now that he was close to entering Dehanlair Province, he had second thoughts. Every time he and Mendehan met, they argued over their different viewpoints. They'd fought a few times over the years, and shared a deep hatred of each other. Histrun scrubbed a hand through his hair.

Zehala nudged her horse closer to Histrun's. "What's wrong?"

"This isn't a good idea. Why did I let you talk me into this?"

"We're here to save lives." Zehala patted his forearm. "Our method does that. I'll put up with Mendehan's condescending attitude if I can save even one life from being lost unnecessarily."

"That part I understand. I can't fathom why Mendehan insisted we're the only ones he'd allow to teach his clan?" Histrun indicated himself and Zehala with a finger.

The technique was mostly Zehala's and Layhalya's work. Histrun had simply made a few suggestions on how to use the warriors more effectively and ensured they had the resources they needed. Somehow that had warranted having his name attached to the procedure.

"There are other people capable of teaching it, but he specifically requested the two of us. Why in the Crone's Fires would he do that? He hates me, and the feeling is mutual."

Zehala shrugged, tucking a strand of hair behind her ears. "The minds of men are strange things. Don't worry about Mendehan. He should be on his best behavior. He has to if he wants to remain Dehanlair Clan Alpha. The Supreme ordered him to ensure the safety of his people. If he doesn't, she will invoke her authority and relieve him of his position."

It had shocked Histrun when he'd heard about the Supreme's order. She rarely interfered in clan politics. The Supreme usually allowed the alphas to run the everyday governance of their provinces as they saw fit.

"I still don't trust him. You know he's going to try to goad me into a fight."

"Then you have to remain on your best behavior as well." Zehala leaned over, closing the space between their horses to brush a kiss on his check. "You can do it, my love. Remember, we are under the Supreme's orders, and therefore, under her protection. He shouldn't try to harm either of us. It would jeopardize his position."

"One would think he'd be that rational," Histrun snorted. "But when it comes to me, he loses reason. This isn't going to end well."

Histrun peered over his shoulder at the keep. "Maybe we should eat the midday meal here. It would be rude not to spend time with the Haasneven alphas."

Zehala snorted. "Now, you're just stalling. It will be fine. I trust you to not to do anything stupid. Come on." She kicked her horse into motion and stepped onto the bridge.

Histrun sighed and followed her across.

As they rode into Dehanrolos Keep, the people on the docks and in the streets stared at them. Histrun's uneasiness increased. Their rose and turquoise barding stood out, letting everyone know they were strangers. Rather than riding through, Histrun led his procession toward the central plaza. They couldn't skimp on their manners, especially here. They needed to maintain tradition and pay respects to the keep alphas. He also hoped to find someone who would guide them through the province to the Clan Keep. He'd never been on this side of the Storengher river before.

The keep alphas stood on the keep house's wide porch. The man held his arms crossed over his chest, and he wore a belligerent frown. He had light-red hair and copper-brown eyes. The woman moved to the railing. Her long braid of crimson hair flowed over her shoulder, and a smile lit her yellow-green eyes.

"You are from Strunlair Province," she said, gesturing to their barding. "Are you the ones sent to teach us the new fighting method?" Hope filled her voice.

Histrun inclined his head. "We are from Strunland Keep—"

"Yes," Zehala interrupted. "We're here to show it to you. I'm Zehala, and this is Histrun."

"I'm Freynara." The woman touched her chest, then tilted her chin toward the glaring man. "My co-alpha is Rodehan. Welcome! Salloreen sent word to expect you soon. I'm so happy you're here. This morning, we lost five people battling the damned Malvers' monsters. I don't want to lose any more. What do you require for this method of yours? I'll make sure you get it." She skipped down the porch stairs.

Zehala dismounted and met Freynara. "We'll need a team of at least eight strong Reds and an equal number of warriors, better if it's double. Where's your practice arena?"

"This way." Freynara gestured to the practice area and strode toward a large building beyond the stables, with Zehala at her side. "Your people can leave their horses with our horse-master."

Histrun helplessly watched the women walk away. He hadn't planned on stopping at and training every keep along their path. But Zehala couldn't ride by without helping. He gave Rodehan a rueful smile and shrugged. As he flung a leg over the saddle and slid to the ground, he resigned himself to spending a couple of days with the Dehanrolos fighters. Histrun gestured to his platoon to dismount, and handed both his and Zehala's reins to Maheli, frowning at her already full hands. She also held the reins of Naila's and Lorstriel's horses, as the two women hurried after their alphas. Maheli juggled a bit to add the additional reins before trotting off toward the stable, leading the horses.

Rodehan hadn't moved from the porch.

Histrun jerked his head toward the practice ring. "We might as well follow the women if we want any peace."

Rodehan scowled. "The old way of fighting has worked just fine for hundreds of years. I don't know why we need to change."

"The monster's behavior has changed, is why. More people stay alive and safe during the fight with our technique. Our casualty rate has dropped significantly since we started using it. Now if someone dies, it's usually because they didn't move quick enough or they were in the path of a tentacle or spine. The monsters rarely get a chance to eat our people anymore. Do you want to continue being stubborn like your fool of a Clan

Alpha, or are you going to learn something that will keep your people alive?"

Rodehan stared into the distance with his lips pulled into a tight line. Finally, he huffed and uncrossed his arms. "My people are more important than old traditions, but I will reserve my judgment until I see your method in action." He stomped down the stairs and trudged across the courtyard to the practice arena.

Chapter 4

Histrun raised his eyebrows at the large group of fighters gathered on the practice sands. More than the requested eight Reds and associated warriors stood in a semicircle, listening to Zehala. Even more people filled the stands. It looked like the everyone in a fighting-pack watched the training. Histrun walked to the sands, stepping over the low barrier, and leaned against the railing.

"Our method uses teamwork to surround and cut off individual monsters from the rest," Zehala said, addressing the assembled fighters. "This way, a warrior doesn't have to worry about being attacked from behind or blindsided by another monster. We've found it is most effective at the nest sites. This serves two purposes. It keeps the monsters in the area, and we don't have to chase them down to ensure we've killed them all.

"You need enough Reds on the perimeter to form a strong fire-ring. Eight is the optimum number." Zehala made eye contact with the Reds in the group. "We split the circle using the cardinal directions, placing a pair of Reds in each quadrant. They support each other, and if one has to help in the fight, she can while the other maintains the fire-ring. Naila and Lorstriel will now demonstrate creating a small fire-ring."

Zehala beckoned the two Reds forward. The women stepped away from the low barrier wall and into the arena's center. They stopped about ten paces opposite each other, then lowered their helbraught blades, glowing with fire magic. As they touched the tips to the sands, a thin stream of fire crawled along the ground in either direction until it met in the middle.

Histrun squinted. His minuscule Red Talent allowed him to see the vague outlines of a magic web woven within the flames. It grew into a twenty-foot-high wall curving inward at the top. Most janacks couldn't reach their tentacles over that height. A malicious grin crept across his face as he recalled the numerous monsters attempting to crash through the ring. The intense heat incinerated the monsters.

Keep Alpha Freynara glowered at the fire-ring, her hands on her hips. "Are you trying to pull a fast one on us? That looks simple enough."

"It's more difficult than it appears." Zehala made a chopping motion with her hand. Naila and Lorstriel released the fire-ring, snapping their helbraughts up. "It takes practice to coordinate and merge everyone's magic into a seamless whole. There can't be any holes, or else the monsters will find them and escape. The brechas are especially adept at finding the holes and slipping through them. It requires skill to quickly reweave the inner net if a Red is injured and releases her magic from the fire-ring. This is simply the first part of our method."

Zehala turned her attention to the men in the circle. "You also play an important role." Confusion darkened their faces. "For this technique to work, the warriors must learn a new way to battle the monsters. They can't fight in a free-for-all, with each warrior attacking the nearest monster. Instead, the fighters work closely with their Reds in quadrant teams. Once the monsters leave the nest, the women cut off individuals with their fire magic and drive them to the waiting warriors." She nodded to Histrun.

He pushed off from the railing he'd been leaning on and strode to her side. "Aye, the fire-ring is a genius discovery, but it took longer for us men to master coordinating our attacks with the Reds. We weren't used to staying inside the confines of the circle. We developed new practice forms to learn this new way of fighting." He glanced at the stands and estimated the practice area would hold the assembled fighters. He beckoned to the watching men. "Warriors, follow me, and I'll teach you in the new fighting forms."

"Reds go to the north end of the arena," Zehala gestured with her helbraught, "where I'll work with you to learn the fire-shield."

The stands emptied of people as they joined their respective groups. Histrun and the men tromped to the opposite side of the arena, where the warriors sorted themselves into several long lines. Every warrior practiced the fighting forms daily when they weren't engaged with the monsters. The set of fighting positions and techniques flowed together, training their bodies to move on instinct. Even as experienced as Histrun was at his ripe old age of 91, he still practiced the forms.

He positioned Eidelstrun, his largest fighter, in front of the group. Lestrun, Dorstrun, Alixstrun, and Chestrun, his strongest fighters, took places on the perimeter. He sprinkled his other pack members throughout the lines. With the placements, no matter which direction the Dehanrolos men turned, they could follow someone who knew the new patterns.

The practice began with the familiar sequences, gradually added the new motions. These taught the men to move differently while battling the monsters within the confines of the fire-ring. After several repetitions, Histrun broke the men into groups of four. They needed to learn to coordinate their movements into a cohesive fighting team.

Several octars later, Histrun's stomach grumbled, reminding him he'd missed the midday meal. "That's enough for today," he called. "You've done well. The only way for these forms to make complete sense is to use them on the field while fighting the monsters."

Rodehan wiped the sweat from his face. "As often as the monsters are spilling from their nests, we'll soon have an opportunity to test this out. Too bad we can't simulate a battle in the practice arena."

"What a great idea! It would help mitigate the risk of injury." Histrun grimaced, rubbing at the ache in his lower back. He was getting too old for this. He gazed at the women still training, then shook his head. "Unfortunately, the Reds aren't skilled with making the type of illusion we'd need with their fire magic. Yellows are the only ones I'm aware of who could create such an illusion. But they aren't fighters."

"As if Yellows could fight," Rodehan scoffed as they trudged across the sands toward the door. The two alphas paused to watch the women's training, while the rest of the men wandered from the arena.

Freynara's helbraught glowed, and a moment later flames zipped along the ground, where they met and melded with the fire magic of her teammates. The fire ring formed, and the women grinned, until Zehala walked behind a tall woman and pushed her. She staggered forward several steps with a grunt. The flames flickered, but the other women scowled in concentration, steadying the wall of fire. Zehala continued to knock women out of the circle until only Freynara and one other woman remained. Sweat dribbled into the two women's eyes as they held the fire-ring.

"And release!" Zehala smacked her hands together. The flames immediately died, and Freynara and her partner sagged against their helbraughts, swiping at their sweat slicked faces.

"Good job," Zehala said. "The true test will come when brechas are shooting their spines at you and a janack's tentacles are reaching for you. Enough for today."

The women filed off the sands and out of the arena. Zehala and Freynara joined Histrun and Rodehan at the arena's edge.

"I can see how this new method of yours could work," Rodehan said grudgingly.

"How soon do you think a nest will mature?" Histrun asked.

"One is due tomorrow morning." Rodehan grimaced. "Damn things are regenerating faster and faster."

"Our fighters will go to the nest site with your fighting pack. We can demonstrate it in actual combat and help you eliminate the monsters."

"We'd appreciated your assistance."

Freynara's eyes glazed over as she mind-spoke with someone. She took a deep breath and blinked. "Rooms are being prepared for your platoon. We'd be honored if the two of you would join us at the head table tonight."

"It would be our pleasure." Zehala's stomach gurgled loudly, and she dipped her head, hiding her blush. "I'm famished. We didn't stop to eat our midday meal before arriving here."

"Oh my goodness!" Freynara covered her mouth, and a blush crept over her face. "I'm so sorry. You must think my manners are sorely lacking."

Zehala put a hand on the other woman's arm. "You can make it up to us by pointing us to the bathing room."

"This way." Freynara led them to the keep-house. Inside, she directed them to the stairs leading down to the bathing room. "I'll have someone bring you a change of clothes."

Histrun walked down several stairs, pausing to rub the shooting pain from his right knee.

"You okay?" Zehala placed a comforting hand on his back.

"My knee is still bothering me from landing wrong when that damned janack hit me in the battle where we met Raelhaas."

"You're getting old to let a monster smack you around."

"Tell me something I don't know." Histrun grimaced.

"Soaking in the heat will help it."

Histrun straightened and continued hobbling down the stairs into the large room in the basement. After stripping off their dirty clothes and putting their personal items in a bin, the couple moved to the line of scrubbing buckets. Histrun eased onto a low stool and dragged a container holding soap, brushes, and rags closer to him.

Zehala dribbled water over his back. She chased the water with a rough cloth. His breath caught as she reached around his waist, gripping his manhood and running her soap slick hands up and down his shaft. Her breasts pressed against him as she brought him to hardness. Histrun moaned, twisting to kiss her. His thumb found her nipple, caressing it. Before he climaxed, Zehala stopped. Quivering, Histrun rose to his feet, lifting his bond mate and crushing him against her.

Entwined, they made their way to the rinsing room, filled with huge water barrels, spigots extending from them. They stood underneath a spigot, and Histrun jerked on the attached chain. Water sploshed out in a waterfall, washing the soap from their bodies. He ducked his head, his kisses along her neck trailed the water flowing over her breasts. He caught a nipple in his mouth, rolling it with his tongue and gently nipping it to hardness. With one hand wrapped around her and holding her close, his other hand slid to the juncture between her thighs.

He found her sensitive nub, and it was her turn to shiver with need. Twisting them around, he pushed her against the smooth wood of the water barrel, lifting her ass. The tip of his manhood touched her softness. Bracing his hands over her shoulders on the barrel, he plunged into her, gasping as they climaxed.

Zehala reached behind him and shut off the water. Slowly, Histrun's breathing returned to normal. They hadn't indulged in shower sex for a long time. He gripped Zehala's hand and kissed her knuckles. "We could skip dinner and relax in the tub, alone."

Zehala's eyes twinkled. "Is that all?"

"I'm good for another round, or two." Histrun grinned.

Zehala gave him a sultry smile, kissing him quickly. She whirled away from him and sauntered away, her hips swaying seductively. With a groan, wishing he recovered as quickly as in his youth, he followed her into his favorite part of the bathing room. The soaking tubs.

A low growl escaped him. Several of their pack-mates lounged in the hot water. Lorstriel nudged Eidelstrun to make room for Histrun and Zehala. Histrun gratefully eased his tired, aching body into the steaming water. Leaning his head against the top, he closed his eyes. "I'm can't continue with this frenetic pace," he murmured to Zehala. "This is the last training trip we're taking. I like the idea of you becoming the Strunland keep alpha more and more."

She squeezed his hand. "I'm happy you're finally coming around. I told you, I'm not leaving Rizelya behind any longer. At the next alpha competition, I'm challenge Koriana."

After a quick breakfast, Histrun and Zehala, along with their fighters, hurried to the stables and saddled their horses. A few milcrons later, they joined the Dehanrolos fighting-pack in the courtyard. Histrun did a double-take when both keep alphas arrived dressed in fighting leathers and mounted their horses, apparently ready to go with the fighting-pack. A keep's alphas rarely departed the keep at the same time, especially not to fight a monster battle. They risked leaving their people without leadership. Histrun cocked his head in question at Rodehan.

Rodehan lifted a shoulder. "Yes, I know it's unprecedented, but it's a necessary risk. We must know how your method works in the field. I'm trusting your people to make sure both Freynara and I return."

"We will do our best," Histrun replied. "How far to the nest?"

"Ten measures. We need to leave to arrive in time." Rodehan lifted his arm, and the noise in the courtyard immediately subsided. He dropped his arm as he kicked his horse into motion. Histrun and Zehala fell into line with their fighters as the group exited the keep gates and rode through the surrounding fields. Rodehan led them away from the river, directly east. Once they passed the cultivated areas, he increased the pace to a fast trot.

Within a few measures, the landscape gradually changed from the tall plains grass into sagebrush and wild-rose bushes interspersed with birch and cedar trees. Soon, Histrun grimaced at the loud sucking noise of Telen's hooves pulling from the marshy ground. The monster's nest would be nearby. Swamps always formed around a nest site, or a nest site created a swamp. No one knew which occurred first. They wouldn't have to worry about setting the surrounding area on fire, unlike in Haaslair Province.

The breeze shifted. Histrun wrinkled his nose at the disgusting reek. Even after a lifetime of fighting the Malvers' monsters, he still hated their stink. Sometimes, the size of a nest could be determined by the stench.

"How big is it?" Zehala asked.

"My guess, it's a small one, only a couple of janacks and less than a dozen brechas."

Zehala nodded. "That's a good size for the Dehanrolos fighters to practice the new method. The fire-ring won't be too large. The Reds should be able to handle it easily."

Half a measure away from the nest, Rodehan stopped near a corral. They left their horses in the care of the teenage Reds, including Maheli and Andriel, and two young men, while the rest continued on foot.

Fifty feet from the nest, Histrun held up an arm, signaling for everyone to stop. "Let's go over assignments before we engage. Zehala, you'll work with Freynara to oversee the battle and direct the Reds on separating the monsters. Naila, team up with Norvela and her Reds to hold the fire-ring. Rodehan, you and I will cull the monsters. Lestrun and platoon alpha Tedehan, pay attention and ensure the warriors fight together."

He surveyed the stirring nest. Spiky shapes intertwined with slick tentacles as the janacks caressed the spines on the brechas' backs. Clacks from the janacks answered the brecha's rumbled growls. He nodded to himself. It appeared to be about the size he had estimated.

"Okay, people. Let's rid our world of another nest. Stay alive." Histrun stepped away to change into his warrior form. The other men joined him.

Zehala and the women paced around the nest, forming a circle, their helbraughts glowing with their fire magic. As the last woman reached their place, the air filled with the men's howls, signaling their readiness. At the sound, a janack's bulbous head lifted above the others. Its heat-sensor stalks waving.

"Ready..." Zehala called out. The women's helbraughts dipped to the ground. "Now!"

A low circle of fire surrounded the nest site, demarcating the battlefield. Two brechas boiled from the nest, and the fire blazed high into a semi-dome. Five warriors charged forward and engaged the two brechas just as three more trundled out. Flames separated the monsters into two groups as warriors sped toward them.

A brecha loosed its spines toward Chestrun's back as he ran, but before they could hit him, the fire surrounding the monster flared, instantly consuming the spines. At Histrun's side, Rodehan gasped. Without their method, Chestrun would have been dead.

As the first janack left the nest, Histrun hung back, watching the fight critically. Most of the men utilized the new forms he'd taught them. He growled at the few older men who weren't. A tentacle snaked out and caught an older man around the waist.

Lestrun, help him! Histrun called out in mind-speech. His warrior's jaws made speaking difficult. The younger man leaped on the tentacle, slashing it with his long claws. Two Dehanrolos fighters joined him in the attack. In coordinated moves, they hacked at the tentacle. The old warrior screamed as the janack's hold tightened. Finally, the trio cut through the thick tentacle. As it flopped to the ground, it released the older warrior, who curled into a fetal position, his arms wrapped protectively around his ribs, which were most likely broken.

Histrun stepped forward to check on the man, but stopped short as the second janack, with three brechas flanking it, rolled from the nest directly toward him and Rodehan. Before the brechas could reach them, fire snaked across the ground, flaring high to trap the monsters. Behind them, warriors attacked, outstretched claws dripping with venom.

The janack trundled toward Histrun and Rodehan, the only two fighters left to face it. They exchanged a glance before racing in, their claws dripping with venom. The men slashed and ripped at the janack's tentacles, pumping their venom into it.

A tentacle shot toward Histrun. He spun away, but not quick enough. The tentacle slammed into his side, knocking him to his knees. Doubling over, he gasped at the searing pain from his previously injured knee, trying to breathe through the pain. The grass by his hand sizzled, and he jerked it back. "Crone's Fires!" he swore. Above him the janack's wide-open maw bore down on him, spittle dripping. With a howl, he rolled.

The whistle of a helbraught warned him, and he ducked. It swung toward the janack's head. A gash opened across its beak. The janack hissed, rearing away. Zehala thrust the glowing blade into the janack's belly, ripping it open. Histrun swore as acidic ichor and monster guts burst from the wound directly above him. Tucking into a ball, he prayed his fur would protect him from the deluge of monster ichor. If it touched his skin, he'd suffer from its poison. A wall of flame surrounded him, burning the ichor before it could land on him.

"You need to move faster, Histrun." Zehala frowned at him before holding out her hand.

He gently took it in his large paw, careful not to get any venom or ichor on her skin. *I need to be twenty years younger. I'm too old for this!*

"Ha! You're not that old. I should have you run alongside of us when we ride, to increase your stamina."

My stamina is just fine. I can still make love to you. He grinned as she laughed.

Yes, you can, she said, her mind-voice only for him. She surveyed the battleground. "The fight is over. Only a few are injured, and those aren't serious."

Freynara joined them. She wiped at her cheek, smearing the ash worse rather than cleaning it. "Thanks to your method, no one died. Separating them with fire works amazingly well, and it made a difference. I can't believe we didn't think about it sooner."

Zehala shrugged. "Neither can I. It's only possible because of the fire-ring, which took a lot of experimentation to find the right spell. Now, if I can figure out a way to invert it so we can use in the plains and not cause a wildfire..."

"The way your technique starts the fire on the ground and builds upward to form the dome would make it difficult to use on the grasslands." Freynara's eyes narrowed as she watched the Reds walk across the battlefield, burning the monster carcasses and any debris. Mumbling to herself, she made a small fire-ring, only a foot in diameter. She studied it for several milcrons before letting it go. "What if we weave the fire magic but don't ignite it until it's complete? If we set the spark to start at the top, rather than the bottom, the fire-ring would be inverted. Like this."

She formed another fire-ring.

Histrun stared at it, his mouth dropping open. The top of the dome glowed blue, indicating the hottest part of the flame, and the part near the ground shone a pale yellow.

Zehala stared at it, then whooped. "Sweet Mother! You did it! We'll have to test it on dry grass, but this should work. Once we practice forming the fire-ring this way, it shouldn't take any longer to form it than it does now. You can't believe how many times and ways I've tried to do this."

Freynara released the ring with a wave of her hand. "Sometimes it just takes fresh eyes."

The entire ride back to the keep, the Reds talked excitedly about the new technique to form the fire-ring. Pride swelled Histrun's heart. Zehala's enthusiasm sparked ingenuity in those around her. Her deep desire to keep her people had led to her experimenting to find another way to fight their ancient enemy.

Zehala glanced at him, then frowned. "What are you grinning about?"

"I thought this trip to Dehanlair was going to be a waste of time. But this new discovery makes it worth it." He rested his wrists on the saddle pommel. "Maybe we can change the name of the method to the Zenara method. I haven't done much to deserve my name attached to it."

"But you have! Without your belief in me and your support, I never would have continued after that first disastrous attempt."

"You mean the time you nearly burned my eyebrows off?" He rubbed his right eyebrow, still sure it wasn't as bushy as his left one.

Zehala laughed. "Yes, that one."

Later that night—after Histrun demonstrated his stamina was just fine—he cradled Zehala in his arms. *Great Mother, thank you for this wonderful woman to share my life as my bond-mate. He kissed her gently, so as not to wake her. I can't imagine what my life would be like without her in it, and I don't want to know. Please, Goddess, keep her safe.*

Chapter 5

Histrun's forehead crinkled in confusion when the next morning he and his people arrived at the stables. More than the expected guides saddled their horses. While he waited for Maheli to saddle his horse—sometimes rank had its privileges—he counted several platoons. Alarm flared in Histrun's belly. He stalked to Freynara and Rodehan, where they stood by the railing with the platoon alpha, Norvela.

"What's going on?" Histrun interrupted their conversation. "Is there another nest? It must be gigantic for this many fighters."

Rodehan shook his head. "No, nothing like that. We're sending Norvela's and two other platoons with you. Along the way, you'll encounter several nest sites. We want our fighters to continue practicing your new method under your guidance."

"On their way back," Freynara added, "they'll stop at our smaller keeps to train them. The more fighters who learn it quickly, the safer our territory and people will be."

Histrun grunted in approval. "It's a good plan. We've done the same with the other provinces we've trained. Dehanlair is the last one to accept it." He nodded to Zehala as she joined them.

"After experiencing how effective it is," Rodehan said, clenching his fist, "I can't believe our Clan Alpha took so long to approve it. How many lives did we lose because of Mendehan's foolishness?"

"More than we should have." Freynara grimaced and crossed her arms across her chest. "Even after the Dehanreen Territory alphas told Mendehan how effective it was, he still refused. They aren't fighting any Malvers' monsters crossing the border between them and Ronanlair Province anymore, because the Ronanlair fighters take care of them in the nest. I'm sure they're not fond of our beasts making their life more difficult because we're not stopping them."

"What made him change his mind?" Zehala asked, leaning her chin on Histrun's shoulder.

Rodehan snorted. "He only did so after we and the other territory alphas banded together and demanded Mendehan to allow us to openly learn the method. The Dehanreende Keep, as the closest keep to Ronanlair, already secretly learned the technique. Before we met with him, we decided if he didn't listen to reason, Wendehan, the Dehanreen Keep Alpha, would challenge him, authorized or not by the Supreme. This would count as extenuating circumstances."

"The Supreme would understand and support such a move. She has also put pressure on him." Histrun grinned at the idea of the old coot losing his position. He'd been the Dehanlair Clan Alpha for thirteen years. Long enough for him to believe himself entrenched—and entitled—to the position. He'd have a rude awakening at the Alpha Competitions next summer.

Freynara gazed at the Temple next to the Alpha House with a troubled expression. Finally, she blew out a breath. "It's good to know the Supreme wouldn't censor Wendehan for doing what is right."

Histrun glanced at Zehala, whose forehead crinkled, reflecting the same uneasy confusion he felt. *Is there something going on they aren't telling us?* he asked in mind-speech.

She lifted a shoulder. *It seems like it. Maybe we'll discover more on the way to the Clan Keep.*

"Thank you for coming and teaching us," Rodehan said, holding out his hand. "Goddess bless your journey."

Histrun gripped his wrist. "May She keep your people safe. Until we meet again."

He and Zehala rejoined their pack. Maheli handed them their horse's reins. Norvela nodded to them, then gave the order to mount. She and Tedehan led the three platoons out the gates, and down the road of crushed sheadash stone. The sound of over two hundred horses trotting over the roadway made conversation difficult.

They soon left the keep's fields and pastures and rode through flowering bushes and trees. Birds chirped overhead and squirrels scolded their passing. The warmth of the summer sun relaxed Histrun's sore muscles. But by midday, when they entered a forest, he welcomed the cooling shade. They stopped in a clearing where a small stream fed into a pond. Yellow, purple, and white flowers dotted the surrounding field, and tall cattails bordered one side of the pond.

Histrun eased out of his saddle, groaning at the ache in his knees. He strolled around the clearing, enjoying being off his horse for a while, and the area's beauty. Zehala joined him, slipping a hand into the crook of his elbow. He patted her hand and smiled down at her. The sun sparkled off the ruby in the bond-mate torque at her throat.

"This place is lovely." She sighed heavily. "Can you imagine what our world would be like if we didn't have to constantly fight the Malvers' monsters? I imagine it all the time. My greatest hope is we can destroy the monsters for good by killing them in the nest. I want more for Rizelya and our people than this constant struggle to survive."

"The monster numbers have decreased in our territory where we've used our method the longest. It's working, but it will just take time." He shrugged. "I don't know if it will be in our lifetime. Maybe in Rizelya's."

"Goddess, may it be so!"

Lorstriel whistled and held up a package and canteen, reminding them they needed to eat. They wandered back to the others and ate a meal of a cold meat and cheese sandwiches, washed down with lukewarm taevo. Histrun bit into a crisp apple, savoring its sweetness. Before remounting their horses, the group refilled their water canteens in the stream.

They had ridden less than a measure when Norvela slowed. Fresh monster slime cleaved a wide swath through the trees and brush. The noise of chatter, the clinking of horse bits, and the creak of leather ceased. An unnatural quiet reigned. No birds chirped or fluttered from branch to branch, no squirrels scolded, and no rabbits rustled the underbrush. A crash of a tree broke the silence. The raucous cry of a crow was cut short.

Tedehan signaled to several people, who peeled off from the group and headed into the forest toward the sounds. Histrun sent a team with them. They would circle around to come at the marauding monsters from behind. Half of Tedehan's and Histrun's platoons followed the slime trail on foot, while the remainder stayed where they were. In the forest's tight confines, too many fighters would become tangled. Eidelstrun, Histrun's best tracker, shifted into his wolf form, leading the way. The sun rippled off his dark-blond fur.

The angry squeal of a boar shattered the silence. Several more squeals followed. The fighters broke into a jog toward the noise, stopping at a clearing where a battle already raged between thirty boars, and a janack and its six brechas.

The janack reached over the adult swine's backs to pluck a young one from where they huddled in a circle behind their mothers. An old sow squealed and rammed into the janack, her tusks ripping into a tentacle. The janack flicked her away as it dropped the piglet into its mouth. A brecha loosed its spines into the press of animals, and two sows crumbled to the ground. The brechas pounced on the downed swine, quickly devouring them. It wouldn't take long for the monsters to kill and eat the entire singular of boars.

A glowing helbraught shone across the glade, signaling the arrival of the other team. Zehala whispered directions to Norvela, who relayed them to her people. The men shifted into their warrior forms, waiting for the order to attack.

"Now!" Norvela shouted.

The warriors raced into the clearing as a line of fire zipped behind them, enclosing the battle in a wall of fire. A brecha dashed toward the forest, but slammed into the fire-ring. It screamed as it burst into flames. Another ring of fire fenced in the boars, keeping them out of danger. They squealed in fright and milled inside of it.

Outside the ring, Histrun sat back in his saddle, observing and letting the younger men and women fight. Lestrun and several other warriors paced anxiously next to him. Watching was the most difficult part of training others. They stayed vigilant, ready to stop any monsters that managed to escape.

The Dehanrolos fighters soon destroyed the Malvers' monsters, without Histrun's team needing to chase any escaping beasts. An angry squeal came from the corralled boars. They were still battle-maddened and would attack the Posairs at the first opportunity.

"Clear the northern quadrant," Norvela ordered. "We'll drive them out that direction."

People scurried to move out of the way. A wall of fire blossomed on either side of the indicated path, creating a passageway into the forest. Slowly, the women opened a section of the fire-ring surrounding the boars. The pigs didn't need much urging and ran through the corridor. The fire-ring collapsed behind them until it bordered the clearing. Even after the boars disappeared into the forest, the fighters remained watchful and ready. Finally, a howl rose in the distance, alerting them the boars had passed the watch point. Histrun blew out a breath, relaxing. When the women finally released the fire-ring, they sagged with exhaustion. Several men stayed in their warrior form, keeping guard in case the boars returns, while the rest shifted back into their normal form.

Still fresh from not fighting, Naila, Maheli, and Lorstriel took over the job of burning the monster remains for the exhausted Dehanrolos Reds.

Norvela, Tedehan, and Zehala joined Histrun on the sidelines. Fatigue pinched Norvela's face, but her eyes danced with joy.

"That was exhausting and exhilarating!" Norvela bounced on her toes. The beads on her tiny braids clicking together. "We never would have saved those boars without your fire-ring method."

Tedehan nodded in agreement. "Your method is useful for more than fighting the monsters. I plan to talk to the keep alphas. Before the end of the lunadar, every Red in my territory will be able to form the fire-ring. I'm tired of having my territory destroyed by those monsters. It's time to take back our land."

Histrun clapped Tedehan on the back. "Good for you! It certainly is a good feeling. In Strunland Territory, the billocks and ducorn herds have grown without the monsters constantly hunting them."

When the women finished burning the monster debris, the group returned to their horses and continued on their way.

Several octars later, Tedehan paused on a hill. Below them the forest thinned into the marshy lands of a swamp, with a nest in the center. It writhed with monsters nearly mature and ready to burst out and begin hunting.

"We have to stop them before they leave the nest," Tedehan said.

"Of course we do." Histrun waved them forward. "Well, have at it. You wanted the practice. I'll watch from here."

Zehala glared at him. He crossed his arms over his chest and sat back in his saddle. "What? I'm old and tired."

She snorted and threw him Kylara's reins before loping down the hill with Norvela. This time, though, Zehala stayed on the sidelines and let Norvela take the lead in directing the fight.

When they stopped at the safe house for the night, the Dehanrolos fighters celebrated their success. They hadn't ever destroyed a nest before the monsters caused damage to the surrounding landscape—and without any injuries.

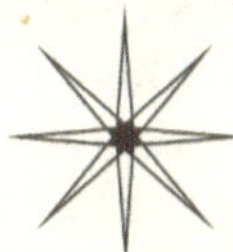

Over the next three days, the fighters fought battles at ten different nest sites, and stopped four more marauding groups. After the third nest, Histrun suspected Norvela and Tedehan were taking a circuitous route in order to get more training, and to finally take the battle to the monsters. He didn't blame them or stop them. He'd have done the same thing.

Besides, it prolonged his dreaded meeting with Mendehan.

"We'll be crossing into Dehanlair Territory tomorrow," Tedehan informed Histrun and Zehala as they ate dinner. "Norvela and I will ride with you to the Clan Keep. The other platoons will stay in Dehanrolos Territory and travel to the other keeps."

"They certainly should be able to teach others the method by now," Histrun grumbled, putting a hand over his mouth to hide his grin. "They've had plenty of experience after the roundabout route you've taken."

"You knew about that?"

"Of course I did."

"And you didn't stop us or say anything?" Norvela shook her head. The beads on the ends of her tiny orange-red braids clicked together with the movement.

"I didn't see the need." Histrun rolled his mug of taevo between his palms. "Your people needed the practice, and we'll arrive at Dehanlair Keep within the specified time frame."

The next morning, Histrun's and Tedehan's platoons left the safe house and headed northwest, while the remaining Dehanrolos fighters turned back the way they'd come. After a few dozen measures, they crossed a bridge over the Tregano River, and Tedehan kept them on the road of crushed sheadash stone. They moved quickly, without stopping at any nest sites.

By midmorning, the trees thinned, and they rode through the cultivated lands of Dehanlair Keep. Histrun frowned at the broken stone fences surrounding the empty outlying fields. Straggly, forlorn plants grew in the fields, and only a few scrawny sheep and cattle grazed in the pastures. The handful of workers looked up at the platoon's passage with tired eyes and shoulders slumped in despair.

Histrun's gut clenched, and he gripped his saddle pommel so hard his hands hurt. "Is it always like this?"

Tedehan's eyes widened. "No. Something must be wrong." He swiveled his head from side to side, taking in the poor conditions. "Why didn't he tell us it was this bad? With the fences in such disrepair, how many people have been lost?"

"If they don't have any other crops or livestock," Norvela said, "they won't be able to survive the winter. The fields look like monster slime has poisoned them. The fighters should have stopped them long before they reached the fields. No one has come out to clean it, either."

"This explains why Mendehan finally requested our help." Histrun flexed his hands and shook his head. "Damn fool. He should have called us in sooner. But why hasn't he asked for reinforcements from his territory keeps?"

"Maybe he's been ill," Zehala said, "or injured."

"We'll soon find out."

Telen snorted and danced in agitation. Histrun pulled him to a stop, twisting in the saddle to take in the entire area. He breathed in deep and gagged. "Monsters!"

"Where? Why isn't the alarm ringing?" Norvela released her helbraught from its holder on her saddle.

Histrun pointed to their left. "There."

A middle-aged man and a woman straightened from the field they tended. Together, they levered an older woman, her face lined and her green hair nearly colorless with age to her feet.

Anger burned in Histrun's throat. "Why in the Crone's Fires is an elder working in the fields?"

"Monsters!" Tedehan yelled at the workers, pointing behind them. "Get out of there and to the keep. Hurry!"

The workers screamed as a janack's tentacle quested over the broken fence. They ran toward the gate, but the old woman tripped and tumbled to the ground. Histrun dug his heels into Telen's flanks. The horse leaped forward, galloping toward the fence. Histrun prayed he'd reach the woman in time. Other fighters thundered behind him. Using a trick from his younger days, Histrun kicked his feet from the stirrups and climbed onto the saddle. Balancing precariously on the galloping horse, he waited until it reached the fence. He leaped off, shifting in midair to his warrior form, grasping for the fence. His claws caught the top of it. He scrambled over and dropped to the ground. Histrun ran to the old woman.

"I twisted my ankle," she cried, as she struggled to stand. "I think it's broken."

A brecha sailed over the fence, tossed by the janack, and it raced toward them. Histrun howled and stood over the woman, bracing for an onslaught of spines. Instead, a wall of flames erupted in front of him. Zehala ran to his side. Her helbraught glowed with orange flames licking the blade. The rushing spines hit the fire-shield, sizzling into ash. With Zehala standing guard over the injured woman, Histrun ran toward the oncoming brecha, flexing his claws to activate his venom.

He swiped across the brecha's flat muzzle and nostrils. It shrieked as green ichor poured from the wounds. It slashed out with its claws, and Histrun jumped back before swiping at it again. His claws caught its side, ripping open a large gash. It stumbled, but reached for Histrun. Its movements grew slower as his venom worked its way through the monsters' system. Histrun easily evaded it, clawing the back of its head, nearly severing its neck. It shuddered as it crashed to the ground. Histrun leaped from its flailing legs.

Claws held ready, he quickly scanned the field. No other monsters had invaded it. He relaxed, crouching to grab some dirt to scrub away the few drops of monster ichor on his warrior pelt before shifting back to his natural form.

The sounds of battle continued behind the fence. He limped to join Zehala, who still stood over the injured woman. Sometime during the fight—or his leap from his horse—he'd tweaked his knee again.

Sweat bathed the old woman's face, and she panted in pain. "She okay?"

"Yes. We need to get her to a healer." Zehala scowled at him as she slapped his shoulder. "What were you thinking? You aren't a young man anymore. You could have been killed!"

He shrugged. "She needed help."

"You could have let one of the younger men play the hero."

"Perhaps." He frowned, looked at the fence, then back at Zehala. "How did you get in so fast?"

"I was smart. I came in through the gate, like a sane person would do."

"Oh," he said sheepishly. "I didn't think I had time to go all the way around. Let's get her to the keep and a healer." He bent down and picked up the woman, grunting with the effort. He staggered after a couple of steps, his leg threatening to give out on him.

"Here, I can take her." Tedehan hurried to Histrun and took the woman from him. Admiration shone in his eyes. "Sweet Mother! Your leap off your horse was something! I haven't ever seen anything like it before."

"I don't recommend it. It's only for emergencies." Histrun limped across the field and to his horse. *What was I thinking?*

Histrun slumped in his saddle, grimacing at the hero worship exhibited by the two platoons of young people as they remounted their horses. He wished they'd quit talking about his incredible maneuver to save the woman. In his day, it had been a common practice. During the battle, the other field workers and herders had run to the safety of the keep. The fighters rode directly to the keep-house, where Mendehan and his co-alpha, Salloreen, waited on the porch.

Mendehan scowled, his thick forehead shadowing his pale-yellow eyes. He rubbed a hand over his extremely short, light-brown hair before re-crossing his arms over his paunch. Red splotches covered his face, a strange black spot marked his neck, and gray tinged his skin. Mendehan barely topped five-and-a-half feet tall, much shorter than most Posair men. Histrun believed Mendehan's short stature gave him an inferiority complex.

Salloreen stood several feet away from her co-alpha. She'd pulled her burgundy hair into a high ponytail, and her gentle brown eyes crinkled with laugh lines. At sixty-five, she was over twenty years Mendehan's junior, and as far as Histrun knew, the two weren't lovers. Based on their posture, they barely tolerated each other.

"What in the Crone's fires are you doing here, Histrun?" Mendehan growled. "I didn't invite you."

"I did," Salloreen said, backing up a step, then straightening her shoulders. "We've lost too many people. We need help."

"No, we don't. I'll deal with you later." He glared at her. His eyes filled with hate and malice.

Salloreen cringed away from him.

Histrun felt off-balance, unsure what his team had stepped into. *What is going on?*

"So, Histrun, still trying to be the big man?" Mendehan ground out. "I heard about your 'heroics.' Only a fool would do such a thing."

"If you'd protect your people like you're supposed to do, I wouldn't have had to." Histrun leaned on the pommel of his saddle. "Where were your sentries? No one was watching for monster attacks. Where were the alarms so your workers had time to return safely?"

Zehala put a placating hand on Histrun's arm. "Now isn't the time, Histrun," she murmured. She pointed to the woman sitting in front of Tedehan. "Where is your healer? This woman needs attending to. I believe she broke her ankle."

The color drained from Salloreen's face. "The healer is on her way. Were there any other people hurt—or killed?"

Zehala shook her head. "No. She's the only one injured."

"The Zehis method works, Alphas," Norvela blurted. "We've seen how effective it is."

"Really?" Salloreen took a step forward. Hope lit her eyes.

Norvela nodded. "Yes, Alpha. We even used it to save a singular of boars from a group of monsters."

"Boars?" Mendehan scoffed. "Filthy beasts."

"They provide meat and are the Goddess's creatures," Salloreen said. "They are just as deserving of life as any other creature." She turned her head from him and mumbled, "Besides, what else are we going to eat?"

Mendehan's fist slammed into Salloreen's cheek, causing her to stumble. "Watch your mouth, bitch!"

Histrun sat back in his saddle, stunned and unable to move. An alpha attacking his co-alpha was unheard of and went against their laws. Only a rogue would commit such a horrific act of hitting a woman in the clan.

Mendehan bared his teeth at Histrun, his fists still clenched, daring him to do something. If Histrun answered the implicit challenge in Mendehan's eyes, Histrun would become the new Clan Alpha—the last thing he wanted to do. He shook his head and turned away.

"I always knew you were a coward," Mendehan snorted. "I want you out of here tomorrow."

After what Histrun had observed already, he wasn't leaving before he found out what Mendehan's problem was, and how to help the Dehanlair people. Histrun narrowed his eyes, glowering at Mendehan, and shook his head. "I can't do that. Did you forget the Supreme's orders?"

Mendehan's head snapped up. He didn't expect Histrun to know of the Supreme's directive. "Then stay. But keep out of my way, Histrun, and we won't have any trouble." Mendehan stomped into the keep-house, slamming the door shut behind him.

Histrun stared at the closed door, trying to make sense of what had happened to Mendehan. Even for him, this was strange behavior.

The healer arrived, and after a quick examination, she gestured to the two strong men who accompanied her. They gently picked up the injured woman and carried her away.

"My apologies." Salloreen bowed, wiping a trickle of blood from the corner of her mouth. "May I start over? Welcome to Dehanlair Keep. Thank you, Histrun, for saving Betsia."

"Zehala helped."

Salloreen inclined her head toward Zehala. "My gratitude to you as well, Zehala. Come. Come in and refresh yourselves and tell me about your journey here. Norvela and Tedehan, after you've shown Histrun's people to the guest quarters, please report to my office. I want to hear about your experiences using the Zehis method."

Chapter 6

Salloreen led them to her office, where a platter of sandwiches and a steaming pot of taevo waited. Histrun gratefully sank into a comfortable chair, took the offered cup, and sipped it. The light streaming through the windows highlighted Salloreen's black eye and the bruise blossoming on her cheek. Other bruises marked her face and arms. Anger ripped through him. He gritted his teeth and carefully set the cup back down. *How dare he? An alpha's duty is to protect his people, not hurt them!* Histrun clamped his hands around the chair arm to keep from rushing from the room and exacting justice on Mendehan by tearing out his throat.

Zehala leaned forward, her eyebrows knitted together. She pointed at Salloreen's black eye. "Did he also do that to you? Does he beat you often?" she asked quietly.

Salloreen covered her face with her hands and nodded.

"What happened?"

She slowly lifted her head, her eyes glistening with unshed tears. "He fell off his horse last year, injuring his back, and he started drinking to ease the pain. It turns out he's a mean drunk. He drinks all the time. This spring, things became even worse. At first he only hit me, but now he beats anyone who displeases him. Mendehan's paranoia reached new heights. He doesn't let anyone leave the keep, which has allowed the Malvers' monsters to run amok. You can't imagine how bad it's here."

Histrun exchanged a look with Zehala.

What in the Crone's fires have we walked into? she asked in mind-speech.

He shrugged. *No matter what it is, we have to help these people.*

Salloreen, oblivious to the exchange, continued, "He's become more belligerent and violent over the past few lunadars. You're our last hope. In fact, I'm surprised you received my message." She stared at her hands in her lap. "We can't lose any more people, any more life, because he's too stubborn to use something you developed." She huffed. "It's stupid."

"Why haven't you let anyone know it was so bad?" Zehala asked.

"And why hasn't someone challenged him, like your second, Lodehan?"

"We've tried!" Salloreen threw her hands up in the air. "He formed the Black Guard, a goon squad, loyal only to him. They stop anyone who tries to leave the keep. After two of my men turned up dead, I stopped sending people out. No one here is strong enough to challenge him. Lodehan certainly isn't. I think Wendehan, the Dehanreen Keep Alpha, or even Rodehan, the Dehanrolos Keep Alpha might win. But they don't know they need to."

"Well, we'll take care of it," Histrun said. "When Norvela and Tedehan return to Dehanrolos Keep, they'll take word with them what has been happening."

"If Mendehan allows them to leave." Salloreen didn't sound hopeful. "If they try leaving without his permission, he'll have his goons kill them."

Histrun's stomach heaved as he slumped in his chair. "A whole platoon? I doubt it."

"You don't know Mendehan's depravity."

A knock on the door interrupted them. Norvela and Tedehan entered, and their talk shifted to discussions on using the Zehis method and stories of how Zehala and Layhalya had discovered making the fire-rings.

Histrun paused on the threshold to the dining hall. *Something feels off,* he said in mind-speech to Zehala.

The hall is strangely empty, but I can't put a finger on why.

Salloreen led them to the front, but chose not to sit at the head table. Histrun didn't blame her for not wanting to share dinner with Mendehan. He didn't want to either. As they waited for the servers, Histrun scanned the room, attempting to discern the problem. The hackles rose on his neck. He bumped Zehala's arm, tilting his head at the armed men stationed around the room in black uniforms—the Black Guard Salloreen had mentioned.

There aren't any fighters in here, Zehala observed. *Our people and Tedehan's are the only fighters eating, if you don't count the Black Guard rogues.*

Histrun's eyes widened. *That's why it's so empty in here. Where are the fighters?* He leaned forward to ask Salloreen, but paused when Mendehan staggered into the room, weaving his way to take the only seat at the head table.

Mendehan banged his metal goblet on the table. "Where's the food?" he slurred. "Bring me food!"

The side door opened, and the serving staff filed into the dining hall, balancing platters of steaming food. Mendehan reached out and snatched the young serving girl walking past by her waist, pulling her to him. She shrieked, spilling the platter she carried onto his lap. Roaring in anger, he pounded her face and body with his fists.

Histrun and Tedehan surged to their feet, their chairs clattering to the floor. But before either one stepped toward Mendehan, six large, brawny men surrounded them. Their hands on their helstrablade handles and menace burning in their eyes.

According to custom, no one carried weapons into the dining room. Histrun's people would be at a disadvantage against these brutes, unless they broke with tradition and fought in their warrior forms. A fight could hurt too many innocent people. Histrun growled at the untenable situation.

Swallowing his pride, he motioned for Tedehan to sit as he fumbled to right his chair. As the poor girl crumbled under Mendehan's blows, Histrun fisted his hands under the table, vowing he *would* end this atrocity. If Mendehan wasn't the Clan Alpha, it would be easy to declare him a rogue wolf. Then Histrun could kill him and be done with it. He couldn't do either to a Clan Alpha. He pinched the bridge of his nose and huffed out a breath. To stop Mendehan's corruption, he might have to issue an alpha challenge. Goddess, he hated the thought!

The next morning, Histrun paced across the floor of his and Zehala's room. Their rank as alphas meant they had one to themselves. Zehala sat on the chair by the desk, her eyes following his motions.

"We have to do something!" Histrun clenched his fist, remembering the cowering girl.

"You heard Salloreen. No one here can challenge him. Do you want to?"

He stopped his pacing for a moment. "No. I'd easily beat the mangy cur, especially in his current condition. But that isn't what this clan needs. They need a strong leader from their own clan, not an outsider like me. We'd have to stay here, and I don't want to."

"Me either." Zehala grimaced.

"We need to get word to Rodehan. From our interactions with him, he'd be a good replacement."

"It will be a risk to whomever we send, if they even make it out of the territory. You saw those goons doing Mendehan's bidding last night." Zehala rubbed her face. "I still can't believe they'd follow his madness. I've never heard of anyone killing people in their own clan before. It's like something has poisoned their spirits."

Histrun shook his head and sank onto the bed. "Neither have I, except for stories about the Great War."

After a soft knock on their door, Tedehan and Norvela slipped into their room.

"We have to do something about Mendehan," Tedehan said as soon as the door closed. "I can't sit by and watch a rogue control this keep. Those are people of my clan that he's hurting!" He took Histrun's place in pacing the small space.

"I know," Histrun agreed. "He needs to be challenged. But I don't want to be your clan alpha."

"No, no." Tedehan made a negation motion with his hands. "We need a Dehanlair warrior as our alpha. I've talked to my people, and tonight a small squad is going to slip from the keep and go to Dehanrolos to bring Rodehan here to make the challenge."

"No one travels after dark!" Zehala's brows furrowed with concern. "There's too much danger of being attacked by narhili beasts or paether."

"They're willing to take the risk," Tedehan said. "It's worth it to put an end to this madman's control."

"Does anyone know what happened to the Reds and warriors?" Zehala asked. "There weren't any at dinner last night."

"I did some asking around," Norvela said from her perch on a clothes chest. "Thankfully, they aren't dead. They're being held prisoner in store rooms below the keep-house. The Black Guard confiscated the women's helbraughts, and Mendehan made sure there wasn't anything they could burn or use their fire magic on. They even replaced the doors with stone. He's ensured the fighter's good behavior by threatening to kill their loved ones and families, going so far as to hold the keeps' children hostage. No one will challenge him. He's already killed one child to prove he's serious."

Histrun surged to his feet. "He's what?"

"How could he do such a thing?" Tears glistened in Zehala's eyes. "How could anyone kill a child?"

Tedehan slumped against the door. "He's depraved and mad. It's the only explanation."

"Send your people out tonight," Histrun said. "In the meantime, we'll make other plans in case they're stopped. As a last resort, I'll challenge the cur to end this."

"We should talk more with Salloreen," Norvela said. "She brought you here to help. We need her input."

Zehala leaned her elbows on the desk. "We do. But she's just as terrorized by Mendehan as everyone else. We came to train the fighters here in our new method, so we can at least show it to her. I doubt Mendehan will deign to appear in the practice arena. Norvela, your people could use more training, anyway." She paused, her hand on her fist and gazing at the ceiling. "I'm going to have our Reds practice using their magic without the aid of helbraughts. We've become too dependent upon them to focus our magic."

Histrun rubbed his hands together. His spirits lifting with something productive to do. "While you train, I'll wander around the keep and do some snooping. Are the children held in the crèche?"

Norvela nodded, frowning. "But there isn't any way to get to them. The crèche is the most heavily protected place in the keep, for good reason. Though this time, it's working against us."

"Guards for the crèche," Histrun said, his forehead creasing. "Guards on the fighters, and guards to block the gates? That's a lot of people. Surely he can't have that many goons following along with his insanity. We have strong fighters. We should have the superior forces."

"Wait a minute." Tedehan stood straight and held up a hand. "We can't fight our own people."

"You just might have to, Tedehan, to free them from this tyranny. We'll attempt to subdue them rather than hurt or kill them. But they probably won't give us the same courtesy. Remember, they've already killed several people."

Tedehan's shoulder's slumped. "Too bad Mendehan doesn't go out fighting the monsters any more. A lot of things can happen during a monster battle."

Histrun snapped his fingers. "That is an idea. I can use our rivalry to shame him into doing his duty. Let me think about the best way to nettle him."

Zehala laughed. "It shouldn't be too hard. As long as I've known you two, he has always resented you, and does everything possible to prove he's better than you."

"Ah, but I want him to fight the monsters, not me." Histrun stretched and rubbed his belly. "It's way past breakfast time, and my stomach's grumbling. Pay attention as we move through the keep. Perhaps we'll discover something useful. We'll reconvene tonight and compare notes."

The others agreed, and together they crossed the strangely empty courtyard to the keep-house.

When they entered the communal dining hall, an odd quiet greeted them. No fighters sat around chatting while they waited for the next monster alarm. No children ran in to beg a snack, and no workers wandered in on their break. In all the other keeps Histrun had ever visited, the dining hall was always a bustling, busy place where people gathered throughout the day. He'd never seen one as empty as this.

The dour kitchen staff brought them bowls of thin gruel and weak taevo. Histrun choked on the lumpy, tasteless stuff. "Do we have any travel bars left?" he whispered to Zehala.

"Yes, in our packs."

"Good. They're better tasting than this slop." He dropped his spoon back into the bowl and pushed it away from him.

Zehala sighed and did the same thing. "Norvela, while you gather our people for training, I'll go ask Salloreen to join us." She and Norvela left the dining hall.

Histrun glared at the bowl of inedible gruel as he put a hand over his stomach. "It's still growling. The first stop on my wanderings is my room to get a travel bar." He pushed away from the table and stood.

"I'd like to accompany you on your inspection," Tedehan said. "We shouldn't all be in the practice arena at the same time. Besides, two sets of eyes may see things one set misses."

"Come along, then."

Histrun's unease grew deeper as they walked the quiet streets. He'd been so enraged over the monster attack in the keeps' field, he hadn't paid much attention yesterday when they'd arrived. Dehanlair Keep was smaller than Strunlair, housing about four thousand people to Strunlair's six thousand or more. However, the size difference didn't explain the strange lack of activity.

Citizens should fill the streets as they went about their business. Normally, vendors would be setting up in the two plazas and doing a brisk trade of their wares, with children romping and laughing through the crowds. But only a few people scurried about, their heads bowed, throwing furtive glances at Histrun and Tedehan as they passed.

On every corner stood a black-clad man watching the light foot traffic. Their hands rested on their helstrablades, their eyes glinted with hardness, and brooding scowls darkened their faces. Danger oozed from them. After last night's events, Histrun decided to defy custom and wore his helstrablade inside the keep. As did Tedehan. The number of Black Guards surprised him. They outnumbered his and Tedehan's platoons.

The men glared at Histrun and Tedehan, but didn't stop them as long as they stayed on the main streets. They turned down the side street leading to the crèche, and a guard stepped in front of them, blocking their way.

"This way is restricted," he said. "Only residents and the Black Guard are allowed on this street."

"The Black Guard?" Histrun raised an eyebrow. "Never heard of them before. What exactly is your purpose?"

The man's scowl deepened. "We make sure the people keep Mendehan's laws."

"What? That's blasphemy!" Histrun shook his head. "The only laws ruling the Posairs are those of the Goddess. The White Priestesses and Clan Alphas work together to ensure people follow those laws—not any 'Black Guard.'"

Few lawbreakers or criminals existed in their society. Most people had enough to do to simply survive the Malvers' monster's continuous onslaught. For a Clan Alpha to make their own laws was unthinkable, and yet, Mendehan was doing it.

"We'll be on our way." Tedehan tugged on Histrun's arm.

"Let me go!" he hissed, jerking his arm free. "This is—" Histrun stopped, bile filling his throat. The guard pointed his drawn helstrablade at him.

"The only reason you're still alive, old man," the guard growled, not lowering his blade, "is because Mendehan wants you for himself. Go on, get out of here." He made a shooing motion.

"Yes, we'll just be on our way." He backed slowly away and crossed to the other side of the street.

"I can't believe he threatened you!" Tedehan exclaimed. "You're an alpha!"

"I didn't think he would," Histrun admitted. He changed course to return to the main courtyard. "We'll have to find another way to check on the children. But first, I want to visit the White Priestesses. I'm now worried they are in trouble, too."

Tedehan's face blanched, and his step faltered. "No... he wouldn't harm a White Priestess!"

"If he's hurt a child, a White Priestess isn't much more of a leap." Histrun quickened his pace. As they neared the main courtyard, the temple bells rang, announcing afternoon services. His heart stuttered when only a group of five old people tottered across the square. Normally, people who could break away from their work streamed toward the Sanctuary.

A Black Guardsman stood next to the temple's doors, glaring as the elders climbed the stairs. Histrun lengthened his stride, not quite running, not knowing what to expect from the Black Guard. He reached the temple a few heartbeats after the elders.

"Go home, old ones," the guard grumbled. "You know you're not supposed to be here."

A woman whose red hair had faded to a pale pink leaned on her cane, her back hunched with age. "Young man, step aside. It is my right to worship when the Goddess calls. Mendehan can't take it away from me."

"Please, Granny," the guard pleaded, "I don't want to hurt you. Go home."

"Now, look here, son." A man stepped forward, his back still straight even though his once-brown hair was so pale as to be nearly colorless. "We're going to attend services."

"Please," the first old woman said, her voice softening, "we don't want to cause trouble. Let us go in. We enjoy hearing the priestesses sing, and at our age, we don't have much to look forward to."

Histrun shook with anger as he climbed the last stair. No one had the right to deny a citizen from attending worship services. He eased around the group of elders to stand in front of them, his hands on his hips—and near his helstrablade.

He exchanged glares with the guard. "I don't know what they've taught you here in Dehanlair Keep, but preventing someone from attending services is against our laws. It is our divine right to commune with the Goddess, and no one," he shook a finger at the young man, and his voice took on a growling tone. "No one can take that away. Step aside, and let these people enter."

"And if I don't?"

"I will go through you." Histrun raked him with his eyes. "How fast can you shift, youngster? Because I can shift and tear out your throat before you blink."

"But... Mendehan—"

"Mendehan, nothing! I'm not afraid of him. Whatever he thinks he can do to me, you'd still be dead. So, what will it be?" Histrun growled, the sound more warrior than man. He lifted a hand, which was now a warrior's paw, his claws glistening with venom. He'd never threatened another Posair before, but this situation was unlike anything he'd experienced in his long life.

The young man gulped, his face losing color. "Sorry, sir," he stammered, as he stepped away from the door. "Please, go right in."

Histrun moved in front of the guard, maintaining his partial shift. With his other hand, he beckoned for the group to enter the temple. After the last person walked through the door, he released the magic and gripped the guard's forearm. He looked him in the eye and lowering his voice. "I don't know what Mendehan has promised you or threatened you with, but you know this is wrong. Grow a backbone, and do what's right. You don't have to be afraid any longer. Help us overthrow him."

The young man lowered his eyes and nodded slightly. Histrun released him, hoping he hadn't made a mistake. He slowly entered the temple.

The dim interior welcomed him after the brightness outside. The familiar scent of kehani flowers and frankincense wrapped around him, easing his mind and soul. He took a deep breath and consciously let go of the altercation with the guard and the issues with Mendehan.

The small group of elders gathered around the central altar, where a White Priestess quietly lit candles and another laid fresh flowers on the altar. Histrun paused as he debated which aspect of the Goddess he needed to connect to the most. The Mother's fierce protectiveness appealed to him as he strove to defend the innocents of this keep. He took a step toward the table dedicated to the Mother aspect filled with unlit votive candles. His gaze swept over the Crone's mural, pausing on the scene of the Crone's judgment fires. *Yes, Mendehan and this keep needs Her purifying fires to erase the evil pervading this place.*

Histrun changed direction and walked instead to the Crone's altar. As he chose a candle from the selection, he glanced up at the Crone's eyes, and remembered Her other aspects: wisdom, patience, and love. He bowed his head at the reminder to temper whatever he did to right the wrongs Mendehan had committed with the same qualities.

He approached the main altar and reverently placed the votive offering on it. Carved in the center was an eight-pointed star, each point inlaid with tiny glass tiles in the color representing one of the eight Talents. The tip of each star-point held a gold symbol for the corresponding Talent. When everyone in attendance placed their offering on the table, the White Priestesses began the ceremony.

Histrun relaxed, letting the sacred words wash over him. His thoughts returned to the Crone's judgment as he contemplated what he could do to stop Mendehan's madness. A plan tickled his mind, but before it could completely coalesce, the ceremony concluded, pulling him out of his meditation. Keeping his eyes closed, he frowned, trying to hold on to the thought, but it trickled away. With a huff, he opened his eyes and found the others had moved from the altar. Only the head priestess and he remained.

"I sense you are troubled." Compassion filled her turquoise-blue eyes. "Are you Histrun de Strunlair?"

"Yes, Priestess, to both. Everything I see in this keep distresses me, but I'm unsure how I can help."

The priestess glanced at the elders still in the temple sanctuary. "Walk with me."

Histrun joined her as she ambled toward the door in the rear of the sanctuary. Her long, silvery-white hair peeked from under her white veil.

"I'm Wylara," she said. "I've been waiting for you. The Goddess showed me our salvation would come from outside our clan."

"What happened to Mendehan? He's always been a stubborn fool, but nothing like this."

She ushered him through the door, down a short corridor, and into a small parlor. A small white couch and two winged-backed chairs surrounded a low table, holding a pot of steaming taevo and two cups. As Wylara settled on the couch, Histrun poured each of them a cup of taevo. He handed her one, then sat on a chair.

"The changes came slowly. First, with his increased drinking, which led to a general decline in keep maintenance. But then he started responding slower to monster attacks, not dispatching the fighters out quickly enough, until he finally stopped sending them altogether."

"So his drinking is the problem?"

"No, it isn't the real cause of the calamity endangering our territory." She placed her cup back on the table and clasped her hands together on her lap. "Did you notice the grayness of his skin? Or the black mark on his neck?"

Histrun nodded. "I thought the drinking caused it."

She pulled her lips into a tight line and shook her head. "One day, nearly six lunadars ago, he disappeared into a swamp after a monster battle. He claims he chased a brecha, but nobody else saw one escape. When he finally returned three days later, he had a black splotch on his neck, although not as big as it is now. Afterward, things changed from bad to worse. He set curfews and claimed all the best the keep had for himself. When people complained, he formed the Black Guard, giving known bullies the power to do whatever they wanted.

"He ordered the fighting-packs to stop leaving the keep to fight the monsters. They, of course, refused. His goons tossed the fighters into the storage level, which they'd converted into a prison. After a janack killed the first field worker, the Browns and Greens rebelled, refusing to work the fields or tend the livestock until they received protection from the monsters. The Black Guard struck at night, seizing all the children and locking them into the crèche."

"I heard he killed a child," Histrun ground out, his hand forming a fist.

She held up three fingers.

"What!" His eyes widened. "He's killed three children?"

"Yes. And one of my priestesses when she tried to stop him. We are effectively imprisoned here in the temple. We're not allowed to leave, or we risk death ourselves. You saw the guard barring our doors?"

"I did. I had to threaten him before he allowed the elders entry."

"They're there to keep us here as much as to dissuade people from coming in. Only the old ones dare to come to services anymore," she said, her voice rough with grief. "He's also killed several other people. He executes anyone caught attempting to escape the keep."

Histrun put his cup back on the table, unable to drink any more taevo. Bile coated his throat from the news. "How could he do such things? When we become Clan Alphas, we swear to protect and defend our people."

"I think whatever happened to Mendehan in that swamp infected him with evil. He hasn't allowed me close to him, perhaps knowing I would sense the evil in him and drive it out."

"If I can get him in here, could you? Could you cleanse him?"

Wylara shrugged. "When it first happened, most likely I could have. But now..." She shrugged again and shook her head. "My spies tell me the blackness covers most of his chest and extends to his mid-back. I fear it is too late for him, and only death and the Crone's cleansing fires can save him now."

Histrun slumped in his chair, unsurprised that the priestess echoed his earlier thoughts. He would have to challenge Mendehan or find some way to kill him that didn't result in Histrun becoming the new Dehanlair Clan Alpha. But how? Again, the beginnings of a plan tingled in his mind but wouldn't fully form.

He cocked his head and examined the priestess. "You seem to hear an awful lot of what goes on around here for someone locked inside these walls."

A slow smile formed on her lips. "I have my ways. The kitchen staff has more freedoms than most. His many prisoners have to eat, after all, and they can't go to the communal dining hall." She quirked an eyebrow at him.

A piece of the plan clinked into place.

"Thank you, Priestess Wylara. I need to get back to my people and stop this madman." He eased out of his chair and knelt in front of the White Priestess. He clasped his hands in prayer over his heart and bowed his head.

"Blessings, my son." She laid her hands on his head.

A moment later, the warm presence of the Goddess washed over him and filled him with determination. His mind cleared.

"Free my people, Histrun."

He swallowed. The priestess's voice had changed and echoed with an otherworldliness. The Goddess had spoken to him!

"I will, Your Grace. I will."

Trembling, he stood, strode from the room, and back into the sanctuary. As he walked to where Tedehan waited by the door for him, ideas swirled through his mind. He'd fulfill his vow to the Goddess and free the Dehanlair people from Mendehan's tyranny and evil.

Chapter 7

Histrun stopped on the temple steps, blinking in the noon sun. The same guard still stood by the doors, his face impassive except for a brief flick of his eyes to his left. Another guard, barely out of his teens, paced nervously in front of the temple.

When he noticed Histrun and Tedehan, he let out a huff of annoyance. "Finally! What took you so long, old man?"

Histrun pulled himself up to his full height, and looked coldly down at the youngster, unused to such disrespect. "I have no need to explain myself to you, whelp. My business with the Goddess is none of yours. What is it you want?"

"Mendehan wants you to join him for the midday meal. Mendehan sent me to escort you there."

Histrun silently swore. He'd wanted to share his plan with Zehala and the others while they ate. And he needed to speak to the kitchen staff.

"Gordehan, let me take him," the first guard said, stepping forward. "I need to stretch my legs and take a necessary break."

"I don't know, Deldehan," the younger guard whined. "Mendehan gave me the order. You know how he is."

"Yeah, I know. I'll take the blame. You stay here and guard the temple."

"It's your skin." Gordehan shrugged, sauntered to the doors, and slouched against them.

"Come on, I'll show you."

"He only wants the old man," the guard called out as they walked down the stairs.

"Got it." Deldehan waved his hand.

They tromped across the courtyard. Deldehan furtively glanced around. "Are you sure you can help us?" he whispered. "Mendehan's turned mean and scarily strong. You're an old man, no disrespect sir, and I doubt if you could take him in a challenge fight."

"I won't be challenging him. Rodehan will."

"But he isn't here—"

"He will be in a few days," Tedehan said. "That is, if you can help my people sneak out of here tonight."

Deldehan's face paled. "If I get caught, he'll kill me."

"Then it's imperative we succeed." Tedehan narrowed his eyes.

"The Black Guard closely watches every exit, and at night, they set a double guard."

Histrun frowned. "Can you arrange to get guard duty at a side exit? Maybe with a friend who is also tired of the way things are around here?"

Deldehan lifted his shoulders slightly. "Possibly. Mendehan will probably punish me with extra guard duty for escorting you rather than Gordehan. I'll be lucky if I don't also get a few lashes."

"He punishes his elite guard, too? And that severely?"

The young man nodded. "No one is exempt. Many in the Black Guard are like me, only in it to protect our families. They're held captive with the others. It binds us to him."

Histrun shook his head.

"I'll send word to you about which exit," Deldehan whispered as they approached the stairs leading to the keep-house. He strode ahead of Histrun, and with a fist, saluted the guard, who barred the door. "Mendehan is expecting him."

The guard smirked. "He sent Gordehan to fetch the old man, not you. You sure have a knack for finding trouble. Haven't you pulled enough night duty yet?"

"I like the dark." Deldehan shrugged. "The night is quiet."

"You'll go too far someday and wind up dead."

"Hopefully not today, my friend." Deldehan pulled open the door. "We're already late. I don't want to get into more trouble."

The guard let Histrun through but blocked Tedehan. "Not you." He slammed the door behind Histrun.

Deldehan led the way up the stairs and down the long hall, stopping at a closed door. He straightened his tunic and smoothed his trousers before knocking on the door. They waited several milcrons until they heard a growled, "Enter." Deldehan opened the door and ushered Histrun inside.

Histrun halted mid-step, gaping at the scene in front of him. A young girl—no older than ten—sat on Mendehan's lap. He held a fistful of her hair in one hand, pulling her head back and suckling her exposed neck. His other hand fondled her, where no man should be touching her at her tender age. Terror glazed the girl's eyes.

Histrun's face flushed hot, his forehead furrowed, and he dropped into a slight crouch, flexing his hands, attempting to keep them from shifting. He'd never wanted to rip out someone's throat as badly as he did Mendehan's at that moment. Deldehan's hand flew up to over his mouth and his eyes widened with horror. Then they narrowed, and he emitted a low, angry growl. They couldn't attack Mendehan, but Histrun could put a stop to this atrocity.

He breathed deeply several times to regain control of himself. When his hands were back to normal, he stalked across the room and pulled the little girl out of Mendehan's grasp.

He handed her to Deldehan. "Take her and get out," he growled, "while I deal with this caitiff scum."

Deldehan nodded, gently holding the terrified girl.

Histrun turned his full attention to the creature in front of him. As soon as the door closed, he leaped across the few feet that separated them and wrapped his hands around Mendehan's throat, throwing him against the wall.

"Tell me why I shouldn't kill you, right now, right here?" He ground out.

"You can't kill me. I'm the Clan Alpha."

"You are a sick bastard, no better than a rogue. I would be within my rights after this." He squeezed a bit harder, enjoying the sight of Mendehan's eyes widen in fright. Then he remembered why he couldn't kill the man like this. He didn't want to become the Clan Alpha of Dehanlair. "Argh!" he yelled, slamming his fist into the wall.

Mendehan rubbed his throat and sneered. "You're as weak as ever, Histrun."

A stench wafted from Mendehan, making Histrun's eyes water. He stared at the black splotch on Mendehan's neck and chest. The smell seemed to come from it. The stink turned his stomach, and he stepped back to lean against the door, unwilling to sit in case he needed to move quickly.

"You really are sick. Why don't you let the White Priestess heal you?"

"That fake? Never!" Mendehan crossed his arms over his chest and glared at Histrun. "Besides, I'm not sick. I'm finally in my right mind."

"What happened to you, Mendehan? You used to respect your obligations and responsibilities. You honored our traditions. The Mendehan I knew would never think about abusing an innocent child like that or beating a young serving girl. He'd be the first one to condemn those types of actions."

"My eyes have opened!" Mendehan flopped down onto his chair. "I've finally seen the light and refuse to be subservient to that bitch Goddess. Unlike you, I'm no longer afraid to hide who I truly am because of her silly rules and traditions. *I* make the rules now. I can finally do whatever I want, to whomever I want, whenever I want."

"You sound like a spoiled child. Or worse, a rogue wolf." Histrun stared at his hand, allowing it to shift. Glaring at Mendehan, Histrun pointedly flexed his claws. "You do remember what we do to rogue wolves, don't you? We put them down."

"But you won't. You can't. You'd have to leave your precious Strunlair Province. I can't see you doing that. And you can't simply kill me, claiming I'm a rogue wolf."

Histrun raised his eyebrows. "After what I just witnessed? Sure I can, right now, and be fully within my rights. But you're right. I won't challenge you for the Clan Alpha position. I don't want it."

"Why? Isn't it good enough for you?"

Histrun let go of his magic, allowing his hand returning to normal. He dearly wished to kill the man without waiting, but Histrun's and Tedehan's people were outnumbered. They needed to neutralize the Black Guard and free the fighting-packs. He wondered how they could accomplish that when another piece of the plan fell into place.

Histrun shrugged, then smirked. "You're getting fat and lazy, Mendehan. Malvers' monsters overrun your land. What? Are you too old to fight anymore? I've killed twenty—in your province. The latest one right on your own keep's grounds. How many have you killed lately? One? None?" He shook his head, clicking his teeth in derision.

"I'm better than you!" Mendehan roared.

"Prove it."

"All right, I will. Tomorrow we'll hunt monsters, and I'll kill more of them than you."

"Tomorrow it is." Histrun saluted and left the room, hiding his smile of satisfaction. His grin faltered at the enormity of the project in front of him. They had to free the fighters. Afterward, Mendehan would receive the death he deserved for his crimes against his people.

Histrun hurried from the keep-house to the communal dining room, hoping Zehala and the others would still be there. After what he'd witnessed, Dehanlair Keep needed rescuing and put back into order, immediately. The first thing they'd do was ensure Mendehan couldn't molest anymore little girls. He paused at the dining hall's entrance, surveying the room. A small group of workers sat with their heads bent over their food, talking in hushed tones. His people and the fighters from Dehanrolos filled several tables, attempting to ignore the loud, boisterous group who all wore the distinctive Black Guard uniforms.

He spotted Zehala's wavy, dark-auburn hair in the crowd and strode over to her. He paused a moment to massage her neck. She glanced up, her eyes widening. She opened her mouth, but he stopped her with a slight shake of his head. Too many Black Guards occupied the space for them to talk openly.

You look like you're ready to tear someone's head off, Zehala said in mind-speech.

I am. We can't wait for Rodehan to get here. We have to move against Mendehan soon. I'll tell you, and everyone, when we don't have an audience. He indicated the watching Black Guards as he sat in the empty seat next to her.

She reached under the table and squeezed his hand. "I heard you attended services. I wish I could have gone with you."

"The priestesses gave a good ceremony." He returned the gentle pressure. "Did you have a nice practice?"

"Yes, we did." She sipped her taevo. "We can, of course, use our magic without our helbraughts. The other Talents do it all the time. But we have fallen into the habit of relying too much on them to focus our magic. It was good practice to go back to the basics."

"I hadn't thought about those exercises in a long time," Naila admitted, putting down her fork. "Once I started fighting, I've rarely used my magic without my helbraught. I think it would be a good idea to require all the Reds to continue with the basics in our normal training."

"I agree," Norvela said. "When I return to Dehanrolos, I'm going to suggest we do the same thing. We don't want to become so dependent on them that if something happened to them, we can't access our magic. We're almost at that point now." She flicked her eyes to the tables holding Black Guards, and she lowered her voice. "Look at what befell the Reds here."

Those close by nodded in agreement.

A server brought a bowl of soup and a slab of brown bread and placed the fare in front of Histrun. As he glanced up, nodding his thanks, he remembered Priestess Wylara's comment about the kitchen staff.

The soup was mostly broth, with only small bits of vegetables and no meat. The bread was tough and chewy. After seeing the conditions of the keep that morning, Histrun appreciated that the people even had this much to eat. As he ate the thin soup, he thought about dinner the night before. The only plates filled were those sitting at the table with Mendehan—and the Black Guard. Everyone else's plates held very little. Shame warmed his face for complaining about the breakfast gruel. If his plans worked, the Dehanlair clansmen would eat decently again.

Soon, only Histrun's people and the Black Guards remained. They'd positioned themselves to watch Histrun's table. He grimaced. It seemed he had a surveillance team. He picked up a pot to pour himself some more taevo and found it empty. Sliding out of his seat, he headed toward the kitchen. One of the guards stood as if to accompany him. Histrun held up the pot. "It's empty." The guard rolled his eyes and sat back down.

Histrun sauntered into the kitchen. He hadn't taken more than a couple of steps inside when a large woman with pine-green hair and brown eyes stopped him. An air of authority wrapped around her.

"Alpha, we would have brought you a new pot. You didn't need to come in here." She reached for it.

"Lady," he said in a lowered voice as he handed it to her, "I need more than taevo." At the woman's raised eyebrows, he hurried to add, "I need your help. Priestess Wylara mentioned your staff has the freedom to go everywhere in the keep."

"Aye, we do."

"Are you ready to stop Mendehan's madness?" He held his breath, hoping he hadn't made a mistake.

She tilted her head, considering him. "Aye, we are. What are you suggesting, Alpha?"

"Histrun, please. And you are?"

"Helvia, the head cook." She handed the pot to a staff member and led him to a desk in the corner, where they sat in relative privacy. "Tell me what you need us to do."

"Do you have an herbal mixture that will put people to sleep?"

"Of course I do. The children needed something to relax them. Mendehan's goons won't allow the healers into the crèche, so they created an herbal tea for us to give the little ones." A corner of her mouth lifted. "But for your purposes, you'd need something stronger to knock out the blasted guards."

Histrun nodded.

"I can ask the healers to wrap a sleep spell on the taevo strong enough to knock out even the burliest man for several hours. When do you need it, and which guards are you targeting?"

"Tomorrow. I have a plan to get some of them out of the keep, so it shouldn't be too difficult."

Helvia snorted. "Things are never easy. I'll plan on serving all of them. What time tomorrow?"

"An octar after Mendehan and I leave the keep."

"We'll be ready." She stood and motioned to a young woman, who hurried over and handed Histrun a fresh pot of taevo.

He took it and returned to the dining hall. A guard scowled at him, but didn't bother to move from where he slouched at his table. Histrun slid back into his seat and poured taevo into his and Zehala's cups.

Zehala leaned against him. "You have a plan."

I'll tell you later, he said in mind-speech, tipping his head toward the guards. Out loud, he said, "Did Salloreen join you in your practice?"

"Yes. She's quite impressed with our method and can't wait to share it with her fighting-packs. That is, if Mendehan would release them to do their jobs." Zehala's mouth pursed in disapproval.

"Since we can't teach them, why don't we adjourn to the keep-house's recreation room and relax?" Histrun made a show of stretching and yawning. "I could use the rest after our long journey."

Zehala rolled her eyes at him as she stood. Norvela and Tedehan's faced scrunched in confusion. Zehala surreptitiously indicated the guards. Norvela raised an eyebrow and elbowed Tedehan.

"How about a game of keshe?" Norvela asked in an innocent voice as she vacated her seat. "I'll invite Salloreen. I'm sure she could use an afternoon to relax, too."

Histrun and Zehala left the dining hall, their people trailing along behind them. As they walked through the doors, the Black Guards followed them. He'd have to find a way to stop them from eavesdropping while he explained his plan to the others.

Inside the recreation room, Histrun and Tedehan chose a table in the back corner. Tedehan opened a cupboard and took out a keshe board and pieces. While he set it up, the room slowly filled with their people. A few groups also pulled out keshe boards, while others found cards to play. On the far side, a group of younger people started a jelehan game. Histrun smiled. The sticks would cause plenty of noise as the players threw them around the circle and people encouraged the players.

When Zehala entered with Norvela and Salloreen, he motioned for them to join him and Tedehan. Unsurprisingly, the same guards took up positions near the door and stared at Histrun. The jelehan game would drown out most of their discussion, but he needed something to distract them. As the three women settled into chairs at the table and chose their keshe game pieces, his youngest pack member caught his attention. He'd watched Maheli start arguments—debates, she called them—with Lestrun and Lorstriel that lasted hours and usually involved raised voices and wild gestures.

Maheli, Histrun called in mind-speech. *I need a loud, boisterous distraction. Can you do that?*

Yes, sir! Maheli grinned. A few moments later, a debate about the merits of multiple partners raged. Soon, a large crowd gathered around Maheli, joining in the discussion. Histrun smirked at Maheli's topic choice as the guards leaned forward, mouths open, no longer observing Histrun. Sex always caught men's attention. Maheli further impressed him, adroitly guiding the crowd to stand between the doors and Histrun's table. He'd have to remember to praise her later.

While playing keshe, he filled in Zehala, Naila, Norvela, and Tedehan in on what he'd learned from Wylara and Helvia. When he told them about the young girl, Zehala's face contorted with fury.

"Did you know he was molesting children?" Zehala hissed at Salloreen.

The color drained from Salloreen's face, and she vehemently shook her head. "No. I swear I didn't know! He and I aren't lovers. We never have been. The last lunadar, I suspected he was doing something worse than the beatings and killings. But what could I do? By then he'd formed the Black Guard and imprisoned the fighting-packs. Even if I had proof, I didn't have any way to stop him."

Zehala turned on Histrun. "Why didn't you kill the caitiff?"

"We can't yet." Histrun reached across the game board and grasped her hand tightly. "He'll be punished, I promise. And soon. We need to get the children to safety first and rescue the fighting-packs. That's what I want your people to do, Norvela, while we're out battling the Malvers' monsters. The healers and kitchen staff will help." He told them about the plan to slip a sleeping potion to the guards.

Salloreen scrunched her eyebrows. "How will you convince Mendehan and his guards to leave the keep and fight monsters with you?"

"Mendehan demanded we go monster hunting together tomorrow morning."

"He hasn't fought for years!" Salloreen gaped. "He hasn't let anyone fight for the last three lunadars. How did you manage that?"

"I challenged his manhood." Histrun smirked. "He's always claimed he was the better warrior than me. This is his chance to prove it."

"Or kill you." Zehala glared at him. "Did you think of that?"

"Yes, dear, I did. I don't plan on allowing him to do that. I have something he doesn't. You. I trust you and Naila to keep me safe. If we're lucky, a monster will kill him during the battle, and no one will have to challenge him. Especially not me."

Salloreen moved her keshe piece to capture three of Histrun's. "Even so, someone strong needs to take command of the clan until the next Alpha Competitions. I can't run it by myself. No one in this keep has the necessary strength. Besides, after what we've gone through, it would be best if it was someone outside this keep. My first choice is Rodehan or Wendehan."

"I have a team ready to leave tonight." Norvela frowned at the board. She captured Tedehan's major piece. "We're keeping it small, just two men in wolf form. They'll be faster and more nimble on four paws. They'll bring Rodehan here."

Salloreen removed Tedehan's last piece from the board. "It would be safer to send another team to Dehanreen Keep, as well, to ensure at least one team makes it through."

"Do we know if that Black Guard, Deldehan, is going to help us?" Tedehan slumped in his chair, out of the game. "He seemed ready to grow a backbone."

"We'll find out tonight." Histrun took his turn, moving a key piece in danger of being captured by Zehala. "I saw his face when we caught Mendehan molesting that little girl. He was furious. It's clear he didn't know it was happening before. I suspect he'll spread the word to those guards who are working for Mendehan to protect their families, and not because they're bullies."

"There are many like that." Salloreen made a move, taking five of Histrun's pieces. "At least, I hope there are, and Mendehan's madness hasn't infected them all."

"We can only hope." Zehala moved her piece, and Histrun lost another three of his pieces, including the one he thought he'd saved.

He'd be out of the game in a few moves if he didn't pay more attention. Plans laid, they could only wait until later that night, when they found out if Deldehan was on their side or not.

Chapter 8

At dinner, Histrun sat at the high table next to Mendehan. His stomach clenched at being so close to the sick miscreant. The stench coming off Mendehan was even worse than it'd been earlier. It interfered with Histrun's appetite, and he swirled his fork through his mashed tubers rather than eating them. His mind went over the plan for getting the teams out of the keep again. If they failed, he could end up the Clan Alpha. He sighed in disgust at the thought. He wanted a more active leadership role, but in Strunland Keep, not this place far from home.

While he pretended to eat, he studied the Black Guards stationed around the dining hall, as well as those eating. He easily spotted the bullies, who were belligerent and antagonized the kitchen staff. Unlike the previous night, all the servers were male. Histrun didn't blame the women for refusing to serve the ill-behaved men, especially after Mendehan beat the young girl. The guards standing along the wall wore stony expressions and helstrablades at their sides.

He caught a whiff of the awful smell of Mendehan's sickness. His gaze slid across Mendehan's chosen compatriots, sitting at the high table. Did they have black marks as well?

The man two seats away from Mendehan lifted his flagon of wine to his lips, his shirtsleeve sliding up to reveal a black spot on his forearm. Another man farther down stretched. His shirt rose, showing a large black mark covering his stomach. *Is this an illness? Even if it is, it isn't an excuse for their crimes. But what is causing it? Is it contagious?* His fork clattered onto the table at the thought. His appetite gone, Histrun sat back and surveyed the room. Here and there, black splotches peeked from collars or shirtsleeves. Every single one of Mendehan's henchmen wore a black mark somewhere on their skin.

A young man weaved around the tables, carrying a platter of dirty dishes. A goon reached out and knocked the platter out of his hands. The men with black splotches roared with laughter; however, a few Black Guards tightened their jaws and clenched their fists. They all lacked black marks and wore thin blue bands around their right wrists.

He scanned the dining hall again, searching for Deldehan. Histrun hoped his absence didn't bode ill for their plans. A server, also wearing a blue wristband, refilled Histrun's taevo, bumping Histrun's arm in the process. When Histrun reached for the cup, a small square of paper laid next to it that hadn't been there before. He palmed it, tucking it into his waistband.

Mendehan's burst of loud laughter filled the hall. Another server stumbled, sending the drinking flagon he carried flying as he sprawled face down on the floor. The flagon crashed, flinging wine in all directions. A red-faced goon jumped to his feet, bellowing in fury, and kicked the hapless young man's side. Eidelstrun tackled the guard before his foot landed again. The goon swung a fist at Eidelstrun, but the bigger man easily sidestepped the oncoming punch. He slammed his fist into the other man's jaw. People at nearby tables quickly vacated their seats. The guard threw a front kick, which Eidelstrun blocked. His fist snaked out, striking the man on the bridge of his nose. The man's eyes watered.

"Oh, ho! A fight!" Mendehan chortled. He turned to Histrun. "Want to bet who wins? My fighter against yours?"

Histrun rolled his eyes.

"If my fighter wins," Mendehan continued, "you and your people leave here tomorrow morning and don't come back."

"And if Eidelstrun wins?"

"Why then, I won't have him killed for interfering. The slave had it coming for his incompetence."

"Your man tripped him. Eidelstrun is doing what we teach every warrior—to protect the innocent."

"Innocent, ha! We're superior. They exist only to serve us. Get him, Meldehan! So, is it a bet?"

"I have no doubt Eidelstrun will win."

As the fighters exchanged blows, Eidelstrun's greater experience in fighting monsters became apparent. Histrun doubted the other man had ever fought more than sparring matches or brawls. He folded his arms over his chest, affecting unconcern.

"Slave?" Zehala hissed, leaning against him and clenching his arm. "Did he call the server a slave? The kitchen staff aren't slaves."

"He did," Histrun whispered back. "And no, they aren't."

"We have to stop this monster."

"We will, dear." He patted her hand. While Mendehan avidly watched the fight, Histrun pulled out the note and surreptitiously opened it. "Good news. Our friend is going to help us." He tucked the paper back into his waistband.

Eidelstrun threw a punch into Meldehan's sternum. As the guard bent over, gasping for breath, Eidelstrun grabbed the man's head, and smashed his face into Eidelstrun's knee. A crunch echoed, and blood poured from the man's broken nose. Meldehan crumpled to the floor, not moving.

"Damn!" Mendehan swore. "Your man won. I guess I can't kill him, since we had a bet. I can wait. When you're dead tomorrow, I will execute him and everyone else in your party." He gave Histrun an evil grin.

"Why wait? Why not now?" Histrun's face burned with fury. His hand balled into a fist under the table.

"The monster battle competition, of course. It's time we had it out and proved who is the better warrior—and man." Mendehan leaned forward to leer at Zehala. "Maybe I'll show your bond-mate what a real man is like before I have her torn into pieces."

Zehala's leg muscles bunched against his as she sputtered expletives. Several Black Guards reached for their helstrablades, their eyes hard. Histrun quickly clamped his hand around her thigh, keeping her in her seat. *Not now.* He flicked his eyes at the guards. Under his hand, her thigh shook with suppressed anger. She jerked, and he loosened his grip as he struggled to keep himself from punching the man.

"Have a care, Mendehan," Histrun said through clenched teeth. "Your time is coming to an end, and you'll have to face the Crone's fires. You'll burn for an exceedingly long time for all you've done and ordered to be done. I can't wait to send you to meet Her." Histrun pushed to his feet, pulling Zehala up with him. "Until tomorrow."

"But you'll miss tonight's entertainment," Mendehan pouted.

"The entertainment is over." Histrun motioned to his people. They all stood at once and quietly escorted the serving staff and everyone who was not a Black Guard from the dining hall. Histrun waited until the room cleared of all the innocents, then stiffly marched out.

When they reached the courtyard, Zehala released her pent-up fury. "I can't believe that caitiff! How dare he threaten me to rape me? If he comes near me, I'll slit his throat." Sparks flew from her fingertips and formed a small ball of fire a few feet in front of her.

Histrun stared at it. In all the years he'd known Zehala, she hadn't ever lost control of her fire magic like that.

"Damn!" Zehala shook her hands and walked in a circle, taking deep breaths as she tried to regain control of her emotions.

"It won't come to that," Histrun said, gently gripping her arm and guiding her around the courtyard. The two men tailing them had stepped back and now gave them a wide berth. There was a good reason people avoided upsetting Reds. They were taught from a young age to control their tempers because they could hurt others if they lost control of their fire magic. After a few milcrons, he grinned at her. He suspected Zehala wasn't nearly as out of control as she'd let on. Her outburst was giving them the perfect cover for wandering the streets after dark.

They left the courtyard and strolled toward the pack house they were staying in. When they passed a side-street, Lestrun and Eidelstrun nodded to them from the darkened doorway of a pack-house. A few moments later, a scuffle sounded behind them. Histrun looked over his shoulder and chuckled as the two guards following him slid to the ground.

The door opened, and a yellow-haired woman leaned out and waved at Eidelstrun. "Hurry, bring them in here," she whispered. "We'll hide them."

As Eidelstrun and Lestrun dragged the men into the house, another woman slipped out and approached Histrun and Zehala.

"I'll show you to the gate," she said. "Deldehan is waiting for you."

"What about Norvela and her teams?" Zehala asked.

"Someone else is guiding them to the appropriate gates."

Histrun raised his eyebrows. "Gates?"

"Yes, gates. This way, they have a better chance of getting out. Hurry, we don't have much time." The woman took off at a jog toward the keep walls.

Histrun's gaze darted from side to side as he and Zehala followed the woman. They reached the small gate on the eastern wall without seeing anyone.

"Where are all the guards?" he asked.

"All those on duty are with us," Deldehan said, holding up his right hand, showing them his blue wristband. "After what I witnessed today, and after your prodding, we've decided we can't continue to turn a blind eye to what's going on around here. It's time to fight back. If someone doesn't have a blue wristband, don't trust them. Some of our people are still too frightened of Mendehan to go against him."

"Noted."

Norvela stood off to the side, talking quietly to three young, strong men. Histrun recognized two as from her platoon. "Who is that?" He indicated the third man with his chin.

"Nevdehan," Deldehan said. "He will guide the others through the territory. This team's destination is Dehanrolos, while the other group will go to Dehanreen Keep. They're leaving from the north gate. I'd go, but after today, Mendehan would notice me missing."

Histrun and Zehala joined Norvela and the brave men taking on the dangerous mission.

"Run swiftly," he said, gripping each one's shoulder. "You know how important this is."

The men nodded.

"Go with the Goddess and may She keep you safe." Zehala brushed a kiss of blessing on each man's cheek.

They shifted into their wolf forms. Deldehan eased opened the gate, and the men slipped out, disappearing into the night with a flick of their tails. He quickly shut it again.

"Is everything set for tomorrow?" Histrun asked.

"Yes. We'll be ready. By then, we should have more people with us, and will outnumber the Black Guard rogues."

Histrun patted Deldehan's shoulder. "Until tomorrow. Stay safe." He and Zehala hurried back to the keep-house, hoping to return before Mendehan could miss them.

The guard at the keep-house door saluted them as they slipped in, his blue wristband peeking from under his sleeve. Histrun blew out a breath of air, relieved his plans were falling into place. But as he readied for bed, a sense of foreboding hounded him. He was determined only one man would return from the monster battle alive, but would it be him? He believed the Goddess was on his side and wanted him to enact justice for all the wrongs Mendehan had committed. But would it be enough to overcome whatever evil was infecting Mendehan?

Histrun made love to Zehala passionately, almost desperately, as if it were their last night together. He held her tightly, wanting to infuse his essence into her soul so she would remember him. Just in case he was wrong, and it wasn't him who walked off the battlefield.

Histrun's nerves jangled as he dressed. He held a hand over his gurgling belly, frowning at the unusual sensation. This monster battle would be different from any other he'd fought in his long life. After they killed the janacks and brechas, Histrun would deal with another monster.

During his time as Alpha, first for Strunland and then as the Strunlair Clan Alpha, he'd put down a dozen or so rogues. Usually, the Alpha Competition tests weeded out those with any such tendencies.

"In all my years, I've never seen anyone who abused their power like Mendehan has." Histrun paced, clenching and unclenching his fists. "I would never guess Mendehan would flaunt our laws so blatantly."

Zehala paused in lacing her boots. "I agree. He's always been a stickler for tradition. I wonder what happened to him?"

Histrun shrugged. "The White Priestess believes it's some sort of illness. We can't wait for the others to arrive." He swung his arms back and forth across his chest. When that didn't help release his trepidation, he shook out his hands. The trouble he'd witnessed, and Mendehan's open threats last night, meant they had to remove him immediately. As much as Histrun would like to turn the responsibility for exacting justice to someone in the Dehanlair Clan, he knew they didn't have time.

It was up to him to stop Mendehan. He skirted the laws by not officially challenging Mendehan. This way he wouldn't end up as Dehanlair's Clan Alpha.

Zehala stood, moving into his path. She took his hands in hers. "Easy, love. Don't get yourself so worked up that you second-guess yourself. This has to be done, and you're the only one available to do it."

He gathered her in his arms and held her close, breathing in her scent. His nerves immediately calmed. "What would I do without you? You keep me sane. Be careful today."

"You too. I don't trust Mendehan. I'm afraid he'll attempt something underhanded."

"I expect him to try. But I trust you and our people to watch my back. You're my secret weapon. You care about me. Mendehan has lost that. His goons will be out for themselves."

"Be extra wary, my love, and return to me." Zehala raised onto her toes and kissed him.

He placed his hands on either side of her face and discovered moisture on her cheeks. He deepened the kiss. The foreboding he experienced the night before slammed into him, weakening his knees. *Please Goddess, let me return to her. Help me defeat Mendehan.*

Histrun finally pulled away. "Goddess, how I love you."

"And I you. Come back to me, my love."

Hand-in-hand, they exited the keep-house and walked to the dining hall. The full room quieted when they entered. Both his and Tedehan's platoons stood and bowed to him. The dozen or so Dehanlair field workers still eating tipped their heads. One furtively lifted his sleeve, showing Histrun his blue wristband. The worker nodded meaningfully at the others sitting with him. A flush of pleasure washed over Histrun. Many people here were willing to stand up for their rights, once they had a leader. On the other side of the room, the Black Guards glared at him.

As soon as he sat at the table next to Naila and Leistral, Helvia, the head cook, brought out a tray of food and served him.

"All is ready," she whispered, leaning forward to place a bowl of thick porridge in front of him. She'd artfully arranged several slices of juicy pears on top of it.

"Thank you." He gripped her forearm. His stomach clenched as his nerves assailed him again, but he forced himself to eat the cereal. He'd need all of his strength for the fight to come. An alarm clanged. The scouts had sighted a band of monsters. Histrun shoveled the last bite of porridge into his mouth. Benches scraped across the stone floor as the fighters pushed to their feet and hurried from the dining hall.

"It sounds like a big nest." Norvela brushed back her braids, striding next to Histrun. "Are you sure you don't want us to go with you?"

Histrun shook his head. "We'll be fine. Your job is too important. Get the children out of the crèche and into the temple. Release the fighting-packs. They can help you subdue any Black Guards left in the keep. Mendehan won't take them all with him."

"Yes, sir."

Tedehan saluted him. "Stay safe, sir."

"You too." Histrun returned the salute.

Chaos filled the courtyard with the horses being led from the stables, allowing Norvela's platoon to quietly ease away. The horse-master handed Telen's reins to Histrun. The already saddled horse danced in place and reared, sensing Histrun's nerves.

"Easy, boy!" Histrun ran his hand over Telen's neck, soothing his horse. Once Telen had calmed, Histrun checked the saddle girth and other buckles. He doubted the horse-master would do anything to harm a horse, but it didn't hurt to double-check the fit. Zehala made the same checks to Kylara's saddle. Soon their fighting-pack gathered nearby, standing by their horses' heads, ready to mount. Histrun surveyed the courtyard. Besides his thirty-five fighting-pack members, another forty men—all dressed in black—stood waiting for Mendehan. Histrun's eyebrows furrowed.

"What is he thinking?" He murmured to Zehala. "Where are their Reds?" Even before the fighting method he and Zehala had developed that used the Red's Talents more effectively, the Reds had always been an integral part of battling the monsters.

Zehala raised on her tiptoes to look around the gathered people. Her eyebrows lifted in surprise. As she settled back down, dread crossed her face. "How can they expect to destroy the monsters without any Reds? I don't like this, Histrun. Salloreen sent a message that this is a huge nest—six janacks and at least thirty brechas. Our eight Reds will be hard-pressed to contain all the monsters and protect you."

"Just do your best," Histrun said, patting her shoulder. His hand trembled slightly. *Did I make a mistake in challenging Mendehan to a monster battle?* He'd expected the nest would be normal sized, with only one or two janacks. But with six—six!—he and the warriors would be busy killing the monsters and trying to stay alive. He doubted he'd have the opportunity to also fight Mendehan. His plans depended on Mendehan not returning from this battle alive. Perhaps he should reconsider and have Norvela and Tedehan join them. He shook his head. They needed them here to free the children and rescue the fighters. The seventy-five people in the courtyard should be enough to tackle the monsters.

They continued to wait for Mendehan to show up to lead the group to the fight. Histrun fidgeted, alternating between slapping the end of Telen's reins in his hands and pacing in a tight circle. If they didn't depart soon, the monsters would leave the nest, making it more difficult to contain and fight them. Mendehan finally sashayed from the keep-house to his horse and stepped into the saddle.

"Well, what are you waiting for?" he said. "Let's go kill some monsters!" He jabbed his heels into his horse's side and struck its flanks with a whip. The horse reared slightly before leaping into a gallop. The fighters scrambled onto their horses to follow him, while the guards scurried to throw open the gate before Mendehan barreled into it.

Chapter 9

Histrun swore under his breath as he climbed into the saddle and urged Telen into a gallop. If Mendehan intended to throw Histrun off-balance, he'd misplaced his efforts. This only made Histrun even more determined to put down the rogue.

In an effort to reach the nest site in time, they rode to the swamp's edge. Normally, they'd leave the horses a measure or more from the fight. Histrun swore again as he leaped off his horse, condemning Mendehan to burn an eternity in the Crone's fires for waiting so long to leave the keep. The nest lay empty, and the monsters trundled away in different directions.

"That Crone-cursed imbecile! Maheli, Andriel, Dorstrun, you're in charge of keeping the horses safe. I'm not allowing Telen and Kylara to be monster bait."

The young people shouted, "Yes, sir!" and quickly gathered as many reins as possible. They drew the horses toward a thicket of trees that would provide some protection from the monsters. The Strunlair horses they hadn't grabbed followed them, but the others milled in confusion, with the whites of their eyes showing and nostrils flaring. Maheli and Andriel worked to build a fire-ring around them while Dorstrun herded the Dehanlair horses toward the center, with mixed success. One horse—Histrun thought it was Mendehan's—squealed in terror and bolted. A long tentacle snatched it and dragged it to the janack's waiting maw. The last horse entered the make-shift corral, and Maheli closed the fire-ring behind it.

Zehala, Naila, and the remaining Reds raced around the marshy glade, attempting to surround the monsters. A wall of fire burst into existence in Naila's direction Naila, stopping a janack and six brechas from escaping. Eidelstrun and five other warriors ran to attack them, while Lestrun led a second group of seven warriors toward Lorstriel. Her fire blocked another janack and its attendant brechas from leaving.

On the nest site's far east side, Kehali finished forming her portion of the fire-ring to complete the circle. Alixstrun and his team slammed into the now milling monsters with flashing claws. Chestrun and his squad-pack fought the janack and brechas blocked by Zehala's section of the fire-ring.

"The big one is mine!" Mendehan cried, pointing toward the largest of the two remaining janacks. "You can have the little one. Ha, ha, ha, I win."

Histrun shook his head. The challenge meant nothing to him. He'd only used it to push Mendehan to leave the keep's safety and give him an opportunity to deal with him—without becoming the new clan alpha. He boiled into his warrior form and loped to meet the janack. Once he destroyed it, he'd deal with Mendehan. He needed to kill this janack quickly.

He jumped on a tentacle with a roar, slicing through it with his claws. Another slash sent a chunk of tentacle flying. A few milcrons later, Zehala joined him, slicing into the thick hide with her helbraught. Together they tore through another tentacle, making the janack weave lopsided. With each swipe of his claws, Histrun pumped more venom into the tentacle.

Zehala vaulted onto a tentacle and ran up it to the head-bulb. Balancing on the bucking monster, she drove her helbraught into its skull. Fire blazed, burning away its brain. As it collapsed, she leaped off, landing in a roll at his feet. Histrun helped her up. They turned toward Mendehan's janack.

Mendehan danced in front of the janack's head, waving his arms and yelling at it. Only a few hunks of tentacles lay strewn around, and the janack didn't act like any venom affected it. The janack snapped at him, and he leaped back, laughing. A tentacle whipped at him, and he rolled away, not even trying to cut it with his claws. Frowning at the strange behavior, Histrun ran toward the janack, Zehala on his heels.

Unexpectedly, a brecha bowled into Histrun, knocking him onto his back. Only his well-honed reflexes saved him. He raked his front claws across its snout while his rear feet clawed its belly. Zehala stabbed it in the side, pulling her helbraught through the tough hide to open a long gash. It shuddered. Histrun heaved with his feet, trying to toss it off him before it crumpled on him and trapped him beneath it. The brecha's weight pressed his knees into his chest, cutting off his breath. The brecha's body flew off, and Chestrun grinned down at him.

"Gotcha, sir," Chestrun garbled. He switched to mind-speech. *All of my group's monsters are dead. Mendehan's men were responsible for this one. But...* He shrugged.

Histrun climbed to his feet and quickly surveyed the battlefield. He sucked in a breath at the number of bodies lying on the ground. Brecha spines stuck out from most of their backs, while others had great, gaping holes from bites. He said a silent prayer. None of his people had died. All the corpses—which had, in death, reverted back to their natural forms—wore black uniforms. He shook his head at the waste of life. Those men had been bullies, not fighters. They shouldn't have been out here without more experienced warriors guiding them.

A familiar yelp caught his attention. His heart leaped into his throat. A tentacle wound around Zehala's waist, lifting her into the air and to the janack's waiting maw. She struggled, hacking awkwardly at it with her weapon. The janack shook her violently, her head wobbling, and she lost her grip on her helbraught. She yelled and threw a fireball at the beast.

Howling with rage, Histrun ran toward her. Naila reached the tentacle first and plunged her helbraught into it, cursing. Histrun crouched, jumped, and gouged the tentacle above where it gripped Zehala.

The tip of another tentacle snaked around Naila's neck. Her eyes bugged as she gasped for air. Chestrun frantically tore into it, finally cutting through it. Naila grappled with the piece of tentacle still clenching her throat, shoving and squirming as she attempted to remove it. Her face slowly turned purple, and her fighting grew feeble as it strangled her.

Histrun couldn't help both Zehala and Naila. Blinking away tears, he yelled at Chestrun to help Naila, while Histrun swiped furiously at the tentacle holding Zehala. A chunk flew off, then another. The janack shook her again. A loud snap cracked, like a whip. Zehala's cries suddenly quieted, and her body hung limp. With renewed frenzy, Histrun scratched, tore, and bit the monster, furiously pumping venom into it. He had to help Zehala. He had to save her.

With a spray of ichor, the tentacle dropped to the ground, still wrapped around Zehala's motionless form. He raced toward her, but another tentacle slapped in front of him, blocking his way. Howling, he tore through it, poured venom into the janack. The remaining tentacles moved sluggishly, and the janack finally crumbled in a heap.

Histrun fell to his knees next to Zehala. Her eyes stared unseeing at the heavens, a trickle of blood dripped from the corner of her mouth. He threw his head back and howled. It ended in a human cry of anguish as he shifted into his natural form. He cradled her head in his lap, rocking back and forth, crooning, "No, no, no... she can't be gone," over and over.

"Mother...?" Naila croaked, crawling toward Histrun. When she saw Zehala's body, she screamed, "Mother!" Great, deep sobs wracked her, and tears flowed down her face as she bent over her mother.

This shouldn't have happened! This wasn't supposed to happen! Histrun surged to his feet, his hands balled into fists. He spun in a circle, searching for the filth called Mendehan. If he had fought properly, rather than goading the janack, Zehala would still be alive. He found the object of his rage, back in his natural form, doing a jig in front of the dead janack as if he'd killed the large monster.

"Mendehan!" Histrun thundered.

The other man paused. His mouth gaped open when Histrun barreled into him.

Histrun's fist landed squarely on the bridge of Mendehan's nose. He shook his head, flinging bloody snot, and threw a counter-punch, which Histrun easily blocked. Histrun threw his hips into a front kick to Mendehan's chest, knocking him back several feet. He followed with a roundhouse kick to the side of his head. Mendehan stumbled and, with a howl, shifted to his warrior form, swinging long claws at Histrun's face. He growled at the cowardly display. They always fought alpha challenges in their natural forms, or in their wolf forms, never as warriors. Histrun leaped out of the way, but not fast or far enough. His growl turned into a yip of pain as the tips of Mendehan's claws slid across his chest.

He stepped in with a one-two punch to his opponent's jaw, then swept his leg behind Mendehan's knees, knocking him off-balance. As the other man fell, Histrun wrapped an arm around his throat, the other hand on the side of his head, and twisted. A loud snap sounded as he broke Mendehan's neck.

He flung the corpse away from him and stumbled back to Zehala, his vision blurry from tears. He didn't care. His bond-mate, the love of his life, was gone, killed to protect a foolish, sick man. If he could kill Mendehan again, he would.

Their fighting-pack surrounded around her body, but they parted to let him through. He had just enough presence of mind to notice Lestrun, Eidelstrun, and several other warriors guarded the few surviving Black Guards.

Histrun gathered Zehala into his arms, cradling her head against his chest in a parody of all the times she had rested it there after they'd made love. He staggered away from the battlefield. Maheli met him before he'd gone far, leading his and Zehala's horses. Unable to bear Zehala's body draped over Kylara's back, he instead awkwardly climbed into Telen's saddle, still holding his beloved close. Like this, she appeared to be just resting.

Grass rustled and leather creaked as his people mounted their horses.

He urged Telen forward into a walk. If he didn't hurry, he could continue to hold Zehala a little while longer, and pretend she was holding him back.

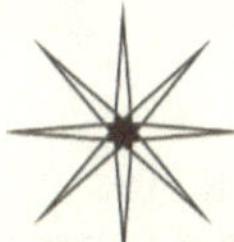

Histrun rode back to Dehanlair Keep in a daze. Over the years, the monsters had killed many of his friends and lovers, but none of them had held his heart like Zehala had. No one else made him feel so alive, so competent, or so loved. He felt lost. He kept hoping to hear her laughter at one of Naila's jokes.

Behind him, Naila rode in front of Alixstrun, unconscious and barely alive herself. Already the skin around her neck and chest was turning a sickly gray from the monster toxin. The Reds hadn't dared burn the poison from her, terrified they'd kill her in the process. Even though he wanted to linger in order to hold Zehala longer, he couldn't continue to dawdle, or he'd risk losing Naila as well. Reluctantly, he kicked Telen into a faster pace.

Soon the keeps' gates came into view—the closed gates. Despair rippled through him. *As if this day couldn't get any worse. Norvela and Tedehan didn't take control of the keep.* Histrun slumped deeper in the saddle. Although he wasn't mentally capable of a dominance fight, he took a deep breath and tried to mentally prepare for yet another battle.

A shout went up from the watchtower, and the gates creaked open. Norvela and Tedehan stood just beyond them, bloody and bruised. Salloreen, a bandage wrapped around her right biceps, leaned against a young man with the same burgundy-red hair as she had.

"Where's Mendehan?" Salloreen craned her neck, peering behind Histrun. "Is he dead?"

Histrun nodded.

"Good riddance!" Salloreen pumped her fist into the air. "Thank you, Mother!"

"Is that Zehala?" Norvela took a step forward, her brow furrowed in concern. "What's wrong with her? Is she injured?"

Histrun shook his head. "She's gone," he croaked past a tight throat. "We need a healer quickly for Naila. She has a bad case of monster poisoning."

"One's coming now. Zehala's dead? How?" Salloreen's voice quavered.

"A janack crushed her."

Alixstrun gently handed off Naila to Eidelstrun. A slim woman with dark brown hair ran to them. Her taevo brown eyes widened at Naila's injury. She motioned for Eidelstrun to kneel so the much shorter woman could reach Naila. The healer placed her hands a few inches above Naila's throat.

Bronze light spread from them, surrounding Naila's wound. The light deepened to a dark, mud-brown as she drew the poison from the monster's ichor out of Naila's body. The healer made a swirling motion and gathered the noxious light into a tight ball. Maheli jumped forward and sent a tendril of fire from her helbraught to the ball. It flared, and fine ash trickled to the ground.

The healer stepped back. "I removed the worst of the poison, but she isn't out of danger. You," she gestured to Eidelstrun, "follow me to the infirmary." She turned on her heel and Eidelstrun hastened to catch up to her.

"I'm so sorry about Zehala." Salloreen placed a comforting hand on Histrun's shoulder. "One of my men can carry her to the temple to be prepared for her final rites."

Histrun hugged Zehala's body closer to him and pulled his shoulder away from Salloreen. "No! I will take her." He stalked toward the temple.

"But—"

He didn't stop, not caring what happened to Dehanlair Keep anymore. The moment Zehala lost her life, he'd stopped caring about anything. As Dehanlair's Clan Alpha, it was Salloreen's responsibility to clean up the mess she'd allowed Mendehan to cause.

Histrun stumbled up the temple steps. Lestrun's gentle hand helped him catch his balance. Lorstriel steadied him on his other side. Together, they would give Zehala to the White Priestesses, for them to usher Zehala's soul through the veil and into the Summerlands, where she would reunite with the Goddess.

Wylara waited inside the temple, her eyes bleak. "My condolences, Histrun. We will ensure she crosses over and is embraced by the Mother." She moved to peer into the courtyard behind him. A hand flew to touch her parted lips as she gasped. "So many dead! Is Mendehan with them?"

Histrun nodded. "He won't hurt anyone else again. Someone should have taken him down long before... before she died because of his foolishness." Fresh tears pricked his swollen eyes.

"Come," Wylara gestured, her eyes filled with compassion. "Come and bring her into the temple to be prepared for her final journey in this life, and you can ease your burden."

"She's no burden," Histrun mumbled as he followed the priestess. Zehala's body seemed so light without the force of her personality.

When they reached the preparation room, several other bodies already lay on the tables with white sheets draped over them. Wylara led Histrun to an empty table.

"You can lay her here," she said kindly.

Histrun shook his head, pulling Zehala tighter to him.

Wylara laid a gentle hand on his arm. "You have to let her go, Histrun. It's time she returned to the Mother. She's ready. I can see her soul, waiting to cross the veil, wanting to go. But she can't while you're holding her back. Do you want her to become a ghost?"

That finally got through to him. *How can I condemn her soul to wander the world rather than find peace with the Goddess?* With great reluctance, Histrun lowered Zehala onto the table, closing her eyes and arranging her arms as if she were simply sleeping. He bent over and kissed her lips, surprised to feel a lingering warmth.

"Goodbye, my love," he whispered. "You take my heart with you as you cross into the Summerlands. Keep it safe. I'll join you soon." He kissed her again and stepped back.

Two White Priestesses covered her with a white shroud.

Histrun turned to Wylara. "Please don't burn her with Mendehan or any of his filthy followers. I don't want their sickness to contaminate her. I'll take her ashes home. She'll only rest in her beloved mountains."

"I'll make sure it is done," Wylara promised. She guided him from the preparation room. "While we attend to the dead, you need to deal with the living. Go. Take care of your people." She paused at the temple door's threshold. "We still need your strength, Histrun. Watch over my people until one of the other alphas comes. There isn't anyone strong enough to lead in the vacuum of power. Mendehan saw to it."

Outside, a crowd packed the area in front of the keep-house. A cacophonous roar of voices raised in anger rang through the courtyard. Salloreen stood on the Keep house's top step with the same young man at her side. One step below her, Norvela and Tedehan watched the crowd. Twenty or thirty men lined up below them, all wearing Black Guard uniforms. Their hands were tied behind their backs and bruises purpled their faces. A few had bloody noses or other wounds oozing blood.

Histrun frowned at Deldehan and several other men who had helped them with them in the group. A nasty cut slashed his left eyebrow and a gash on his biceps dripped blood.

Salloreen raised her hands, and the crowd quieted. "Mendehan is dead," Salloreen announced. "His sickness and madness are gone with him."

"How can you be sure?" a woman yelled. "I don't want to be imprisoned again just for being a Red!"

"I don't want my children locked away from me," another woman cried. Histrun picked her out from the crowd. She hugged two small children to her chest as if she'd never let them go. "They need to be punished!"

"Kill the rogues!" Someone yelled. The chant echoed through the courtyard as others took it up.

Salloreen held up a hand and tried to yell over the noise, but no one paid any attention to her. Something had to be done before the crowd turned into a mob.

Histrun pushed his way toward the front, using his fists as necessary to get through. Finally, he reached the keep-house stairs and ran up them. "People!" he cried, holding up his arms. "Quiet! Listen to me!"

The chant died to quiet murmurs as the people pointed and stared. He glanced down at himself, realizing for the first time blood covered him. Splotches of monster gore spattered his sleeves, and his pants leg near the hem had a ragged hole where the acidic blood had eaten the fabric away. Luckily, his boot protected his skin.

"I can assure you the rogue, Mendehan, is dead!" Histrun shouted. "I killed him myself." He gazed at his hands, imaging Mendehan's neck in them as he broke it. It had been too easy of a death. The crowd quieted. "He took most of his personal guard with him to the monster battle, and they are also dead."

A tall young man with mouse-brown hair and a bruise on his cheek pushed to the front. He slammed his hands onto his hips and glared at the alphas on the steps. "Why would Mendehan go to a monster battle? He hasn't fought the monsters, or allowed anyone else to fight, for over six lunadars."

Histrun quirked an eyebrow. "It wasn't too difficult for me to goad him into it."

"And who exactly are you?"

"Podehan, don't you recognize him?" An older man stepped forward, elbowing the younger man. "He's Histrun de Strunlair, Mendehan's nemesis. I've seen them fight over just about anything, with Histrun always coming out on top. It infuriated Mendehan." He frowned and looked around. "Hey, where's your bond-mate, Zehala?"

Grief washed over Histrun anew. His throat grew tight with unshed tears. These weren't his pack. They didn't need to see him weak. "She…" he swallowed. "She was killed by a janack."

"Who cares who he is?" Podehan growled, pointing at the bound men. "Those men deserve to be punished! How many people did they hurt? How many women did they rape or worse? They're rogues! And rogues need to be killed."

"Put them down!" someone yelled, while someone else screamed, "Kill the rogues!"

Many in the crowd took up the chants again. Histrun grimaced. He'd almost had them under control, and now they were turning into a mob again. He glared at the young man before turning his attention to the former Black Guards. *How can we separate those who were part of it because they liked hurting people from those who were there to protect their families, like Deldehan?* A prisoner struggled against his bonds, his shirt slipping off his shoulder, revealing a large black splotch similar to Mendehan's.

Histrun stalked down the stairs, grabbed the man, and dragged him up the stairs so all could see him. He ripped off the man's shirt. The ugly black splotch covered his shoulder and chest.

Histrun pointed at the markings. "I believe this marks those who willingly followed Mendehan. He wore a similar one that stank of evil."

"Jaedehan is one of the bad ones, all right," the older man said. "He beat me before throwing me into the prison. I watched him whip a man to death, a grin on his face the whole time."

Eidelstrun and Dorstrun hurried up the stairs and hauled the former guard to the side.

Histrun pointed to Deldehan. "There are those, like him, who were in the guard to protect their families. They aren't rogues, just men trying to do the best they could in an impossible situation. They shouldn't be punished—or killed."

"Prove it!" The younger man crossed his arms over his chest.

"You know he never hurt anyone, Podehan," the older man said.

"Bring him." Histrun hated what had to subject Deldehan to. Even with the man's testimony, only proof would satisfy the crowd.

Alixstrun hurried to obey, keeping hold of Deldehan's arm as he stumbled up the steps.

"Strip him."

Alixstrun cut off Deldehan's shirt and pants with a few quick slices of his helstrablade.

Deldehan stood nude, shivering slightly. Without urging, he turned in a slow circle with his arms held wide. His body was free of any black blemishes.

"Satisfied?" Histrun asked.

Podehan jerked his head, while the crowd murmured assent.

Soon, they'd stripped all the former Black Guards and segregated them into two groups. Those without black marks outnumbered those that had them.

"Take them," Salloreen ordered, "and confine them up in the jail until we can put them down like the animals they are."

Several men stepped forward to obey the command, but Podehan stopped them.

"Why should we listen to you?" he sneered at Salloreen. "You did nothing to stop Mendehan or to help your people. We should lock you up with them."

"I was as much his victim as you were!" Salloreen cried. She lowered the top of her dress to reveal dark bruises.

A woman with mussed up, bright-red hair stepped forward. "You're not much of an alpha, Salloreen, if you let him beat you and intimidate you."

"You didn't stand up to him either, Verdara."

"It wasn't my job. It was yours. You are, or were, the Clan Alpha, Salloreen. Your job was to balance Mendehan, and make sure he treated your people right. You failed. I don't believe you are fit to lead us. Step down."

"Are you challenging me, Verdara?"

Verdara shook her head. "After lunadars locked up with little food, I'm not strong enough. But when I've recovered my strength, then yes, I challenge you."

"We can't be without alphas for that long," the young man standing next to Salloreen spoke up. "I'll lead."

"You!" barked Podehan. "No. Salordehan, you're not an alpha. You hid behind your mother's skirts. This is the first time I've seen you in chedans, if not lunadars. Where have you been?"

"Locked away, just like you, Podehan. Mendehan hated me more than anyone else."

Podehan looked the younger man up and down, then sneered. "You don't look like you suffered much."

"Why, you... you..." Salordehan sputtered, his hands balling into fists.

Histrun stepped in before the two could come to blows. "Neither of you are qualified to be Keep Alphas, let alone Clan Alphas. Wendehan or Rodehan will hold the interim position until the formal Alpha Competitions next summer. They should be on their way here." Histrun glanced at Norvela.

"Both teams passed beyond my reach late last night," she said, "unharmed. I believe they made it through. As soon as we gained control of the keep, I sent larger packs to help them."

Histrun groaned inwardly. The White Priestess was correct. No one in this keep was capable of leading. He'd have to step in. "Until they arrive, and it's determined which one will become the interim Clan Alpha, I'm in charge. I killed Mendehan, and I was the Clan Alpha of Strunlair for many years.

"You all have jobs and know what to do. This keep is in disrepair, the fields lie fallow, and the herds are untended. Malvers' monsters roam unchecked. I want the fighting-packs to gather in the practice arena in one octar. Dismissed!"

The courtyard quickly cleared as people scurried away. It surprised Histrun at how little grumbling he heard. Right now, they were still in shock from the past lunadars of terror. It wouldn't last. He hoped the two Dehanlair alphas arrived soon to take over. All he wanted to do was leave this dung-heap and take his beloved back home.

Chapter 10

That evening, the Dehanlair citizens marched from the keep carrying the white draped bodies to a field far from the living spaces used for the funeral pyres. The high stone fences surrounding the field protected it from narhili beasts, and the Malvers' monsters went into a stupor at night. Behind the main group, the Strunland contingent followed Lestrun, Alixstrun, and Chestrun, who carried Zehala. It took all of Histrun's strength to stagger along in the procession. When they reached the burning grounds, Priestess Wylara directed them to a pyre built as far from the others as possible.

"Wait here," Wylara instructed. "After we've started the fires for the Dehanlair people, we will come to send Zehala on her way."

The pallbearers carefully lifted their burden onto the pyre. Each member of the fighting-pack solemnly laid a flower or some other token on or around Zehala's body, and said their final farewells. Naila's absence broke Histrun's heart further. Still unconscious from her injuries, she couldn't send her mother to the Summerlands.

After everyone else had stepped forward, Histrun approached the pyre. He held both his and Zehala's bond-mate torques. The matching thin, gold wire twisted together with a ruby set in the center was the symbol of their unification.

"Goodbye, my love. May you rest in the arms of the Mother." Tears streamed down his face as he placed the one he'd given

Zehala on her chest; he'd never give it to anyone else. It would go with her to the afterlife, where perhaps she would remember him. He clasped the one she had given him around his neck, vowing to never remove it. With his helstrablade, he cut off a lock of Zehala's dark-auburn hair. Later, he would weave it into his torque.

When he finally stumbled away, Wylara and her priestesses moved into position. Wylara stood at Zehala's head as one priestess poured sweet oil over Zehala and another one sprinkled the sacred incense made from kehani flowers and frankincense on her. Finished, they stepped back to join the other priestesses, surrounding the pyre in their snowy-white gowns, veils covering their faces.

"Great Mother," Wylara intoned, lifting her hands toward the sky, palms upward, "accept your daughter, Zehala, into your loving embrace. Hold her close and give her comfort as she releases the burdens and joys of this life. Gentle and wise Matriarch, guide your daughter through the Summerlands, where she may remember and learn from the lessons gifted in this life. Gracious Crone, may your purifying fires be gentle as they burn away the dross accumulated during Zehala's life. And may her next life begin in pure love and joy. Zehala, you brought many gifts into this life and shared them with all you met. You lived a good life, and your loved blessed all those who you touched. Go with love and grace."

Maheli, Lorstriel, and Kehali stepped forward and touched their glowing helbraught blades to the pyre. Their magic quickly lit the wood, and in milcrons, the fire burned high. The sun set with a glorious display of purples and oranges. Histrun took it as a sign Zehala peacefully crossed the veil.

He and the others stayed until the wood collapsed into a heap of glowing coals, and the fire immolated everything on the pyre. A priestess, with water as her secondary Talent, lifted her hands and a cooling mist settled over the coals. Steam billowed into the night air, and the coals sizzled until they were nothing but ash. Another priestess, this one with Yellow Talent, created a hot, dry funnel of air, and swirled the ashes together into a neat pile. Histrun stepped forward with a carved wooden box, and the priestess used the air to scoop the ashes into the box.

The final rite concluded, the priestesses and the fighting-pack walked back to the keep. Histrun stood alone for a long time, staring at the small box holding all that remained of his beloved Zehala. He couldn't stop the tears. By now, he shouldn't have any left. When he finally lifted his head, sunrise brightened the sky. It stained the few clouds a pale rose and gold, and a light breeze caressed his face. He put his hand on his cheek and closed his eyes, pretending it was Zehala's touch.

But it wasn't. He had to go on living without her. Wiping away the wetness on his cheeks, Histrun straightened his shoulders, and marched back to the keep.

Bypassing the Keep House, he strode to the building serving as a jail. He frowned at the absurdity of it. Never before had a clan needed a dedicated space for miscreants.

The same healer who had saved Naila met him outside the cell doors. She tucked a stray strand of dark brown hair behind her ear as she pushed away from the wall opposite the cell. She held out her hand in greeting. "Thank you, Histrun, for freeing our people, especially the children."

Histrun gripped her wrist. "I only did my duty..."

"Flothera," she supplied.

"How is Naila faring?"

"She's healing. I'm keeping her unconscious for now. Her throat is badly damaged, and I don't want her talking until it heals more. I've done all I can, but I'm afraid she may never talk well. She's lucky to be alive."

"Flothera, I'd like you to determine what, if anything, we can do about Mendehan's followers infected with the strange black splotches. It would be better if we can heal them rather than cull them as rogues. Have you treated any of the men for the strange skin illness?"

Flothera shook her head. "No. Mendehan wouldn't let me heal him or any of his men. He threatened me with incarceration if I came near them. I couldn't help my people while locked away, so I obeyed. I wish now I had insisted on treating him. Perhaps we could have avoided the past few lunadars."

"I'm not so sure."

Tedehan and several of his bigger men arrived, each one carrying thick cudgels in case the prisoners became violent. Eidelstrun, Chestrun, Lorstriel, and Kehali followed a moment later. Although Tedehan had shown himself to be trustworthy, Histrun preferred to have his own people at his back. The two Reds carried their helbraughts to further deter the prisoners from any rash moves.

"We're ready." Histrun nodded to the young man guarding the door, who pulled out a key and unlocked it.

Inside the cell, Histrun grimaced at the thick chains shackling the most pugnacious men to the wall. *What did Mendehan use those for? Why would he need them?* Histrun turned his thoughts away from that terror with a shudder. Tedehan's men filed into the cell, hefting their heavy cudgels threateningly at the unchained men. Eidelstrun and Chestrun took positions on either side of the door. The two Reds waited in the hall, alert to danger. Finally, satisfied no one would harm the healer, Histrun gestured for Flothera to enter.

She examined the men with the smallest markings first, working her way to the last man, Jaedehan, who had the largest. Her brow furrowed into a deeper frown, and her eyes grew bleak as she moved around the room. Once finished, she motioned for Histrun to follow her outside.

"I don't know what it is or how to heal it," Flothera said, wringing her hands. "It reminds me of gangrene, with the tissues putrefying, but there isn't any infection I can discern. It's like they are rotting from the inside out. Priestess Wylara needs to see this. Perhaps it is a soul sickness."

The young guard ran to fetch the priestess. While they awaited her arrival, Histrun re-entered the cell and studied the infected men. Almost to a man, they sneered at him. Jaedehan pulled against his chains and spat at Histrun. After a short interview with them, their responses confirmed his suspicions they were men who enjoyed hurting others and believed the world owed them for some imagined slight. If this was a soul sickness, it had found fertile soil in their selfish, brutal hearts.

"Histrun," Kehali called softly, "the priestess is here."

He abruptly cutoff his questions and hurried from the cell.

"Flothera filled me in." Wylara's pale skin was dull, and dark circles smudged her eyes.

Guilt fluttered in Histrun's belly. As the head priestess, she had stayed at the funeral pyres the entire night, guiding the souls of the departed across the veil. She deserved her rest, and here he was, asking her to push herself further.

"Don't fret so, Histrun." Wylara laid a soft hand on his arm. "This is my calling and my duty."

Embarrassment warmed Histrun's ears. She had sensed his thoughts. "Sorry, my lady. What do you need?"

"Just a moment of quiet."

Wylara went to the first man and placed her hands on his head. He tried to jerk away, but thin cords of white light shot from her hands and wrapped around his head, holding it in place. After a couple of milcrons, the light receded, and the man slumped on the ground. The black spot oozed from his skin like pus. It pooled on the stone floor, then turned and flowed toward the closest man, as if it sought a new host.

"Burn it!" Wylara leaped back, horror on her face.

Lorstriel jumped inside, her helbraught flared, burning the inky mess. A noxious stink filled the room as it burned, making everyone cough and gag.

Fanning away the smoke, Histrun peered at the floor. "Is it gone?"

Wylara nodded.

"What was that?"

"Some type of malignant magic." Wylara's voice shook, and her hands trembled. "It acted like some sort of parasite, attaching itself to its host's soul and eating it. It's highly contagious."

"Why isn't everyone affected by it, then?"

"It needs hosts predisposed toward wickedness and ill-intentions. It feeds on those feelings, exacerbating them until all that remains of the person's personality and soul is a craving for more evil-doing." Wylara blew out a breath, and, uncharacteristic of priestesses, swore. "Had I insisted on treating Mendehan when he first became infected, I might have stopped this."

"What-ifs and hindsight don't solve problems." Histrun awkwardly patted Wylara's back. "We can only move forward with the information we have available now. Can you treat the others?"

Wylara's gaze lingered on the chained men with the largest splotches. "If the infection isn't too far advanced, I can. But those who are too far gone, we can't do anything to help." She turned to the infected men, taking a step toward them, compassion showing in her eyes. "I'm sorry, there's nothing I can do to help you."

"Bitch!" Jaedehan spat out, lunging at her, his hands grasping for her throat. "Plague bearers! We'll purge you and all your kind from this world. It will be as if you never existed." Spittle flew from his lips as he continued to rant.

Tedehan leaped forward and clubbed the man. He dropped like a stone, finally silent.

"Sadly, his humanity is gone." Wylara strode to the door. "Bring the lesser infected to the temple where my priestesses can cleanse them of their illness." She pointed to the shackled men. "Keep them chained until you or the next Clan Alpha puts them down so they can't harm anyone else. No one enters this room without a White Priestess to ward them."

"It will be done," Histrun promised.

Tedehan's fighters prodded the men to their feet and out the door. Histrun sent a mental command to Alixstrun to clear a path from the building housing the prison to the temple. If the illness was as contagious as Wylara implied, he didn't want any new cases.

Histrun accompanied Wylara back to the temple to make arrangements for men to guard the temple. He wanted to ensure the priestesses' safety while they treated the infected men. The untreatable men could wait until one of the Dehanlair alphas arrived. It wasn't Histrun's responsibility to kill the rogues.

Late afternoon shadows skittered across the courtyard when Histrun left the temple. His feet dragged, and his stomach growled. He needed food and rest. Instead, he hurried away from the temple to the keep-house, avoiding eye-contact and ignoring anyone who called his name. Unable to face going back to the room he had shared with Zehala, he found an empty room and fell into the bed. Behind his closed eyes, he relived the last excruciating moments when the janack squeezed the life from Zehala, and he'd been incapable of saving her. If only he'd been faster, stronger, younger, she'd still be alive. Finally, exhaustion carried him into oblivion.

Histrun's busy schedule kept him from thinking about his loss and succumbing to the grief threatening to overwhelm him. During the day, he focused on returning order and justice to Dehanlair Keep. However, he lost the battle to the lonely nights and empty bed. Finally, to fall asleep, he raided Mendehan's supply of whiskey, drinking himself into a stupor every night.

The Dehanlair fighters insisted on going back to work, even though they were weak and underfed from their time locked away. Lorstriel, Kehali, and Norvela taught them the Zehis fighting method. The next day, the fighting-packs left the keep for the first time in lunadars. In a testament to their determination to overcome Mendehan's laxness, they cleaned out two nests in the area without any deaths. Within a few days, the herders and farmers returned to the fields without fear of being attacked by marauding monsters.

Histrun refused to lead any monster battles, claiming he had too much work to do inside the keep. In the moments he was truthful with himself, he acknowledged he was reluctant to jeopardize anyone else's life from his inability to move fast enough.

The morning of the fourth day, Histrun sat in his borrowed office, dealing with a fight between Argodehan, a former Black Guard member, and Salordehan for the second time.

A breathless messenger burst into the room. "Sir!" The man saluted, then leaned over to catch his breath. "A platoon of fighters is racing across the territory, led by Keep Alpha Rodehan. They should arrive at the Clan Keep by early afternoon."

Histrun let out a whoop of relief. "Blessed Warrior, thank you!" He could finally hand off this mess to someone else and take his beloved's ashes home.

When the messenger left, the two men in trouble tried to sidle out with him. "Where do you think you're going?" Histrun growled, stopping them in their tracks. He glowered at them. "I'm not finished with you yet. Since you two can't seem to let go of past misdeeds, perhaps if you work together to rebuild this keep, you'll learn to like each other again. The fence in the south multa pasture needs to be mended. I'm assigning you to fix it. Just the two of you—no one else."

The men groaned and glared at each other.

"That's not fair!" Salordehan howled, pointing at the former Black Guard. "He's the one who followed Mendehan and made us slaves."

"I only did what I had to do to survive!" Argodehan sputtered. "Mendehan told me if I didn't become a guard, he'd rape every woman in my pack. What else was I supposed to do? I couldn't allow that to happen."

"Enough!" Histrun roared. "I don't care. You have been at each other's throats, disturbing the peace we're trying to reestablish. You're both in the wrong. Go fix the fence. And while you're at it, fix whatever is going on between you two. The south field is far enough from everyone that you won't bother anyone or pull them into your feud if you continue to bicker and fight. Now go!"

The men tromped out, grumbling. Histrun sat back in his chair, put his hands over his stomach, and scowled at the door. These weren't his people. He didn't know their history or their personalities and was bumbling in the dark, trying to solve their problems.

Histrun leaned forward and pulled the top report from the stack on the desk, scowling at the bad news from the kitchens. The fresh food was gone and the grain stores were low. They would have to petition foodstuffs from the other Dehanlair Territories to survive. Report after report continued in the same vein. Supplies of ore were low, wood for fires needed to be gathered, hay and grain for the livestock were nearly gone, and very little grew in the pastures. By the time he finished reading the last report, he was ready to kill Mendehan all over again for his mismanagement. Salloreen was no better for allowing it to happen. The poor state of the keep spoke of more than a few lunadars of mismanagement. This had been happening for two years or more. This clan needed a new set of alphas, not just a new male alpha. How had this happened?

A knock on the door broke into his musing.

"Sir," the same messenger said, coming into the office. "Rodehan's platoon is approaching the gates, and Wendehan's party will arrive within the octar."

"Good, thank you." Histrun stood and straightened his tunic. Soon, he could turn over the keep's management to someone else and go home. He followed the messenger through the Keep-house and out onto the porch. Norvela and Tedehan joined him, along with Lorstriel and Eidelstrun. Histrun searched for Zehala before remembering she wouldn't be joining them. He touched his bond-mate torque. He missed her advice and wisdom. Naila was still recuperating and confined to the infirmary.

The Dehanrolos keep alphas, Rodehan and Freynara, stopped their horses in front of the Keep House. Road dust and grime covered them, and fatigue pulled on their faces. They had ridden hard to reach the Clan Keep so quickly.

Rodehan searched the people assembled on the porch. "Where is he? Where's the caitiff Mendehan!"

"He's dead." Histrun leaned against the railing. "I had to put the rogue down. Wendehan is on his way, so there will be a fair challenge for Clan Alpha."

"And Salloreen?" Freynara asked. "Is she also dead? I don't see her."

Norvela stepped forward, her tiny braids clinking together. "We removed her as alpha due to her incompetency, so we also need a female Clan Alpha. If I hadn't seen the situation with my own eyes, I wouldn't have believed how far Mendehan had fallen, and how awful he'd treated the people of this keep. Histrun is right. Mendehan was a rogue and a sick madman and needed to be put down. When Wendehan arrives, we'll tell you both the story. For now, welcome. Come in and rest."

Freynara wearily slid off her horse. She frowned as she studied the group on the porch. "Where is Zehala?"

Histrun's heart stuttered at her name. He swallowed. "She's... she's..." His thoughts froze and the words wouldn't pass his tight throat.

Norvela came to his rescue. "A janack killed Zehala. It's part of the sad story we have to share with you."

"Oh, I'm so sorry, Histrun." Freynara hurried up the stairs and wrapped her arms around him.

He stood there, arms at his sides, not knowing how to react. People hugged Zehala, not him.

An octar and a half later, the group returned to the Keephouse porch to welcome Wendehan, his co-alpha, Marlora, and his platoon. Once Wendehan and Marlora had cleaned up from their journey, the alphas gathered in a small parlor. Norvela and Tedehan filled them in on all the happenings in Dehanlair Keep.

"So it's important for the new leadership to go into effect immediately," Histrun said when they were up-to-date. "This keep, and this clan, haven't had good alphas for quite some time. The Alpha Competitions aren't until next summer. Until then, someone has to act as the interim Clan Alphas. And that person isn't me. My home is in Strunlair Province."

Wendehan and Rodehan looked at each other for a long time. Finally, Rodehan broke the silence. "How do you want to do this, Wendehan? Either one of us would be better for our clan than what we've recently had. I'm prepared to take on the responsibility. I know my keep will be in fine hands with Norvela and Tedehan taking over as the alphas." He smiled at them. "This situation has proved they are quite capable leaders."

Norvela blushed with the praise, and Tedehan straightened his shoulders.

"The messenger warned me this is why I was called here," Wendehan said. "I too am ready. I left my seconds in charge of Dehanreen Keep, knowing there was a possibility I wouldn't be returning." He turned to Histrun. "You have been a Clan Alpha for many years and have gone through several challenges. Would it be possible for you to devise a set of challenges for us to complete, and the winner will determine the new alphas?"

"Could you, Histrun?" Rodehan's his eyes lit up. "Something to simulate the Alpha Competitions would make the choice fair for us and our people. It'd ensure we've chosen the best candidate available. "

Histrun leaned back in his chair, studying the two alpha pairs. Their willingness to test themselves was an encouraging sign they would be good leaders, thinking more about the needs of their people than their own desires. He had hoped they would suggest it, and had already thought of several tests, and the tasks would also solve some of the keep's immediate concerns. He sent a mental command to Maheli to bring him the papers off his desk.

"Yes, I can do that." He inclined his head. "I think testing problem-solving, management skills, leadership in battle, and adaptability will suffice. Rodehan and Freynara, you recently learned the Zehis fighting method. Have you led any monster battles using this method?"

Freynara shook her head. "No. Like most Keep Alphas, we've stayed in the keep, letting our fighting-packs go out."

"Good, it'll be a fair test. We'll teach the two Dehanreen alphas the Zehis method as well. Afterward, you'll go to the nearest nest site and test your ability to use this method in actual conditions. You will have to adapt your fighting styles to this new method." Maheli's soft knock on the door interrupted him, and he called her in, taking the papers from her. When she departed, he handed one to each alpha pair.

"Those are your problem-solving and management tests," he explained. "Those are just a few of the problems and shortages Mendehan and Salloreen left this keep with. Your test is how to fix them. You will be helping your clan while proving your capabilities." He let them review the lists, each one containing five of the keep's most pressing needs.

Marlora raised her eyebrows at the list. "All of this is wrong with the keep?"

Histrun nodded. "That and more. You have three days to complete your tasks. Wendehan and Marlora, your training begins within an octar. Good luck to you all. May the best people prevail."

Over the next two days, Histrun observed the alpha teams as they threw themselves into proving which would make the better interim Clan Alphas. The results showed Histrun either pair would serve the people of Dehanlair well.

On the morning of the third day, Salordehan and Argodehan were brought into the alpha's office for fighting—yet again. This time they'd thrown food at each other in the dining hall. They hadn't made much progress on their fence mending because they'd been too busy arguing. Based on their bruised faces and bloody knuckles, they'd also been beating up each other.

"You, sit there," Histrun ordered Salordehan to a chair by the window, then pointed Argodehan to the chair on the opposite side of the room. "Both of you, quiet!" They slumped in the chairs, arms folded over their chests, and glared at each other. He called in the competing alpha pairs.

"I've had it with these two," Histrun growled. "They've done nothing but fight since Mendehan fell."

"But—" Salordehan started.

"He's a—" Argodehan sputtered.

"Auck," Histrun held up a hand, "did I give either of you permission to speak?"

They shook their heads and sank lower in their seats.

Histrun turned his attention to the alphas. "Both of you are doing exceptionally well with the tests. At this point, it's a toss-up which set would be better than the other. Whichever one of you can solve this problem—" he pointed between the two young men "—will win the competition. Good luck." He pushed away from the desk, stood, and marched out of the office.

He hurried down the stairs to the recreation room and flung open the door. Naila sat in a comfortable chair. "Oh, it's so nice to see you up and about," he said. Bandages still covered her throat, and she was thin and pale, but otherwise she looked well. "Glad to have you back with us. Are you ready to go home?"

Naila nodded, then answered in mind-speech, *Yes, very ready. When do we leave?*

Histrun surveyed the room and found Lorstriel and Maheli playing a game of keshe. "Lorstriel, Maheli, go find everyone and let them know we'll be leaving this afternoon."

"Yes!" Maheli shouted, pumping her fist in the air. "I'm so ready to go home. Come on, Lorstriel." Maheli scooped the game pieces into the wooden box.

"Hey, I was winning!" Lorstriel shrugged and hurried out the door with Maheli to spread the word about their departure.

So who won the alpha competition? Naila asked.

"Don't know. Don't care. Either pair will do well. They'll know which one solved the final problem I gave them. I don't have to be here to tell them which one won. While they're working on it, they can manage the keep between them."

What was it?

"The Salordehan and Argodehan problem. I've been dealing with those two idiots for the last seven days. I doubt their issues can be solved in the next chedan or even the next lunadar."

Naila chuckled, the sound rough and scratchy. *I've heard those two have been at each other's throats for years. That was mean, Histrun.*

"Perhaps." He shrugged. "I'm not going to change the final challenge now."

He left her and went to his room, where he quickly packed his few belongings. He carefully took down the carved box holding Zehala's ashes from the shelf over the desk and cradled it in his arms. "Soon, my love," he whispered. "Soon we'll be home."

Chapter 11

Later that afternoon, Histrun waited in the courtyard for Maheli to bring Telen to him. His people filled the area as they finalized their preparations to leave.

Rodehan hurried from the keep-house. "Histrun!" he called. "You can't leave yet."

Histrun raised an eyebrow and crossed his arms across his chest. "Of course I can."

"But you haven't decided who won the Alpha Competition yet."

"The winner will be whoever solves the problem between Salordehan and Argodehan. You don't need me here to tell you the obvious. I've stayed here longer than I wanted to in order to help your people recover. The rest is up to you and Wendehan. You're both quite capable of turning this clan around."

"Thank you for that vote of confidence. But please, stay until the morning, when you can start out fresh."

"No." Histrun shook his head. "Norvela assures me we can reach the first safe house before dark."

"If I can't convince you to stay, at least wait for Norvela and Tedehan to gather their people and accompany you back to Dehanrolos Keep." Rodehan's gaze took on the look of someone communicating via mind-speech. "They will be ready in half an octar."

"That's too much time," Histrun huffed out. "They can meet us at the first safe house and continue the rest of the way with us. But we will be pushing hard, and we won't be stopping long at Dehanrolos Keep."

"That is acceptable. I'll tell them." He put a hand on Histrun's shoulder. "I am truly sorry about what happened to Zehala. Dehanlair Clan will always be in your debt. If you need anything in the future, just ask, and we will do all we can to help you."

Histrun gripped Rodehan's wrist. Maheli approached him, leading Telen. After she handed the reins to Histrun, she scurried to her horse. Kylara kept searching the courtyard for her rider, rearing when Maheli tried to tie her lead reins to the back of her saddle. *Poor horse, she doesn't understand Zehala will never ride her again.*

Once the animal calmed, Histrun gave the signal to mount and led his people toward the gate. As he passed under it, he said a fervent prayer that he'd never set eyes on Dehanlair Keep again. He had lost too much here. He kicked Telen into a quick trot, and as soon as they rode past the fields and pastures, he quickened the pace into a canter.

The sun was setting when they rode through the safe house's gates. Not long after, Norvela and Tedehan's platoon clattered into the courtyard. True to his word, Histrun set a grueling pace back to Dehanrolos Keep. Fortunately, they didn't run into any monsters to slow them down, and they arrived in the late afternoon two days later.

He declined Norvela's offer to stay the night and crossed the bridge into Haasneven Keep. He sent Lorstriel and Lestrun to the docks to inquire after a boat to take them back upriver. Meanwhile, he, Naila, and the others went to the keep-house to pay their respects to the alphas.

A wave of grief sweep over him when he started to make a comment to Zehala, only to remember Naila rode at his side. *It should be Zehala riding next to me.* He looked away and swallowed the lump in his throat.

"Histrun," Naila croaked.

When he raised an eyebrow in question, she continued in mind-speech, *I know I'm not her, but don't shut me out, Histrun. I loved her as well. She was my mother. I'm grieving too. We all are.*

Histrun bent his head, shame filling him. He was acting like he was the only one suffering from Zehala's death. "I'm sorry. I'll try."

She nodded once in acceptance. Before they left, the healer removed her bandages, revealing a nasty, ridged scar encircling her neck where the janack's tentacle had wrapped around her.

"Does it hurt?"

"Talking does," she croaked, and swallowed hard several times. *It's easier this way.*

Sir! Lorstriel's mind-voice interrupted. *You'll never believe who is here. Captain Daelena with her barge, the Dawn Sister. She says she can take us upriver. She'll be ready to shove off once we're all loaded on. Give her an octar.*

"We have a ride upriver." Histrun blew out a relieved breath as he turned his horse back toward the docks.

I heard. It gives us time to meet with the Haasneven alphas. She reined in her horse, then twisted in the saddle. *Maheli, take our horses to the barge. The rest of you, go with her and help Daelena and her crew.*

Naila slid off her horse without waiting for Histrun. Maheli saluted her and held out her hand for the reins.

A smile played at the corners of his mouth as Naila took charge and assumed the role of alpha. With Zehala gone, they had been missing a female alpha. Not anymore. She would make a good keep alpha someday. He threw his leg over Telen's back, dropped to the ground, and handed his reins to Maheli.

Naila straightened her shoulders and her jacket, and together they went to visit the keep alphas. When the alphas saw her injury and heard about Zehala's death, they didn't prolong the meeting or insist they spend the night. Histrun and Naila strode down the dock to the *Dawn Sister* well within the allotted octar.

Daelena met them at the gangplank, her honey-gold eyes full of compassion. "Good to see you again, Histrun, Naila. My deepest condolences for your loss. I really liked Zehala."

Histrun blinked his eyes, willing the tears away. "Thank you. How far up the Storengher River can you take us? I have her ashes and want to get her home as quickly as possible."

Daelena ran a hand through her azure-blue hair. "Normally, we don't go much past Haaslair Province. The Storengher be a feisty beast as it runs through Strunlair Province. But as summer be nearly half over, the river be a bit calmer. I'll take you as far as I can. No guarantees how far into Strunlair we can go."

"I'll take whatever you can give me."

He crossed the springy plank and boarded the barge. Trudging to the cabin house, he claimed a spot out of the sun and wind, and slid to the wooden deck, his back against the cabin. He dug the carved wooden box with Zehala's ashes out from his packs, along with a ceramic jug of hard cider. Holding the box in his lap, he sipped on the liquor, letting it warm his belly.

Zehala love, I miss you. A pleasant buzz fill his head from the alcohol, and he leaned back, closed his eyes, and shut out the noise of the barge getting under way. If any problems came up, he was confident Naila could competently handle them. He was tired, so tired, of trying to act normal when his soul had been so horribly sundered. He only roused from his stupor to drink more and relieve himself.

"Histrun..."

The voice sounded far away.

"Histrun! Wake up!"

Now the voice sounded irritated, and a shove accompanied it.

"Wha... what?" He opened bleary eyes to find Maheli leaning over him and shaking him. He waved her off and fumbled to sit up, then rubbed his eyes, blinking at the bright sun. "What do you need?" he grumbled.

"Ugh, you're a grouchy drunk. Not to mention a stinky one," Maheli said, waving her hand in front of her nose. "We're approaching Haasnelyn Keep. Naila wants to know if you want us to stop for the night. Daelena is willing to send a messenger to tell them we're here."

"Why would I want to talk to them?" He scrunched his face at the awful taste in his mouth.

"I don't know? Because they're friends?"

"Don't get uppity with me, girl. No, no need to stop. We've been gone from home for too long. Let's get Zehala home." With one hand, he cradled the box and with the other, he patted around his spot for his jug. Finding it, he lifted it to his lips, only to find it empty.

Maheli turned to leave.

"Wait! Be a good girl and get me another jug." He held up the empty one, shaking it to show her nothing sloshed inside.

"That's just what you need." She rolled her eyes and stomped off.

He decided she wasn't coming back, and he'd have to go find his own drink. As he staggered to his feet, she slapped a full jug into his hands.

"That's a good girl." He slid back down to the deck.

"It isn't from me," she huffed. "I'd make you dry out. But Naila pities you. Go on, stay drunk. We don't need you any way."

Histrun frowned, trying to make sense of her words. She left before he could ask her what she meant. Shrugging, he gulped more cider, sighing as the fog swept over him, easing the pain in his heart.

Histrun's head slammed against the deck, startling him to awareness. Rain lashed down, soaking him and the deck, and the barge rocked and bucked like an angered stallion. He began to roll toward the railing, and the roiling, white water. He scrambled to grab onto the railing moments before he slid over.

"What in Crone's fires is going on?" he hollered.

Strong hands grabbed him about the waist and dragged him back onto the deck. "Let's get you strapped down." Eidelstrun carried him back to the cabin house.

"What's going on?" Histrun demanded.

"A storm slammed into us before Daelena could find a safe spot to tie up the barge. We're having to fight the storm and the river." Eidelstrun looped a strong rope around Histrun's waist and tied it onto a bolt on the deck. "Here, stay here." He patted Histrun on the shoulder, like a small child, then rushed off.

"I don't need to be tied down!" Histrun yelled. The wind tore the words away as they left his mouth. "At least you could have put me inside the cabin so I'd be dry," he muttered. He brushed the water from his face with his empty hands. The box with Zehala's ashes was missing! "Zehala!" He tried to slide out from underneath the rope binding him to the deck, but it held him too fast. He struggled with cold fingers to untie the knot.

It wouldn't give. "Goddess, no, no. Zehala!" He repeated the desperate cry over and over.

"Shh... Histrun, shh." Naila's rough voice, and mind-speech, penetrated his fog. "I have her."

He sagged against the rope, not caring that tears streamed down his face. "Thank you, Naila. Thank you."

After what seemed like forever, the river under them quit bucking, and the sky above them cleared. Eidelstrun came by and had to cut the ropes to free Histrun from his bonds that had kept him safe on the barge. The days—he wasn't sure how many—of drinking and mourning had left him weaker than he wanted to admit. He stood on shaky legs, and once they stopped trembling, made his way to the railing where Naila stood.

"Where are we?" His voice was as shaky as his legs.

"Almost home," she croaked. *I'm not sure how Daelena did it, but we're in Strunlair Province. Once she finds a place we can moor, we'll disembark.*

"Was anyone injured or lost in that storm?"

She shook her head. "Lucky, and Daelena's a good sailor."

He peered at the sun, but he couldn't gauge how much time had passed. "How long have we been on the river?"

"Eight days."

He whistled in surprise at how long he'd been out of it. He placed a hand over hers. "I'm sorry I've acted like a fool since we boarded."

"It's okay. I understand." She made a face, and a frustrated sound, then switched to mind-speech. *We all grieve in our own ways. At least on the river we didn't need you for any monster battles.*

He gazed at the passing shore and the familiar landscape sliding by. "I can't fight another battle, after... after what happened to Zehala, and you. I'm old and have fought for over seventy-five years. I'm done."

Don't make any rash decisions. Take time to fully mourn and to heal before making such a choice. You still have a lot to offer. "Thank you for that, Naila." He turned to face her. "She would be so proud of you and how, even injured, you've stepped up and taken charge."

Naila smiled. *She taught me well. You both did.*

Histrun returned his attention back to the shore, awkwardly patting her hand. Zehala had always been better at showing affection than him.

Ahead, an outcropping of rocks formed a deep pool alongside the shore. The sailor's shouts rang across the barge as they scurried across the deck. The barge slowly turned into the small harbor and bumped into the banks. Sailors jumped off, tying the barge on the nearby trees. Histrun recognized the area. Strunland Keep lay only ten measures to the northeast.

Once they secured the barge, Daelena joined Histrun and Naila at the railing. "The *Dawn Sister* be as far up the Storengher as she can go. You'll have to finish your journey across land."

"This is much farther than I expected you to take us, Daelena," Histrun said.

"It be farther than I expected! That last white water be tricky, especially going upriver. It should be a blast sailing down." Daelena extended her hand. "I be truly sorry about Zehala's death and wish you and your clan the best. If you need to travel the river again, I'd be happy to carry you."

"Even after I've been a drunken sod this whole trip?"

"Even so. At least you were quiet, except when you tried to sing."

Histrun frowned. "I didn't. I don't sing."

"Oh, we know." Daelena laughed.

Histrun his ears warmed. He had a horrible voice and sang way off-key. Zehala had been the singer. Her voice could charm the birds to sing with her.

He gripped Daelena's wrist in farewell and watched, bemused, as she and Naila hugged. Zehala would have done the same thing. The breeze shifted, and Histrun caught a whiff of himself. While the horses were being unloaded, he found a spot in the river to bathe. Feeling more like himself, he ordered his pack to mount. With a wave to Daelena and her sailors, Histrun led the way from the river toward Strunland Keep.

Home. Almost home at last.

Histrun rode through the familiar landscape. He attempted to not remember the many times he and Zehala had ridden this same route, or had crossed the same streams, or had fought in the same swamps. But the memories kept intruding, and the ghosts of the past haunted his mind's eye. That swamp and monster nest there was the first one where Zehala's fire-ring had worked to stop the monsters. And over there, in that copse of trees, was a hidden glade with soft grass where they'd made afternoon love more than once. He suspected Zehala had conceived Rizelya there.

The thought of the little girl drew him up short. How could he tell her that her mother would never tell her another story, or sing her another song, or teach her a new fire spell? Rizelya looked so like her mother. He doubted he could look at her without remembering Zehala and his pain.

The measures passed quickly under their horse's hooves. The shadows of dusk played across the land when they rode through the gates of Strunland Keep. Home. He was home—but it wouldn't ever be the same without his love and the other half of himself.

People streamed to the dining hall for the evening meal. A gaggle of children ran around the adult's legs, laughing as they played. Histrun caught sight of a dark-auburn-headed little girl chasing a white-headed one: Rizelya and Wisah. Rizelya put on a burst of speed and touched Wisah's shoulder, causing her to squeal in mock fright. His throat clenched, and his stomach dropped. He refused to be the one to ruin Rizelya's joy. He turned Telen away from the dining hall and toward the stable.

"Histrun!" Naila called. A coughing fit seized her. As soon as the attack subsided, she said, "Where are you going? The alphas are inside." She coughed again and held a hand to her throat.

It must still hurt her to talk. But then, it had only been two chedans since her injury. He looked back, and the children had disappeared.

"I can't face everyone right now." As he said it, it sounded lame in his own ears. He'd been an alpha, even a Clan Alpha for years, for most of his adult life. Death and loss weren't anything new. He should be stronger than this.

We need to inform the keep alphas what happened. Naila's eyes flicked to the dining hall entrance. *They're coming. We can tell them about Zehala, and they will tell the others.* She threw her leg over the saddle, slid off her horse, and handed the reins to Maheli. *Take our horses to the stable, then you can go eat dinner.*

"Yes, ma'am." Maheli saluted, shifting in her saddle while she waited for Histrun to dismount and dig out the box with Zehala's ashes from his saddlebag. After Histrun handed her his horse's reins, Maheli hurried after the others to the stables, and within moments, only Histrun and Naila stood in the courtyard.

He clutched the box to his chest, holding it close, as if through it, he could still hold Zehala.

"Histrun, Naila," Kolstrun's gruff voice broke Histrun's reverie. "What's going on?"

"We didn't expect you so soon." Koriana's gaze swept the courtyard. "Where's Zehala?"

Histrun raised his eyes, took a deep breath, and held out the box.

Koriana's hand flew to cover her mouth as she gasped. "No! That can't be her, can it?"

"It is," Naila said. "She's dead..." She swallowed hard and put a hand over her throat. *A janack crushed her. It's a long story.*

Koriana stepped toward Histrun, her arms out as if she wanted to hug him. He leaned back slightly. He'd never been one for public displays of emotion. She let her arms fall to her side. "I'm so sorry, Histrun. I know how much you loved her."

"My condolences," Kolstrun said, folding his arms over his chest. "It is a great loss to lose her knowledge and skills."

Koriana squinted at Naila in the failing light. "Sweet Mother! That looks like it hurts."

"It does, especially when I talk."

"Then don't. Use mind-speech. Come inside." Koriana gently wrapped an arm around Naila. She looked over her shoulder at Histrun. "You too. I understand how difficult it will be, but we need to know what happened."

The keep alphas led them to a small table in the corner of their office. Histrun carefully placed the box on the table. Kolstrun raised an eyebrow at it, but didn't say anything.

A few moments later, two young women brought in trays of food and set it on the table, bowing to the alphas before they left. The smell of spicy lamb and savory tubers made Histrun's mouth water, and his stomach growled. He scowled, trying to remember the last time he'd eaten. He didn't remember much of the return boat trip at all.

After a few milcrons, Koriana put down her mug. "Tell us about your journey, and how Zehala died."

Histrun stirred his tubers with his fork, staring at his plate. He didn't want to admit to them her death was his fault. But it was. She'd be alive now if he hadn't goaded Mendehan into going to the monster battle in an effort to avoid a dominance fight.

"We had a good trip until we reached Dehanlair Keep," Naila started, her voice rough. A coughing fit overtook her.

Histrun grimaced in shame. He shouldn't make her tell the story when it hurt her to talk. And mind-speaking for so long was exhausting. They used mind-speech mostly during fighting, when there was too much noise to hear commands, not for everyday communications.

"Zehala was her usual friendly-self." A smile flitting across Histrun's face as he remembered her joy at seeing a centaur and the wild horse herds running alongside them. "She made friends wherever we stopped."

He told them about meeting the Haaslair clan and Zehala's experiments for a different type of fire-ring, all the while caressing the box. The more he talked, the easier it became to talk about her as he remembered their journey. He shared the wonderful time they'd had crossing the plains and going down river on the *Dawn Sister*. Anger crept into Histrun's voice when he described the deplorable conditions they found in Dehanlair Keep.

"That's appalling!" Kolstrun leaned forward, placing a hand over his mouth. "I've never heard of an alpha letting their Keep become overrun with monsters."

"Mendehan had fallen into some sort of madness that twisted his mind." Histrun haltingly told them about Mendehan's actions with the young girl and about the monster fight. But when it came to telling them about how the janack had killed

Zehala, his throat closed. He couldn't say the words that would reveal his shame.

Naila took up the narrative. *The janack wrapped a tentacle around her. I tried to sever it, but another one caught me. After that, I didn't see what happened. I was too busy struggling to breathe. But the other fighters, who were there, have told me about the fight. Histrun tried to save Zehala, but Mendehan attacked him.*

Histrun frowned. He didn't remember that happening. He only remembered tearing into the tentacle in a frenzy, trying to free Zehala.

"That's despicable!" Koriana said, her hands on either side of her face. "Why would he do such a thing?"

"Because he was a sick caitiff." Naila's voice dripped with scorn. She switched back to mind-speech. *Histrun thrust Mendehan aside to fight the janack, only to have Mendehan attack him again. This time, Histrun knocked Mendehan unconscious. He returned his focus on the janack, tearing great chunks from the janack's tentacles.* She paused and took a drink of taevo. She brushed away the tears leaking down her cheeks.

It was the last monster to go down, and Lestrun, Eidelstrun, and the others joined in attacking it. By then, it had snapped Zehala's neck, and their efforts turned to keeping it from eating her. Together, they killed the beast. Mendehan regained consciousness, and Chestrun finally freed me, so I saw this next part. It was the strangest thing to see him dancing around the janack's head, as if he'd been the one to kill it. Histrun saw him, and a berserk rage overtook him—not that I blame him one bit—and he charged Mendehan. They fought. Mendehan didn't have a chance against Histrun's rage. It was awesome, and frightening, to see, especially after Mendehan shifted into his warrior form.

"No! He didn't!" Kolstrun eyes widening as his fist clenched around his mug. "That's cowardly and disgraceful. We never fight each other in our warrior forms."

Well, Mendehan did. Histrun remained in his natural form. Even then, Mendehan couldn't match Histrun's skill and strength. Histrun nearly tore Mendehan's head off!

"No, I didn't," Histrun said, confused. "I only broke his neck."

Naila raised her eyebrows at him. "I saw the body. You never looked at it again."

"Thank you, Histrun, Naila," Koriana said, "for telling us what happened to our good friend and clan member, Zehala. I know there is more, but that is enough for now." She gazed at the box Histrun still stroked. "We'll have a farewell ceremony for her tomorrow. Afterward, you can scatter her ashes over the land she loved so much. It's late, and you need rest."

At the dismissal, Histrun pushed away from the table and stood. He felt like an old, old man. Talking about Zehala's death had drained him of the little energy he had left. Why hadn't Naila told them it was his fault in the first place that the janack had grabbed Zehala? If he'd just moved faster, he could have saved her. He picked up the box and stumbled from the office.

On his way to his room, he stopped at the recreation room, relieved to find it empty, and grabbed a bottle of whiskey. It was much better for forgetting than the hard cider from Dehanlair. He opened the door to his room, but paused on the threshold. One of Zehala's shirts hung on the back of a chair. The book she'd been reading lay open on the desk, and draped at the bed's foot was the blanket she liked to wrap around her shoulders. He scurried inside, snatching up the blanket and bolting from the room. There was too much of her in it. He wandered to the wooded area by the horse pasture, curled up under a large oak, and wrapped the blanket around his shoulders. He took a swig from the bottle. "Zehala, forgive me, love. I should have saved you."

He drank until the litany of self-incrimination stopped—or he blacked out. He wasn't sure which occurred first.

Chapter 12

Histrun awoke with a start, sputtering at the water splashing on his face. Naila stood over him with an empty bucket, glaring at him. He quickly checked Zehala's box of ashes, letting out a sigh. They weren't wet from his dunking. Zehala's blanket bunched at his feet had escaped the water, too. As he sat up, the bark of the oak tree he'd slept under scratched his back. He blinked at the late afternoon sun.

"The farewell ceremony for Zehala is at sunset," Naila informed him. She rubbed her throat as she held out her other hand. *Give me her ashes. The priestess needs them to prepare the service.*

"No, I'll do it." Histrun hugged the box to his chest.

Naila put her hands on her hips and scowled at him. *You have an octar to get cleaned up. We can't have a farewell ceremony without Zehala's ashes.*

Histrun clutched the box to him and scowled at Naila. "I'll be there."

"Be sure you are." Naila took several steps away from him. She stopped, whirling around and placing her fisted hands on her hips. *There's someone else who's hurting and missing Zehala. You remember your daughter, Rizelya, don't you? She could use you now.*

"Does she know?"

Naila nodded. "I told her."

Histrun watched her tromp down the path. His head ached, and his mouth tasted sour. Making a face, he reached for the whiskey bottle and lifted it to his lips, only to find it empty. Tossing it aside, he used the tree to push himself to a standing position. When the world stopped spinning, he strode back toward his pack's house. He kept to the side streets to avoid coming into contact with anybody, not wanting to hear any condolences for his loss.

He entered his room, snatched some clean clothing, and hustled to the bathing room. The few people already there took one look at his face and left him alone while he bathed and dressed. Histrun noticed himself in the mirror. His blood-shot and puffy eyes stood out from his red hair, noticeably paler with age these days. His scraggly beard attested to his lack of self-care over the past few chedans. He ran his fingers through it. *I should shave. Zehala hates the scratchiness of beards.* He dropped his hand and leaned his forehead against the mirror. *It doesn't matter if I shave or not. Zehala isn't here to care if I have a beard.*

Histrun trudged up the stairs, dreading the emotional turmoil to come of formally saying goodbye to his love. He detoured into the recreation room, poured himself a large glass of whiskey, and downed it in a single gulp.

The setting sun's rays burnished the clouds gold as Histrun hurried into the temple. The White Priestess nodded to him and indicated for him to approach the central altar, already covered in candles and mementos. He carefully placed the box with Zehala's ashes in the empty space in the center. After giving it a loving caress, he stepped back.

A small hand slipped into his. Startled, he looked down. Rizelya stood next to him. Wisah held her other hand, and Naila stood on the other side of Wisah. They represented all the direct family Zehala had left in the world.

Rizelya glanced around the room with wide eyes. She dropped his hand to tug on his pant leg. "Sir?" She swallowed hard when he glowered at her. "Sir, where's Mother? She said she'd only be away a little while, and she went with you. You're back, so where is she?"

Histrun winced. *She doesn't understand! How do I explain to a five-year-old her mother is never coming back?* He turned to glare at Naila. She'd said she'd told the little girl. Naila shrugged. He knelt, trying not to be so imposing. "She's gone to live with the Mother Goddess. We're telling her goodbye now."

"Oh. I didn't believe Wisah." She bent her head, shuffling her feet. "I thought she was teasing me when she told me she'd seen Mother cross the veil."

"Riz! I wouldn't tease you about something like that," Wisah objected, then lowered her voice. "She misses you so much." She raised her eyes to meet Histrun's. "You, too, although she's worried about you. I don't know why."

Histrun gulped and closed his eyes. "I do. Thank you, Wisah, for the message." He gently gripped Rizelya's shoulder. "Would you like to help me scatter her ashes?"

Rizelya nodded.

Histrun straightened. The White Priestess began the ceremony. His eyes burned with unshed tears when the priestess extolled Zehala's many accomplishments. She paused, turning to him, expecting him to speak, and he vehemently shook his head. If he spoke now, he'd fall into a blubbering heap. He had to stay strong—for Rizelya, for Naila, and for his clan.

One-by-one, people stepped forward to say a few words about Zehala, first Naila and their fighting-pack, then other clan members. The temple's candles pushed back the darkness that had settled. The White Priestess picked up the box and reverently led the procession from the temple to the high hill they used for the funeral pyres. She stopped at the top. Only the slightest sliver of the smallest moon, Chelar, shone in the night sky. The priestess handed the box to Histrun. He hesitated. When he opened the lid, the last bit of Zehala would be gone. Finally, he remembered his promise to Rizelya. He scooped her into his arms.

"Together, little one," he whispered to her. "Let's open it together."

Rizelya nodded and placed her hand—it appeared so tiny next to his much larger one—on top of the box. He gave her a small nod, and they lifted the lid.

A breeze delicately delved into the box, turning into a miniature whirlwind which gathered the ashes and lifted them high into the air. It carried them across the keep and deeper into the mountains, falling like a gentle rain on the land Zehala had loved. When the dust cloud disappeared from view, a minuscule pile of ashes lay tucked in the corner. He caught the White Priestess's eye, and she nodded once.

"Is she gone now?" Rizelya asked.

"Yes, little one. She's gone." Histrun set her down. He wasn't used to holding the little girl in his arms, and it made him uncomfortable. He closed the lid on the box so he wouldn't lose the precious ashes.

"It's okay, Riz," Wisah whispered to Rizelya. "Your mama is with the Mother Goddess now. I saw the Mother embrace her, and she was so happy to be home. Don't worry, Rizelya, you still have me. And you can share my mama with me."

Naila gathered both girls into her arms. "That's right, you have me. You also have all the caretakers in the crèche who will take care of you, just like always."

"Oh, okay. I guess that will be okay," Rizelya said.

Histrun watched them leave, unsure of what to say or do. He mentally shrugged. The little girl would be fine.

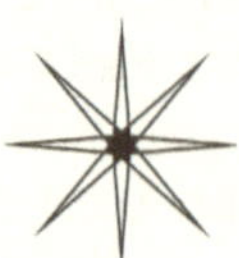

The next morning, Histrun took the precious ashes and his bond-mate torque to the metalsmith's shop. He'd already twisted the bit of Zehala's hair into the entwined metal.

He placed the torque on the table in front of Maehalya. "Can you make the center piece into a locket?"

Maehalya pushed back her dark-brown hair. She picked up the torque and examined the ruby. "This looks like my work. I should be able to modify it for you. What would you like to put inside?"

Histrun carefully opened the box to reveal the bit of ashes.

"Ah, Zehala's?"

Histrun nodded.

"Leave it here. I'll have it for you by the end of the chedan." Maehalya placed the torque on top of the box, then disappeared with the items behind a curtain.

Histrun frowned, perplexed by Maehalya's actions. The Keep provided everyone's basic needs as everyone shared in the upkeep and protection of their community. However, for personal items like the torque, he was expected to give something, or do something for the person doing the work.

Instead of returning to the room he'd shared with Zehala, he stalked to Kolstrun's office. "I need a different room to sleep in," he groused, flopping into the chair across from Kolstrun's desk. "I can't stay in the old one. Too many memories."

"This isn't unexpected. You haven't slept in your old room since you returned." Kolstrun sat back in his chair. "Due to your age and past service, you can have the single on the east side."

"Thanks," Histrun said.

Within the octar, he'd moved his few belongings into the small room overlooking the practice arena and the adjacent woods.

At the end of the chedan, Histrun anxiously opened the door to Maehalya's workshop. The metalsmith stood behind a table spread with a black cloth. Histrun's mate-torque lay in the center. The ruby glinted under the soft lights, and the gold gleamed from a recent polishing.

Maehalya placed her hands on either side of the torque. "With a locket, you'd risk losing Zehala's ashes if it came open when you fought. Instead, I sealed the ashes behind the ruby. They will never fall out, and as long as you have this, her ashes will be close to you."

Histrun gently lifted the torque, his hands shaking slightly, and placed it around his neck. The metal quickly warmed. "Thank you. I will never take it off."

"I hope you can find peace and happiness again, Histrun," Maehalya said quietly as he left.

How could he ever be happy again? His love, his life, was gone. He knew he shouldn't, but he prayed the Mother would take him too, and soon. He didn't want to live with the emptiness in his heart and soul.

Histrun wandered to the storehouse and raided the liquor cabinet, taking several bottles of whiskey, and, for good measure, a jug of hard cider. Drinking was the only thing that allowed him to forget the ache of his loss. Over the next few days, he spent his time leaning against the building across from the crèche, watching Rizelya and her new friend, Aistrun, play. The young boy towered over her. Histrun chuckled when he overheard Aistrun call Rizelya "Little Red," to which she'd call him "Wolf."

Soon, even watching Rizelya didn't stop his heartache. Instead, he found himself growling in rage at the sight of her. Her auburn curls and sunny disposition reminded him too much of Zehala. He wished Zehala were alive and with him, not the miniature version.

He took to wandering in the wooded area within the keep grounds during the day, where he drank until he passed out. Most nights, he'd fall into a drunken stupor under a tree, and not wake up until well past mid-day. On the rare occasions when the drunken daze lifted, he became aware of the pitying looks people gave him as he staggered through the keep.

One day, he stumbled into the storehouse and blinked in foggy surprise. A shiny new lock hung on the liquor cabinet. A few moments later, Kolstrun strode into the room.

"You won't get any more liquor, Histrun," Kolstrun said, harshly.

Histrun swayed, trying to focus on the alpha. "I'll just get it from my room."

"There isn't any there. I had it all removed."

"Can't do that." Histrun wiped the spittle from his chin.

Kolstrun leaned against the cabinet and crossed his arms over his chest. "I'm the keep alpha, and I can do what I need to do to protect my people. And in this case, it means keeping you from drinking anymore."

"My life. I can do what I want."

Kolstrun frowned, his gaze raked over Histrun. "Look at you, man! There are leaves and twigs in your tangled hair. Your beard is straggly and untrimmed. Not to mention how filthy and rumpled your clothes are from spending days in them. I've seen you sleep outdoors more often than in a bed. You won't be able to continue much longer. Summer is almost gone. The nights will soon get cold as autumn arrives." He wrinkled his nose. "And when did you bathe last?"

"Don't know," Histrun slurred. "Don't care. Why do you care?"

"This isn't healthy. I'm worried about you. Crone's fires! The entire keep is worried about you."

"But why?"

"You've been an esteemed leader of this keep and of Strunlair Clan for all of my life." Kolstrun's voice softened as he uncrossed his arms. "I've looked up to you and tried to follow your example and leadership. I can't stand to see you like this. The young ones are beginning to think of you as 'that worthless, drunk old man.' They're forgetting how much you've done for this clan, for our people. You need to snap out of it. We still need you. We still need your skills, your knowledge, and your wisdom."

Kolstrun pushed away from the cabinet. "We've let you mourn, but it's been six chedans since you returned to the keep. And you've spent the entire time in a drunken stupor. You aren't even mourning, and certainly not healing. You're hiding from your feelings and the world. But Histrun, the world still needs you. This keep still needs you."

"There's nothing left for me." Histrun eyed Kolstrun, wondering if he could wrestle the keys to the lock from him.

"Maybe not here," Kolstrun agreed. A few moments later, Naila slipped into the room.

"We have a favor to ask you," Naila croaked. Her voice was still rough from her injury. She cleared her throat and switched to mind-speech. *But you'll have to get sober and stay sober to do it.*

Histrun debated about outright refusing. The alcohol kept him comfortably numb. But she was Zehala's daughter. He'd at least hear what she wanted from him.

Taking his silence as assent, Naila continued. *My daughter, Wisah, is now five and needs to go to the Sanctuary for her priestess training. I don't think I need to tell you how powerful she is. She can't remain here without training much longer. I'd like you to take her for me. I trust you'll get her safely to the Sanctuary.*

"And," Kolstrun added, "you can stay there for a while where there aren't constant reminder of Zehala. Perhaps then you can start to heal. I meant it, Histrun. We really do still need you. But not like this." He waved a hand at Histrun, encompassing his slovenly appearance. "We need you at your best."

"Please, Histrun," Naila implored.

He turned his head away as he considered their words. High in the mountains, there weren't any monsters near the

Sanctuary. He wouldn't have to be terrified of going into battle again and failing, of letting someone else die because he was too old and too slow to save them. Perhaps at the Sanctuary he could find the peace he couldn't find anywhere else, not even at the bottom of a bottle.

"I'll..." He cleared his throat, making a face at the sourness in his mouth. "I'll do it. I'll take Wisah to the Sanctuary. When do you want us to leave?"

"Within a few days," Naila said.

"We need to gather a pack to go with you," Kolstrun added. "It will give you a bit of time to start drying out."

Histrun nodded, glancing at the liquor cabinet again and licking his lips. He resolutely turned away from it and walked out of the storeroom. As he strode to his room, he tried to ignore his shaking hands and the snakes crawling in his belly. He was a warrior. He could defeat this new enemy: the need for alcohol.

Chapter 13

Histrun gathered a fresh set of clothes and descended the stairs to the bathing room. When he passed the mirror, he stopped short, gaping at his disheveled appearance. Kolstrun's description of him had been kind. His eyes were bloodshot and puffy, red blotches mottled his face. He leaned closer to the mirror, fingering the bruise darkening his check above his scraggly beard and trying to remember how he'd received it. He shook his head. The last few chedans were nothing but a blur in his mind. His snarled hair contained numerous leaves and twigs entwined in it, as well as a clump of something unidentifiable. With much gritting of his teeth—and loss of hair—he finally tugged all the leaves out. He left the gunk alone, not wanting to touch it, afraid it was something awful, like horse manure. Peeling off his filthy clothing revealed more bruises and scrapes.

It took several buckets of water and vigorous scrubbing to get all the dirt, and the mysterious crud, from his body and hair. By the time he finished, his hands shook, queasiness clenched his stomach, and a headache throbbed behind his eyes. He climbed into the big redwood tub and slid into the steaming water. He found a bench at the right level to submerge his entire body. Leaning his head back on the tub's edge, he closed his eyes, letting the warmth sink into his muscles. After several milcrons, he finally relaxed. Histrun's mind floated in a place of emptiness. For the first time since Zehala's death, no guilt assailed him, no fear attacked him, and no memories plagued him.

The sound of a scrub brush splashing into a wash bucket startled him awake. He surged out of the water, his eyes searching for the danger, his fists at the ready. His breath came in short gasps, a sudden pain clutched his chest, and his throat closed, causing him to choke. Fur covered the hand he raised to his throat, and the tip of a claw bit into the top of his shoulder.

A teenage boy padded into the soaking area, his wet hair streaming in front of his face. He froze, like a startled ducorn. "Ah, sorry, sir," he sputtered, his eyes wide. "I didn't know anyone else was here."

Histrun sucked in a deep breath and tried to release the magic he'd called unconsciously. It took several tries for his hand to return to normal.

The young man sidled to the far edge and appeared ready to bolt.

"It's okay, son." Histrun's voice shook, and his hands trembled. "I'm sorry. You startled me. I was asleep." He climbed out of the tub, reaching for a nearby towel. "I'm leaving. You can stay and finish your bath."

"Yes... sir," the boy stammered. He didn't move until Histrun exited the soaking area.

Histrun quickly dressed. He picked up his razor to trim his beard, but the tremors in his hands convinced him it could wait, rather than risk cutting his own throat. Standing with his hands braced on the sink, he gazed at himself in the mirror. *Why had I reacted so violently to the young man's entrance? Am I turning into a caitiff like Mendehan to attack children?* He shook his head at the thought and wished he could blame his reaction on a nightmare, but his doze had been dreamless. "I could really use a drink right now," he told his reflection, "to calm my nerves. But I promised Naila I wouldn't drink. I can't let her down."

Back in his room, he slumped onto the edge of his bed, his hands clasped tightly between his knees, trying to stop their shaking. The dinner bell reverberated through the walls—and in his aching head. He pushed to his feet and immediately crumpled back onto the bed. He clutched his head with one hand to stop the dizziness, and his stomach with the other to hold back the nausea. Groaning, he laid still. The thought of food and eating made his stomach roil even more. He curled up on his side in a tight ball, squeezing his eyes shut and gritting his teeth.

Quite some time later, a soft knock sounded on his door.

"What?" he croaked.

A woman with walnut-brown hair and sage-green eyes stepped into his room. She held a steaming mug in one hand and several packets in the other.

Histrun warily eyed the mug, unsure his stomach could handle a nasty-tasting concoction, which seemed like the only thing the healers knew how to make.

"I heard you were trying to dry out from all that alcohol in your system." Andreyan glided to the bedside. "You don't look so good. I imagine you don't feel so well either. Quitting drinking takes a toll on the body. Come on and sit up for me. I have a brew here to help your shakiness, nausea, and headache." She held out the mug.

Histrun levered himself to a sitting position and gingerly took the mug from the healer. Surprisingly, the scent wafting off it had a pleasant, minty, floral scent. He took a sip, then another. It didn't taste so bad either, except for a bit of bitterness under the sweetness. "What is this?"

"A blend of chamomile, hops, lemon balm, peppermint, lavender, ginger, and valerian root."

The last herb explained the bitterness and the hint of dirty socks smell. He took another sip, letting the warmth slide down his throat.

Andreyan watched him. When he started to put the mug down, she stopped him. "Go on, drink it all. Alcohol withdrawal isn't something we can heal with our magic. The Goddess doesn't reward stupidity with an easy fix. The only way to treat it is with herbs and time. Over the next few days, you'll probably feel worse before you feel better. This is more of the herbal mixture you're drinking." She held up a blue packet, the largest of the three. She showed him a red one. "This is for the headaches. You'll want to drink it fast. And this one is for the chills, sweating, and fever that will come." She waved the yellow packet. She placed them on the table next to his bed. "The best thing you can do is drink plenty of water and the brew from the blue packet. Go to the baths and soak, and believe it or not, exercise. You need to get your blood pumping the alcohol from your system. You should feel like eating again in the morning."

Finished with the brew, Histrun set the mug on the table. "Thank you, Andreyan." Already the nausea and headache had eased, and his hands weren't shaking as much.

"It's no trouble," Andreyan waved away the sentiment. "Lay back down and try to get some sleep. I'll come check on you in the morning." She pulled the bedding up and covered him, patting his shoulder before she left his bedside. At the door, she paused. "Oh, Histrun? No matter how bad you feel, don't succumb and start drinking again. I've put a spell on the herbal mixture to make you violently ill if you drink any alcohol."

Histrun's eyes widened. He knew the healer wouldn't bluff about something like that. Now he had an added incentive to stop drinking.

True to Andreyan's prediction, over the next two days, Histrun's withdrawal symptoms worsened. But on the third day, he awoke without any tremors, headache, or nausea. His heart still felt like it had been ripped from his chest, but he could function and go through the motions of living.

Naila joined him at breakfast. "You look better. Will you be ready to leave tomorrow?"

"Yes. The healer's brew has helped."

The next morning, Histrun's eyebrows knitted together when he entered the courtyard. A gaggle of children gathered, waiting to start the journey. When he'd agreed to Naila's favor, it had been to escort one child, Wisah. The passel included five white-haired little girls, including Wisah, three brown-haired teenagers, and two White Priestesses in their late teens. He stomped over to Koriana, who stood off to the side.

"What's the meaning of all this?" He waved an impatient hand toward the children.

"The White Priestesses have finished their training here and are returning to the Sanctuary. The teenagers are metalsmiths and are going to Strunland Keep to apprentice with the helstramiester. The other children are old enough to be sent to the Sanctuary to begin their priestess training. It seemed a waste of an opportunity not to send them with you."

"I didn't agree to babysit," Histrun grumbled. "With all of them along, it's going to take much longer to reach the Sanctuary." Now he understood why Naila had assigned additional fighters to his platoon. They'd need them if they did run into a nest missed by the regular sweeps, or crossed a nest ready to mature.

"You'll be fine." Koriana laughed. "What else do you have to do?" Without waiting for his answer, she turned away, hurrying to help Maheli tie a pack onto a multa's back.

Wisah lingered at the courtyard's perimeter, out of the way. Rizelya stood next to her, a forlorn frown on her face as she watched the proceedings. Her friend Aistrun held her hand. Histrun idly wandered a few steps closer to hear their exchange.

"But Wisah, you can't go," Rizelya pleaded, her eyes shining with unshed tears. "You'll never come back, just like my mama."

Wisah, with a maturity beyond her tender young age, pulled Rizelya into a hug. "I'll be back, Rizelya. You'll soon begin your training to be a Red, and I'm going to the Sanctuary to start mine as a White. Before you know it, I'll be riding back through those gates to do my apprenticeship training at our temple. I won't let the Supreme send me anywhere else, I promise."

"I'll miss you." Rizelya wiped her eyes, then gazed at the horses. "Did you see the one they picked out for you? It isn't a pony. It's a big horse! I can't wait until I can have a horse of my own. She'll be like my mama's horse, Kylara. Poor thing, she misses her friend something fierce. About as much as I'm going to miss you, Wisah."

"Hey, Little Red," Aistrun said, scuffing a toe in the dirt. "I'll still be here. You won't be alone. I'll watch out for you."

"I know, Wolf, but you're not the same as Wisah." Rizelya heaved a sigh.

Naila approached the children. "It's time to go."

The two little girls hugged again. Naila took Wisah's hand and led her to her waiting horse. Aistrun put an arm around Rizelya's shoulder. Histrun thought he should go to the girl and say something to her, but he wasn't sure what to say to a five-year-old. As he made the final checks on Telen's saddle girth, he glanced up. Rizelya watched him longingly. He nodded to her and saluted. She threw back her shoulders and saluted him back with a grin.

He surveyed the courtyard. The children sat on their horses, and the fighters stood ready to go.

"Mount up!" he ordered. The creak of leather filled the courtyard as people climbed into their saddles. "Move out!" He gave the signal and led the platoon through the gate.

The morning sun shone on the fertile fields, and the ripening grain waved in the soft breeze. The field workers had already harvested several vegetable plots and preserved the produce for the coming winter. Various shades of orange dotted the ground as the squashes broke through the covering vines. They passed a crew mending the stone fences to ensure they were strong enough to withstand any monster incursions. At the first fork in the road, he guided his group on the northwest path toward Strunlair Keep. The route took them through Strunland's orchards, where glistening red and yellow apples hung heavily from the tree limbs.

Histrun nodded in satisfaction at the well-maintained fences and abundant fields of Strunland Territory. They contrasted sharply with the desolate lands around Dehanlair Keep.

It would take many years before Dehanlair Keep would flourish as much as Strunland did now. The Dehanlair people would struggle to survive the coming winter, even with help from the rest of the province. Maybe he should mention it to Felstrun and Tylira, the Strunlair clan alphas, when he met with them in a few days.

All of Strunlair Province was prospering, not only Strunland Territory. The province had been the first to implement the new fighting method and to reap the benefits of containing the monsters to their nests and swamps. The land wasn't being constantly attacked by monster slime, and the animals weren't being eaten by the monsters. They had the surplus now to send aid to Dehanlair. Just because Mendehan had been a rogue didn't mean his people should suffer more than they already had.

The sounds of children's giggles broke his reverie. He turned in his saddle and frowned at the gaggle of children riding in the center. It was going to be a long trip with so many children along. Grumbling, Histrun turned back to the road.

They passed the last fenced area into a wide meadow. A sudden whoop, followed by the thundering of a galloping horse—

no, three galloping horses with teenagers on their backs—made Telen rear. They ran past him and into the meadow. Histrun jerked on Telen's reins to keep him from joining in the race.

"Slow down, you imbeciles!" he shouted. He lifted his head skyward, shaking it. *Sweet Mother, this is going to be an extremely long journey.*

"Let them have some fun while it's safe," Lorstriel said, coming to ride beside him. "They'll settle down in a few days."

"Days! You mean I have to put up with their shenanigans for days?"

"Most likely. They're young and full of energy. This is the first time they've been allowed to go beyond the keeps' boundaries, so they're excited."

Histrun swore under his breath. The racers were getting too far away for his liking. "Maheli! Chestrun! Go catch those fools and make sure they're safe. And make sure they walk their horses to cool them down."

The two nudged their horses from the line and kicked them into a gallop. Their plains-bred horses could run faster and farther than the locally bred horses the children rode. Histrun was confident they'd soon overtake the youngsters. He scowled, then ordered Alixstrun and Dorstrun to join them. Although the Strunland fighters diligently eradicated the monsters in their nests, there was always a chance for a nest to mature out of phase.

The faces of the other children were alight with excitement as they took in the new sights. Scratching his head, he turned back to Lorstriel. "So if this is their first time away from the keep, they won't be used to long days in the saddle, will they?"

She shook her head. "Nor are they skilled riders. Those that raced ahead are the older ones, the apprentices. I doubt the younger ones are capable of cantering or galloping, at least not yet."

Histrun swore again. This was going to be an excessively long journey. *Why did I let Naila talk me into this?* He didn't even like children, and now he was going to have to spend chedans with a whole gaggle of them. He patted his jacket, reassured by the flask in his pocket. When they stopped for the night at the safe-house, he'd fill it with something more bracing than taevo.

He'd promised not to drink, but that was before he knew he'd have to deal with not one but ten children.

Histrun breathed out a sigh when the spires of Strunlair Keep peeked over the treetops. Their slow pace had dragged the normal three or four days of travel into seven. They'd covered more measures per day over the past two days because the children could maintain a trot for several measures and even handle a short canter. The journey had been sedate since they hadn't had to battle any monsters. Pride swelled Histrun's chest at how well the Strunlair fighters kept the monsters at bay. It made traveling safer, especially with so many children, than it had ever been before.

The trees parted to reveal the familiar massive stone wall surrounding Strunlair Keep. Histrun's heart squeezed, and his gut clenched. Some of his best memories of Zehala had occurred in that keep. *You can do this,* he told himself.

Histrun's party paused, waiting for the shepherds to herd a flock of sheep across the road toward their night pens inside the keep. Field workers walked along the road, heading back to the keep from their day's work. Some people waved and called out greetings to him. He'd spent many, many years in Strunlair Keep—sixteen as the Clan Alpha and eight of those years as co-alpha with Zehala. He took a deep breath. By the time they reached the keep, someone would inform the alphas of his arrival.

He didn't allow his group to linger and gawk at the massive gates, which were wide enough for four horses to ride abreast. He pushed on to the main plaza fronting the clan-house. Built from granite flecked with mica, the building sparkled in the sun. A sweeping white marble porch skirted the front of the building. Black marble columns held up a balcony. Dark ironwood double doors, polished to a glossy shine, blocked the entrance. They had wide bands of helstrim affixed to them, giving them added strength against the monsters. The vast building could hold more than a thousand people in case of an attack on the keep.

As he'd predicted, Clan Alphas Felstrun and Tylira stood on the porch. A grin lit Felstrun's dark-brown eyes, and he pushed back the cinnamon-brown hair that flopped into his eyes. Histrun lifted his hand in greeting. He'd always liked the tall, lean man. Felstrun had his arm wrapped around the waist of his co-alpha and lover. Tylira's vermilion hair flowed down past her shoulders and her pale-yellow eyes shone with warmth.

Without waiting for permission, Histrun slid off his horse, tossed the reins to Maheli, and approached the stairs.

"Welcome, Histrun." Felstrun gripped Histrun's wrist. He looked over Histrun's shoulder at the cluster of weary children and raised an eyebrow. "I never would have expected for you to travel with so many little ones."

Histrun grimaced. "I was tricked into it. I'd agreed to escort Naila's daughter to the Sanctuary to begin her training, and somehow, it morphed into that!" He waved toward the children.

"Which one is she?" Tylira craned her neck to examine the group.

Histrun studied them, then pointed. "That one. The one with creamy-white hair on the blue roan mare."

"Oh, she'll be a powerful White Priestess when she comes fully into her Talent."

"She already is. Wisah has seen souls cross the veil."

Tylira gaped. "That is unusual for one so young. It's a good thing you're taking her to the Sanctuary to be trained by the Supreme." She glanced to her right.

Histrun followed her gaze. Several women with Brown Talent approached, wearing the uniforms of caregivers. He inwardly sighed in relief. They'd take the children to the crèche and out of his hair while they remained in Strunlair. The women took charge of the children, quickly helping them off their horses, and ushering them away from the courtyard toward the crèche. The three teenagers fidgeted in discomfort until a woman with chestnut-brown hair and wearing a leather smock turned around the corner. They brightened when they saw her and hurried to greet her, then followed her away from the courtyard. The two White Priestesses bowed respectfully to the Clan Alphas, before wearily tromping across the courtyard to the temple.

"Your people will stay in the clan-house," Felstrun said to Histrun, loud enough for them to hear him.

Lorstriel nodded in acknowledgment. She led the remaining group to the stables, each leading a horse or two of the children's horses. The children were too young to be expected to untack the horses and curry them. And White Priestesses didn't do such menial chores.

Tylira turned sad eyes on him. "We heard about what happened to Zehala. We're so sorry for your loss. She will be greatly missed by everyone."

"Dinner won't be served for another half octar." Felstrun put a hand on Histrun's shoulder. "Come, let's share a drink and toast to her memory while we wait."

"That would be good."

Histrun strode beside Felstrun, toward the alpha's study. They settled into comfortable leather chairs, and Felstrun poured a double-shot of whiskey for them both.

"To Zehala! One fine woman," Felstrun toasted.

Histrun held the glass under his nose and inhaled deeply. His mouth watering in anticipation. As he lifted the drink to his lips, the words of the healer floated back to him, telling him she'd spelled her healing brew. He hadn't fixed himself any of the healer's brew while on the road. Keeping track of the gaggle of children kept him so busy and exhausted he hadn't craved a drink. Cautiously, he sipped, enjoying the alcohol burn trailing down his throat. He waited for a few anxious milcrons. When nothing happened, he tossed the rest of the drink down and held out his glass for a refill.

One drink became several as they reminisced. Histrun and Zehala had worked extensively with the current Clan Alphas, and they were old friends. Felstrun ordered dinner brought to them, rather than interrupt their conversation, to go to the dining hall.

Two octars past the midnight bell, Histrun staggered to his bed chamber, and he admitted as he flopped onto the bed, he was quite drunk. The next morning, he lay in bed, groaning from the hangover. *After the last chedan of dealing with children, it felt good to talk with an adult. I deserved to relax for the night and reminisce with my old friend. I'm glad we stayed clear of talking about Zehala, mostly.* He swung his legs off the bed, sitting up and putting his head between his knees. As he gazed at his trembling hands, he knew that was just an excuse.

Even as his head pounded and his stomach roiled with queasiness, he craved a drink. He yearned to forget who he was, forget his inability to save Zehala, and most of all, forget his pain. He'd never been one to bury himself in a bottle, but he hadn't ever lost the love of his life either. Zehala wouldn't approve of his self-loathing, or hiding from his pain in the depths of alcohol. But she wasn't here, and he was. He slipped off the bed and huddled on the floor with his arms wrapped around his knees, holding back the grief. After a long time, he resolved to do better, to be the man Zehala had fallen in love with, not the contemptible failure he was now. Much later, he fixed himself a cup from the healer's herbal tea from the blue packet.

Histrun and his pack spent the next two days in Strunlair Keep, resting and recuperating from the long ride. The next leg of their journey would grow more arduous as they traversed through the mountains.

When they rode out the back gate on their way to Strunhelos Keep, Histrun continuously looked over his shoulder to be sure they had everyone. The gaggle of children was too quiet. The group now included eight more little girls with White and Gray Talents ready to begin their priestess training at the Sanctuary, plus three more White Priestesses. Tylira had given him the same excuse Koriana had used. Why waste the opportunity when he was traveling to the Sanctuary any way? Thankfully, for his nerves, they'd lost the three boisterous helstramiester apprentices. Although, he expected fourteen children to make more noise than the future White Priestesses did.

A narrow sheadash stone road wove its way through orchards with plump fruit hanging from their branches. In a few dozen measures, a thick forest replaced the orchards. They rode under tall pine, bushy spruce, and majestic oak trees. The horse's hooves stomping on the ground littered with pine needles released a fresh, clean scent. The road took them northeast toward the towering peaks of the White Mountains, where the Sanctuary was located. Strunhelos Keep guarded the only pass into those mountains. Once they were through it, they wouldn't have to worry about Malvers' monsters. The mountains were too cold for them, and as far as he knew, no monsters had ever crossed beyond the Strunhelos Pass.

Every measure north they traveled, they climbed higher into the mountains. Even though it was the last chedans of summer, the chilly nights made his knees and hands ache. The distance between safe-houses increased as the land grew more wild. Strunhelos Territory was the most sparsely populated territory in Lairheim. A few minor keeps snuggled in the mountains, not much more than permanent logging and hunting camps.

As they rode deeper into the mountains, Histrun kept a close watch on the shadows near the trail. Although there might not be many Malvers' monster nests in the area, there were other, equally dangerous predators, like paethers and narhili. They would be safe from the nocturnal narhili beasts as long as they didn't travel after dusk. The paether, though, hunted during the day, and this was their territory. Histrun hoped the large group of fighters would deter any attacks, but he also worried that the children would make tempting targets for the beasts. He sat stiffly in his saddle, his eyes darting anxiously at the shadows as he watched for danger. After three days of nothing out of the ordinary happening, his nerves felt strung taunt.

Two measures from the last safe-house before reaching Strunhelos, Telen shied away from a shadow at the base of a spruce tree. Histrun inhaled deeply and caught a musky scent. He narrowed his eyes, searching the brush beside the road. He glimpsed the long, lean body of a paether. Its mottled gray hide was the perfect shade for slinking in the forest's shadows. Long tusks jutted from the lower jaw of a square head. Its four eyes— two in the regular position, facing forward, and two on the top of its head—allowed it to see its prey as it ran under its belly.

"Paether!" he yelled as he drew his helstrablade. "Protect the children. Don't let the beasts get under your horses and ride! Ride like your life depends on it."

Immediately, the ring of helstrablades being drawn from their sheathes rang out. The Reds in the group unhooked their helbraughts from their saddles and fed fire magic into the long blades. The light of the glowing blades penetrated the forest's gloom. They moved to the outside where their longer reach would be more effective against the low-slung paether.

Wisah squawked when Chestrun plucked her from her saddle and plopped her in front of him. The other fighters did the same with the other young children. Histrun knew the men would protect the children with their lives. The fighters kicked their heels into their horse's flanks, and the horses leaped forward into a gallop, with the riderless horses keeping pace. The five White Priestesses leaned low on their horses as they raced toward the safe-house. Histrun debated whether to shift to his warrior form, but he couldn't ride Telen in that form, and Telen could run much faster than he could.

Gray shapes surged from the shadows, keeping pace with the horses. Maheli's helbraught swung through the air, resulting in a yip of pain from the paether trying to weave under her horses' hooves. Telen suddenly kicked out, and Histrun clung to the saddle, as Telen's hoof connected with a thud. The paether dropped behind them with its head caved in. Another one darted toward them. Histrun leaned over, thrusting his blade into the ugly beast's head. He jerked the blade free in time to slash into another beast attempting to slide under Telen's belly.

Histrun risked a glance ahead to see how close they were to the safe-house. The lead riders, those with the children, flew through the gates. A paether snapped at Telen's heels, who kicked out again, nearly unseating Histrun. He turned his attention back to the fight at hand. Only a few beasts remained of the original dozen. Lorstriel drew her horse to a stop at the side of the gate, while Kehali did the same on the other side. Their glowing blades dripped blood. With a swing of her helbraught, Lorstriel neatly decapitated a large male. Its head rolled to the side of the road.

"Go! Go!" she urged. "We'll keep them from getting in."

While the fighters still on the road kicked their horses into greater speed, Histrun held Telen back, ensuring everyone made it through the gates before him. Ahead of him, a horse stumbled, falling to its side and throwing its rider. Alixstrun rolled to his feet. A paether tore into Alixstrun's horse's exposed belly, and another two paethers lunged toward Alixstrun. But before they could reach him, he shifted into his warrior form and howled. He tore into the paether. As soon as he finished destroying the beasts, Alixstrun raced to the gate. Instead of going through, he stopped in front of it, growling menacingly at the last paether. It yipped, tucked its tail, and ran into the forest.

Histrun raced into the safe-house courtyard, followed closely by Alixstrun, Lorstriel, and Kehali. As soon as they were inside, fighters slammed the gates shut and barred them. Telen skidded to a halt, blowing hard.

"Was anyone hurt?" Histrun surveyed the small courtyard. Fighters walked their horses to cool them down before taking them into the stables. None of the children were in sight, already ushered into the safe-house.

"I don't think anyone was seriously hurt," Maheli answered as she walked by. "A few cuts and scrapes are all I've seen."

"Make sure to examine all the horse's bellies. A paether could have slipped under one of them and done serious damage with their tusks."

"Yes, sir. I'll pass the word." She saluted. "Do you want me to walk Telen for you?"

Histrun nodded and wearily slid from his saddle. It had been a long time since he'd fought from horseback. "Let me check him first before you take him." He squatted and peered under his horse. The hand he ran over Telen's belly came away dirty, but not bloody. He sighed in relief and gave a quick prayer of gratitude. He stood, groaning as his aching knees protested. "Go ahead and take him."

Inside the safe-house, the children huddled together near the fireplace. Their faces were pale with terror. "It's okay, we're safe," he said, trying to reassure them. Wisah pulled away from the others and flung herself into him, wrapping her arms around his legs. Histrun blinked before awkwardly patting her head.

"I was so scared," she whimpered, her voice muffled by his legs. "I saw the veil open and was sure it would pull us all through."

"No one died, except the paether and Alixstrun's horse."

"Oh, that must be who the Goddess was welcoming."

Histrun gaped in surprise. He hadn't known animals went to the Summerlands, or even really thought about what happened to them when they died. That was the priestesses' area of expertise. But as he thought about it now, he realized the animals were also the Goddess's children, so it made sense they would return to her in death. He shuddered to think that the Malvers' monsters would also cross the veil.

"No silly," Wisah said, "the Goddess didn't create them."

Histrun stared at her. He hadn't voiced that out loud, and he certainly hadn't said it in mind-speech. It was a good thing Wisah was going to the Supreme for training.

Chapter 14

The next day, the children rode subdued in the aftermath of the paether attack. Even though the fighters surrounded them, they'd jump and twitch at every snap of a twig or the rustle of leaves. But by late afternoon, Histrun huffed in irritation at their noisiness and playful antics.

"They've recovered quickly." Lorstriel waved at Wisah and another girl giggling together.

"Humph. I liked it better when they were quiet. But, it is amazing how quickly the young forget." He gazed at the spires of Strunhelos peeking over the treetops. "Unlike the old," he murmured, "unlike me."

A bend on the road turned and Strunhelos Keep came into view. It squatted in front of a tall, sheer cliff devoid of plant-life. The mica in the sheadash stone shimmered as the late afternoon sun touched the walls. The small, fortified garrison guarded the pass into the White Mountains and the Sanctuary, as it had done for thousands of years. Unlike the newer keeps built after the Great War, Black Talent strengthened the walls to withstand almost any magical attack devised. Enormous black spots marred the thick stone walls, attesting to the magical battles fought during the Great War. Sadly, they couldn't replicate the spell in modern times. No one had been born with Black Talent since the end of the Great War.

Later that night, while everyone else slept, Histrun stood at the window of his room, remembering the numerous times he and Zehala had traversed to the Sanctuary. He doubled over as fresh pain assailed his heart, sloshing the taevo in his cup over his hand. *Will my heart ever heal? Do I want it to if it means I forget her?* His lips twisted as his body burned with craving the release that came from alcohol. After wiping off his hand, he refilled his cup, heavily dosing his taevo with whiskey. Sipping his drink, he stared at the mountain peaks rearing behind the cliff. Even in these last days of summer, snow covered the peaks. His mind wandered to the Alpha Competition when he'd first met Zehala. "Crone's Fires! Even the Sanctuary holds memories of her." He turned away from the window, downed the last of his drink, and crawled into the cold bed. He missed her warm presence at his back while he slept.

The next morning, the cliff overhead shadowed the road through the pass. They rode single-file as they entered a narrow, dimly lit tunnel. It soon opened onto a road only a little wider than the tunnel, meandering through a canyon with steep cliffs towering above them. Nothing grew on the rocky cliffs, and the smooth surface didn't provide any hand holds. The horse's hooves echoed off the walls, and guards patrolled along the top of the cliff, longbows strapped to their backs.

"Wisah!"

The shout startled Histrun, and he reached for his helstrablade. He relaxed with a grimace when he heard the echo and the peals of laughter. He glared back at the gaggle of children, which had grown again when he'd left Strunhelos Keep by two white-headed little girls. Another girl shouted her name, then another as the girls took turns making the canyon echo.

"I liked it better when they were quiet and subdued," he grumbled to Lorstriel. "I'll be glad when we reach the Sanctuary."

"Oh, I love that they're having fun. Who knows what rigors the Supreme will put them through in their training?" She gave him a sympathetic smile. "It will be over soon. We only have a few more days of escort duty."

The cliffs receded abruptly, almost as if their ancestors had hewn them from the mountains to create the pass. The landscape opened to reveal forest and meadow. Trees marched up the slopes with a road winding through them.

Four days later, Histrun's group topped a rise overlooking the Sanctuary grounds. Even here, where Malvers' monsters, narhili beasts, or paether weren't a danger, walls enclosed the living space. Although walls didn't surround the fields and pastures covering the wide valley, like everywhere else.

So close to their destination, Histrun was ready to end this long journey. He increased the pace, not allowing the youngsters to gawk at their new home. In a short time, they approached the gates. At the sight of fifteen girls with White and Gray Talents, the guards waved them through.

They entered a small cobblestone courtyard. A door on one side led to the cloisters, which Histrun, as a male, had never seen. It would be the children's new home. The opposite side held the door leading to the guest area, where he and his people would stay. Several brown-haired women hustled from the stable next to the gate. The two journeyman priestesses jumped off their horses and removed their saddlebags containing their few personal belongings.

"We'll take care of the horses," the horse-master told Histrun. "I've called a girl to guide your people to the guest houses."

"Thank you." Histrun climbed off Telen, patting him fondly as he undid the buckles securing his bags to the saddle. The children also dismounted, staring around the courtyard with wide eyes. The door to the cloister banged open, and a middle-aged priestess with white hair and kind, gray eyes bustled into the courtyard.

She smiled and opened her arms to the youngsters. "Welcome, little ones, to your new home. I'm Blenora, and I'll show you to your dormitory. We're so happy to have more priestesses to serve the Goddess." She turned to the two teenage girls in the group. "We're glad to have you back with us. Before you head to your rooms, could you help me settle these little ones?"

The two teenagers nodded, and in a few minutes, the courtyard cleared of children. Histrun took a deep breath. He was free! He wouldn't have to deal with the inane chatter of little girls any longer.

The door to the guest area opened, and an adolescent girl with pale brown hair stood on the opposite side. Once she knew they'd noticed her, she turned on her heel and headed back into the guest area. Histrun and the others hurried to catch up.

They walked along a cobblestone road lined with trees. Flowers bordered the road and manicured grass led to the various pack-houses on the street. At the first pack-house in the row, the girl stopped and waved for them to enter. As soon as they climbed the steps to the wide porch, she turned and ran away. Several tables and chairs strewn about the porch invited the guests to gather outside. Inside, an older woman with chestnut-brown hair and an air of authority around her waited for them.

"Welcome to the Sanctuary," she said. Her smile crinkled her yellow-green eyes at the corners. "This will be your home while you stay here. We've readied rooms for you, and we serve meals in the recreation room down the hall." She indicated the left hand side corridor.

"You're welcome to explore anywhere on this side of the temple grounds and to attend services in the temple. But please, do not enter the cloisters. They are reserved for only the priestesses. The bell-pulls throughout the house will summon a household staff member if you should need anything." She indicated the one hanging by the door. "Histrun, the Supreme will meet with you in the morning after breakfast. A runner will come to escort you. Please enjoy your stay with us." She bowed, then hurried down the left-hand hall, disappearing through a door.

"The bedrooms are upstairs," Histrun said. "Most are dormitory-style, except the one at the end of the right-hand corridor. I'll take that one. It's reserved for the alphas. Go find a bedroom for yourselves and enjoy the baths, which are downstairs. I'll see you later at dinner."

Histrun detoured to the recreation room and strode straight to the well-stocked liquor cabinet. He needed to relax from the long journey. Grabbing a bottle of brandy and a glass, he climbed the stairs to the room he'd claimed. He tossed his saddlebag onto the desk and sank into the chair. He poured himself a glass of brandy and sighed in pleasure as the warmth crept down his throat. Memories assaulted him of the many times he'd spent here with Zehala, of competing and winning the competitions, and their enthusiastic celebrations.

By the time the dinner bell rang, Histrun had passed out.

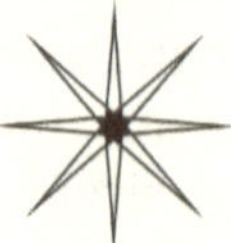

Histrun woke up to someone banging on his door, and Lorstriel's insistent voice yelling.

"Wake up, Histrun!" Lorstriel repeated. "You're going to be late for your meeting with the Supreme."

Groaning, Histrun pried his eyes open, blinking at the bright morning light spilling through the window. He grimaced at the nasty taste in his mouth and his rumpled clothing. When he sat up, he gripped his aching head between his hands.

"Histrun!" Lorstriel banged on the door again.

He pushed himself to his feet and staggered to the door. Lorstriel nearly pounded on his nose as he flung open the door.

"I'm awake. Do I have time to bathe and eat first?"

"Yes. When you didn't come down for dinner last night, we figured you were drinking again. I allowed plenty of time for you to clean up before your meeting."

Histrun patted her on the cheek. "You're a good kid, Lorstriel."

She rolled her eyes. "I'll meet you in the recreation room. For some reason, the Supreme also wants to see me." She tromped down the stairs.

While Histrun finished his breakfast, the same girl from the day before entered the recreation room. She glanced back at the head housekeeper, who stood at the door and made an encouraging motion with her hand. "Sir..." the girl squeaked. She swallowed hard, then tried again, this time her voice stronger. "Sir, the Supreme will see you and Lorstriel now. If you'll follow me, I'll guide you to the audience chamber." She looked again at the head housekeeper, who smiled at her.

"Good job, Raemy," the housekeeper said. "Now, come and wait by the door for them. Remember to walk ahead of them. Don't run."

The girl nodded and fled to the housekeeper's side.

Histrun shoved his last piece of toast into his mouth and washed it down with the remaining taevo in his mug before pushing away from the table. He walked cautiously toward the girl and smiled at her. She gasped and ducked behind the housekeeper. He looked over at Lorstriel, lifted his hands, and shrugged.

"It's your beard," she said, motioning at his chin. "You didn't trim it much. It's all bushy and hides your face."

He smoothed a hand over his beard, frowning. "I think it's thick and full and will keep my face warm when winter hits." He motioned for Lorstriel to go ahead of him. Raemy seemed less intimidated by her.

The girl led them into the main Sanctuary grounds. Histrun chuckled as she kept her pace barely under a sprint. He and Lorstriel lengthened their stride, easily keeping up with her. Inside the temple, the same priestess, Blenora, stopped them.

"It's okay, Raemy, I'll guide them from here." She gave the girl a gentle pat on her shoulder. "You did well. You can return to Naedera for your next chores."

Blenora turned back to Histrun and Lorstriel. "Welcome to the Sanctuary. The Supreme asked me to escort you to this meeting. If you'll follow me."

She sedately walked across the chamber, giving Histrun time to appreciate the beauty of the space. Familiar murals and statues covered three walls, depicting the Goddess's four faces. He turned his attention to his favorite, the fourth wall. Images of the Consort filled it in his life stages. Starting with a small boy, experiencing the joy of shifting to his wolf form for the first time. He grew through becoming a warrior and leading, culminating in a venerable sage with a long beard, wrinkled face, and kind, wise eyes.

Histrun puffed out his chest, proud to be a Posair male. The images reminded him that his power and strength were for protecting his people, and must be tempered with compassion. Mendehan had forgotten these things in his madness. Histrun dipped his head, praying he'd remember the Consort's lessons.

Blenora led them to the rear of the chamber and through a door. Her pace quickening as they moved through the corridors. Finally, they reached a black ironwood double-door barring their way into the audience chamber. On either side of the door, a red-leather clad woman stood guard. They each held a helbraught, and red veils covered their faces. They nodded at Blenora, and the one on the right opened the door for them.

White sheadash and marble formed the audience chamber's floors and walls. Several hundred people could fit inside the enormous space. White curtains hung on the windows and scented white pillar candles were lit, even though sunlight filled the room. At the far end, rose a dais with an aging woman sitting on a crystal throne. She wore a dazzling white long silk gown, and a white veil covered her hair. She had white hair and unusual white eyes. The Supreme. She had been the Supreme Histrun's entire lifetime.

Ten paces from the throne, the group dropped to their knees and made the gesture of obeisance and honor to the representative of the Goddess. Cold from the marble stone floor seeped through Histrun's trousers, making his knees ache. She didn't make them kneel long before she bade them to rise. He groaned as he rose, fighting the desire to rub the chill from his knees.

She surveyed him for a long moment. Her piercing gaze felt like she delved into his soul. He pulled on the expressionless mask he'd learned as an alpha to hide his thoughts from showing on his face. Her scrutiny made him want to fidget like some boy caught misbehaving.

"Histrun," the Supreme finally said, her voice husky and dry. "Thank you for escorting our newest priestesses and keeping them safe on the journey. I understand paether attacked you near Strunhelos Keep."

"Yes, your grace. But the Zehis method is working in Strunlair Province. We didn't have to battle any Malvers' monsters."

"That is a relief and good to hear. And has the last province, Dehanlair, been taught this method?"

"Yes, your grace, just this past Sandar."

"What can you tell me about Mendehan? I haven't received reports from my priestesses in many lunadars. I fear there are problems."

"There were, but no more. An illness infected Mendehan, warping his mind and soul. I fulfilled my duty and put down the rogue, freeing his people from his tyranny."

The Supreme's eyes narrowed at the mention of an illness. "Come closer." She beckoned to him. "I would see into your mind all that transpired with Mendehan."

Histrun stepped forward. His heart beat furiously in his chest. The Supreme hadn't ever needed to scour his mind before. Those who had, reported it was an unpleasant, painful experience.

The Supreme frowned at him. "Closer. I need to touch you. Considering your age, you may sit at my feet rather than kneel." She indicated a stool beside her throne.

He placed it at her feet and gingerly sat on it, anxiously waiting for the pain to begin.

The Supreme put cool fingers on Histrun's face, her fingertips touching his temples and forehead. "Relax," she chided. "I'm not going to hurt you."

Histrun closed his eyes and did the mental exercises to relax his muscles.

"Good. Now, recall the journey to Dehanlair Keep and remember everything that happened." The Supreme's calm, soothing voice put Histrun into a trance.

Unbidden, the memories of laughing with Zehala flowed first. Followed by listening to her sing him a lullaby as she gently stroked his face. Next came the memory of them lying on the ground and staring at the stars sweeping across the vast sky in the plains. The horrors of what he'd seen Mendehan do to his people gradually replaced the good memories. He experienced again the tragedy of losing Zehala, and the foggy chedans of his grief. At last, the Supreme released him. Drained, he slumped against her legs, trembling and holding a fist over his mouth to keep the grief from pouring from him in a sob.

Warm, gentle fingers brushed the hair from his face and pressed a cup to his lips. He sipped the cool liquid, surprised at his dry mouth. He opened his eyes. Blenora leaned over him, and compassion filled her eyes. She helped him to his feet and led him off the dais. She handed him the cup and motioned for him to drink more.

"Lorstriel, did you also witness these crimes Mendehan committed?" The tightness around the Supreme's eyes and mouth belied her calm voice.

"Y-yes, your grace," Lorstriel stammered. She gripped her trembling hands together in front of her.

As soon as the Supreme touched her face, Lorstriel's body went rigid. Her eyes flew wide open, unblinking, and her face became a frozen mask. She remained in the pose the entire time the Supreme held her in her thrall. Finally, the Supreme released her, shaking out her hands. Freed, Lorstriel slumped over and would have hit her head on the hard floor if Blenora hadn't rushed up the stairs and caught her. She reached behind the throne, and another cup appeared in her hand, which she pressed to Lorstriel's lips. After a moment, Lorstriel revived and sat up.

Histrun studied the cup in his hands. The contents tasted like cool water, but there must have been a spell laid on it to help the victims of the Supreme's mind-read to recover quickly.

"Thank you, Histrun, Lorstriel," the Supreme said. Her voice sounded tired, and exhaustion pulled on her face. "I have all I need for now on Mendehan's crimes. Lorstriel, when you and your team have recovered from your journey, you may return home."

The Supreme's gaze fell on Histrun, and he again felt like a naughty child. But instead of judgment, he detected compassion. "Histrun, your heart and soul are broken from losing Zehala. Stay here. Let the peace of the Goddess that lives in this place heal you. Blenora will help you. She is skilled at healing the wounds of the soul."

"Yes, your grace," Histrun and Lorstriel said together, bowing their heads and making the gesture of obeisance again. Blenora touched his shoulder, and he raised his head. The Supreme no longer sat on her throne. Blenora led them back through the temple's inner sanctum and into the sunshine and gardens outside.

He scrutinized Blenora. She stood calmly under his examination, waiting for him to finish. He crossed his arms over his chest. "So, when does this healing of yours begin?"

She smiled. "It already has. Return to the guest house, relax, and enjoy the company of your people while they are still here. Raemy," she called, "you can escort our guests to their rooms."

The girl stepped out from behind a tall flowering bush. This time, she wasn't quite as nervous. She only jogged back to the guest house. It was progress. Perhaps one day he wouldn't terrify her. He'd have time.

Histrun swore. He knew an order when he heard one. He couldn't leave the Sanctuary until the Supreme dismissed him.

Three days later, Histrun watched Lorstriel and the platoon ride out the gates, returning home. He stood gazing at the road long after they disappeared from view. Gravel crunched behind him, followed by the scent of lilac and roses mixed with the prevalent scents of kehani flowers and frankincense floating on the breeze. Only one priestess wore this particular perfume: Blenora.

"Do you miss them?" she asked.

Histrun shook his head. "No, not yet."

"Then why are you standing here, gazing after them with longing?"

He lifted his hands and shrugged. "I'm at a loss at what to do."

"You can do whatever you like."

"Then I'll go back to my room and drink myself into a stupor."

"You can certainly do that." Her forehead crinkled in displeasure. "But you can only hide from your pain in liquor for so long before you must face it. I'll be here when you are ready." She turned around and walked sedately into the Sanctuary.

The guest house echoed in its emptiness. Histrun pulled out a bottle of whiskey from the cabinet in the recreation room and flung himself on a couch. Foregoing a glass, he drank directly from the bottle. The couch made a much more comfortable bed than the leaves he'd used at Strunland Keep.

Water splashed on his face, and he came to with a roar. Naedera stood over him, glaring, her hands on her hips. "Up you go," she growled.

"Why do I need to get up?" Histrun slurred, rubbing his crusty eyes. He squinted against the bright light streaming through the window.

"We're moving you. There's no sense in keeping this house open just for you. And cleaning up after your messes." She said the last under her breath.

Histrun's eyebrows drew together in confusion. "What messes? I've been on this lovely couch all day." He sat up, throwing his feet onto the floor, gagging at the stench of vomit. He lifted his feet from the mess and scrunched his nose at the filth on his shirt. Rubbing his face, he grimaced at the muck in his beard.

When he stood, the room swirled. He clutched his stomach, gritting his teeth against the rising bile, and screwed his eyes shut until the dizziness stopped. "I'm going to go wash up."

"Yes, please do. We'll bring clean clothes to you. We can pack your bags, or do you want to do it yourself?"

"You can." He waved at her and burped.

She shot him a disgusted look before stomping away.

Histrun staggered down the stairs and into the bathing room, quickly washing, and climbed into the soaking tub. *I can't believe I was so drunk that I don't remember throwing up. What an idiot! Naedera has the right to be disgusted with me. I'm disgusting!* He slammed his palm into the water, sputtering as it splashed his face. He hung his head in shame. *Zehala would be so disappointed with me.*

Finished, he found a clean tunic and a pair of trousers in a nondescript beige, neatly folded. He held them up, his forehead crinkling. No embroidery decorated the hem or sleeves with his clan colors of rose and turquoise. At home, everyone's clothing had some sort of decoration on it.

Naedera waited for him at the top of the stairs, his saddlebags at her feet. When he tried to detour into the recreation room, she blocked his way. He shrugged. He'd find something to drink from wherever they were putting him. When she led him away from the guest area, he raised an eyebrow.

"Where are we going? I didn't think I was allowed inside the cloister."

"You're not. We're going to the staff quarters."

Naedera led him across the Sanctuary grounds fronting the temple and the large library. Manicured grass and flower beds in riotous colors bordered the pathway. They meandered around the temple and deeper into the Sanctuary than Histrun had ever been. The wall separating the priestesses's area from the rest of the grounds rose in the west. The path took them in the opposite direction, toward the river which created the Sanctuary's eastern boundary.

They stopped at the edge of a small village of three dozen or more cottages of various sizes. They formed their own little community within the greater whole. Even the largest ones could only house a few people, unlike the large manors in the Keeps where several packs lived together. A short hedge surrounded each cottage's yard and flower beds nestled against the buildings. As he drew closer, he recalled exploring the ruins of ancient settlements as a young man. A multitude of foundations had poked through the ground that he couldn't fathom the type of building had stood on them. But now, seeing this village, he recognized their similarity. This must have been how their ancestors had lived, before the Great War and before the Malvers' monsters forced the population into fortified communities.

Naedera stopped at a tiny cottage with a door painted a cheery red, differentiating it from the others, along with a number engraved on the lintel.

Naedera pushed open the door. "This is where you'll stay. We have enough space right now, so you have it to yourself. If you're still here in the spring, we'll probably give you a roommate as we gear up for the Alpha Competitions in the summer."

Histrun stepped into the cottage. A fireplace filled the west wall. In front of it lay a brightly colored rug, and two comfortable-looking rocking chairs and stools faced it. A small table with two chairs sat nearby. Stairs led to a loft, which held a pair of narrow beds, with matching tall wardrobes and chests for his clothing and belongings. A table with a lamp sat between the beds, and a small window over it let in light and air. A thick fur rug covered the wooden floor. Tucked under the stairs was a small necessary room.

"Where is the bathing room?"

"We have a communal bathhouse. Put your bag down, and I'll show it to you."

Histrun dropped his pack near the stairs, regretting he hadn't taken it up with him the first time. He squinted at the lack of a railing or wall on the stairs. He'd have to be careful not to fall if he awoke during the night to go to the necessary room—or if he was drunk. Histrun snorted at the real possibility.

Naedera gave him a tour of the village, pointing out the communal bathhouse, dining hall, and gathering room. A woman exited a building, brushing wood chips from her clothing.

"Those are the various workshops for the craftspeople who work here to keep the Sanctuary well-maintained and self-sufficient," Naedera explained.

A few men, none of whom seemed to be fighters, nodded to Histrun as they passed. Most of the people living in the village were women, representing all the Talents, except Red. He remembered the Supreme's guard, all of whom were Reds.

"Where do the Red Guards stay?"

"They have a section within the cloister, as they are a type of priestess. Once a woman joins the Red Guard, she serves here the rest of her life."

Their wanderings brought them back to the cottage assigned to Histrun. Naedera stopped at the hedge boundary.

"I'll leave you here to settle in. We serve meals in the community dining hall, but if you choose, you may bring a tray to your cottage. A housekeeper will pick it up in the morning. However, we won't bring your meals to you. The kitchen is open throughout the day and closes after dinner."

Histrun nodded. It was the same at home. Naedera left him, heading toward the temple. She hadn't allowed him time to rummage in the gathering room for a fresh bottle of alcohol. He rubbed his chin, contemplating whether to walk back to grab one or to go inside. A shadow moved in the doorway. Anger flooded him. *How dare someone enter my room uninvited!* He stomped to the door, ready to yell at the interloper. Blenora turned at his entrance, a vase filled with flowers in her hand. He swallowed the words. No one mistreated a White Priestess.

"Greetings Histrun." She gave him a cheery smile. "I was just brightening your room and leaving you a welcome gift."

Under his breath, Histrun growled. He didn't need flowers in his room.

"Naedera told you that you have freedom to wander the grounds and to explore the area around the Sanctuary, didn't she?"

"She did."

"The fresh air would do you good. And your poor horse, Telen, could use a run to stretch his legs. He doesn't like anyone else to take him out of the stable."

"He should still be good. It's only been a few days since we arrived."

"Ah, no." Blenora's forehead wrinkled. "You've been here nearly a chedan already."

Histrun's face scrunched in confusion. "Didn't Lorstriel and the others leave yesterday?"

She shook her head. "No, they left four days ago."

His mouth dropped open. He couldn't believe he'd lost so many days. He didn't remember anything after Lorstriel left.

"You, Histrun, have a drinking problem. If you keep up like this, you're going to kill yourself. Are you going to let it ruin your life? Or do you want to regain control?"

Histrun leaned against the door frame. "I'm not ready to face life without Zehala. The drinking helps me get through the loneliness and emptiness." Drunk, he could forget how he had failed her, allowing the janack to kill her because he was too old and slow. At least here, no one would be depending on him in battle.

"It's up to you. But the Supreme will only allow you to wallow for so long. I'd suggest you don't wait for her to take the choice from you. It won't be pleasant." She turned with a swish of her long white gown. The veil covering her hair floated behind her.

Histrun stomped into the room and slumped onto a rocking chair, but the slight back-and-forth movement made him dizzy. He glanced down at his shaking hands. A sudden clenching of his stomach had him running for the necessary room. After emptying his stomach, he leaned on the sink and rinsed out his mouth. He gazed at his reflection in the mirror. His skin sagged with a ruddy tone to it, which didn't go well with his red hair and beard. If Zehala saw him now, she'd berate him for letting himself go.

He remembered the herbal packets Andreyan had given him before they'd left for the Sanctuary. They had helped him with the alcohol withdrawal enough to allow him to function during the journey. Once he'd left Strunland Keep, he hadn't continued to take them, so he should have a few in his pack. He climbed the stairs and searched through his bags. After dumping out the contents of both saddlebags, he found a single blue packet.

Downstairs, he discovered the cottage came equipped with a kettle to hang over the fire, a pot for taevo, and a couple of mugs. The cabinet by the fireplace held a canister of dark-roasted taevo, and one of a spicy blend. He started a fire, filled the kettle from the necessary room's sink, and put it over the fire to heat. Perhaps the healers here would have something like what Andreyan had given him.

The next morning, he found his way to the dining hall.

"Oh, my," Naedera said, placing a hand over her chest when she saw his bloodshot eyes and shaking hands. "You need to visit a healer. Here, I'll take you."

The healer gave him several packets of the herbal mixtures. This time, it took over a chedan before the tremors, headaches, and nausea left him. The potions helped him resist the craving for alcohol.

As soon as he had recovered, the Supreme sent orders requiring him to meet for an octar each day with Blenora.

The first day, he met Blenora in a small, comfortable room in the temple. A tray with a pot of taevo and sweets sat on the table between their chairs. The porcelain cups were finer than he'd ever seen before, even at Strunlair Keep. Histrun waited for Blenora to do something to him, to use her White Talent on him, but she simply sat quietly, sipping her taevo and watching him.

"Aren't you going to 'heal' me?" he finally asked.

"Do you want me to?" She peered at him over the rim of her dainty cup.

"No. I'm only here because the Supreme has ordered me to attend."

"I can't heal you against your will. We can simply talk if you'd like. You have to be here for an octar."

"Talk about what?" he grumbled.

"Anything you'd like. Tell me about Zehala."

"No. I don't want to talk about Zehala, or our life together, and especially not her death." Histrun slumped in his chair, crossed his arms over his chest, and pursed his lips together.

"That's fine. You can join me in meditation if you'd like." Blenora placed her empty cup on the table, folded her hands into her lap, and closed her eyes.

Histrun wasn't sure what to make of Blenora's healing technique. He glumly waited for the octar to be up so he could leave.

After a few days, he sensed her gentle touch on his mind and soul. It wasn't intrusive, but comforting. He began to relax in her calm presence.

Chapter 15

As the days passed, Histrun settled into living at the Sanctuary and his daily sessions with Blenora. He quickly looked forward to meeting with her. Blenora's serenity hid a quick mind and a humorous streak. Soon, he thought of her as a friend and sought her out to go riding or to play keshe with him.

One day, while returning to his cottage from a session with Blenora, an adolescent boy ran in front of him, nearly running into him. The boy raced across the lawn toward the cloister, with a girl on his heels about the same age. Histrun stopped in his tracks and stared at the children. The girl had unusually dark charcoal hair. He didn't recall ever seeing anyone with that shade before. For some reason, it made him uncomfortable. He blinked in shock when the boy ran through the cloister gate. *Huh? I thought the Supreme sent any boys born in the Sanctuary to their father's clans once they reached five or six. Why did the Supreme allow this boy to stay?*

Over the next few days, he frequently crossed paths with the boy and girl when he walked to the library. Quite often, they were heading to or from the library, usually at a run. The boy's dark-auburn hair with a thin, gray stripe at his right temple reminded Histrun of a precocious little boy he'd met during an Alpha Competition several years ago. The boy had delighted in teasing and pestering Histrun until he'd finally had enough.

He shifted into his warrior form and chased the boy. The child hadn't bothered him again. Could this be the same boy?

After a lifetime of constant battles with the Malvers' monsters, Histrun needed more physical activity than wandering the Sanctuary's gardens. He took long rides on Telen, exploring the wilds surrounding the Sanctuary. Sometimes Blenora accompanied him.

They were on one such ride, but instead of enjoying the crisp fall day, Blenora seemed to be nervous. She'd start to say something, then stop. He worried she was working up the courage to ask him about being in a relationship with him. She was a lovely woman with her white hair and gray eyes, and even in her early-forties she was lean and shapely. But he was more than twice her age and still in love with Zehala.

They stopped at a stream to let their horses drink. Blenora kept running her horse's reins through her hands.

"Ah, Histrun," she said, haltingly. "I have a favor to ask."

He sighed in relief. "Yes?"

"You've seen the adolescent boy in the Sanctuary, haven't you?" At Histrun's nod, she continued, "Well, he's my son, Blazel. He's nearly twelve, and isn't that when boys learn to shift into their warrior form?"

"It is." He now had an idea of the favor she wanted from him. The men he'd met during his stay were either farmers or herders. A dozen warriors served as gate guards and were at the Sanctuary as punishment for unruly behavior. The Supreme supervised their discipline to ensure they return as functioning members of their society. He wouldn't want to trust them to train a young man in the ways of being a warrior.

"Well... could you..."

Histrun took pity on her. "Yes, I'll teach him. The wolf-form is almost second nature for us, and it's easy to shift back and forth. But it's dangerous for boys to try shifting into the warrior form without guidance. They could get stuck between forms."

"I'm not sure Blazel knows how to shift into his wolf form. At least, I've never seen him do so."

Histrun stepped back, putting a hand over his chest, horrified. "It's unusual for a young boy to not know how to shift into his wolf form. It's instinctual. I can't imagine not experiencing the joy of running as a wolf."

Blenora shrugged. "His only friend is Chariel. He's a sensitive boy, and since she can't shift, he doesn't."

"That isn't good. Every man shifts into their wolf form regularly. Even the men who don't choose to become fighters are taught the nuances of shifting into their warrior form. Although, for them, it's in case there is a monster attack while they're away from the keep. Bring Blazel to my place tomorrow after breakfast, and I'll make sure he knows what to do."

"Oh, thank you!" She threw her arms around him and gave him a quick hug. "This is such a relief. There wasn't anyone else to ask. I didn't trust the gate guards to teach him the right way."

The next morning, Blenora and Blazel waited for him in front of his cottage when he returned from eating breakfast. The boy stood with his hands clasped behind his back. He kept his eyes on the ground and shifted from foot to foot.

"Bright blessings, Blenora, Blazel," Histrun said as he approached them on the pathway.

"Bright blessings, Histrun." Blenora gave him a smile. "I hope we're not too early. Blazel was excited."

"Scared mostly," Blazel muttered under his breath.

Histrun clapped a hand on Blazel's shoulder, causing him to glance up. The boy had dark-gray eyes, an unusual combination with his auburn hair.

"It is scary the first few times you shift," Histrun assured him. "But it gets easier with practice. Are you ready to get started?"

Blazel nodded and looked, not at his mother, but back toward the cloister. "Chariel wanted to come and watch, but she didn't think you'd let her."

Chariel must be the girl Histrun always saw Blazel with. The note in Blazel's voice made him think the boy hoped Histrun wouldn't allow her to join them. Perhaps he was afraid he'd fail and didn't want a witness.

"No," Histrun shook his head. "It wouldn't be a good idea right now. After you've had some practice, maybe she can watch."

Blazel's breath came out in a whoosh of relief. A tiny smile lifted the corner of his mouth.

"Now, why don't you and I find a quiet, private place?"

A grin brightened Blazel's face. "I know just the spot. I go there all the time to hide... I mean, to be by myself."

Histrun gestured for Blazel to lead the way. "Why don't you show me, boy?"

Blazel glared at him. "My name is Blazel. Not boy."

"You're a boy. You're my apprentice now, and you can call me either 'master', or 'sir.' Or don't you want to learn to be a warrior?"

"I do."

"I do, 'sir.'"

"Yes, sir. I do, sir."

"Lead the way to your spot, boy."

Blazel's lips pursed, but he didn't say anything. Histrun had been ready to administer some discipline to him, suspecting him of being a spoiled mama's boy. That didn't happen often with the children of fighters, since they lived in the crèches. But he'd experienced it a few times with the herder and farmer packs.

The boy headed toward the river before climbing higher up the slope. They threaded through a maze of brambles, and in a few places, Histrun had to suck in his breath to pass. Finally, they stopped in a shady glade. A stream trickled off to the side near a small pile of boulders. They were far enough from the Sanctuary grounds no one would disturb them, but not too far as to be in danger. Histrun nodded in approval.

Histrun sat on a large, flat boulder. A shaft of sunlight warmed the stone and his back. "Now, boy, Blenora says you don't know how to shift into your wolf form. Let's start there."

"I can shift," Blazel said petulantly, crossing his arms over his chest and sticking out his lower lip.

"Then show me."

Histrun winced in sympathy when Blazel's shift took a long, painful time. It was common for the boys to shift from boy to wolf-pup while running and not miss a step. But no one had ever worked with this poor child or taught him how to access his inner magic pool that made the shapeshifting possible. Histrun sighed inwardly. He had his work cut out for him to teach this boy how to shapeshift safely.

He had hoped the Supreme would release him to leave the Sanctuary before the winter storms blocked the pass. But now, he couldn't leave until he'd trained Blazel properly.

When Blazel finally shifted back to his human form, he leaned over, his hands on his knees, panting. "See? I can shift."

"How often do you shift?"

Blazel hunched his shoulders and shuffled his feet. "Not often. I'm already an outsider as the only boy. Shifting makes me feel even more of an outcast."

"Understandable." Histrun beckoned to him. "Come, sit with me. I'll teach you how to access your magic so you can shift forms properly. You have to be able to shift easily to and from your wolf form before you can attempt the warrior form."

Blazel chose to sit on the ground at Histrun's feet. He listened carefully, asking questions, before attempting to shift again. He practiced shifting the rest of the morning. By the time they ended and returned for lunch, Blazel shifted forms much more quickly and easily.

Histrun paused at the hedge boundary of his yard. "Meet me every morning after breakfast for training."

"Yes, sir!" Blazel thumped a fist to his chest in a warrior's salute, then ran off. A few steps later, he kicked his heels together and whooped, "Yippee!"

Histrun smiled at the boy's enthusiasm. What would it be like to be raised in a place where you were the only boy? Histrun would do what he could to help the boy.

The oak trees blazed orange, and the aspen leaves turned a brilliant yellow in their fall colors. The days started off crisp and cool, warming enough in the afternoon that Histrun appreciated the shade of Blazel's hidden spot.

Histrun began Blazel's training by having him simply practice shifting from his natural form to his wolf form. He made Blazel shift until he could do it from one breath to the next, no matter what he was doing.

After nearly two chedans of this, Blazel plopped his fists on his hips and glared at Histrun. "Is this all you're going to have me do? When am I going to learn how to shift into my warrior form? Isn't this for little kids?"

Histrun settled more comfortably on his camp stool. The boulders had quickly become too hard for his old, bony rear. He'd expected this outburst, and it actually surprised him it had taken so long.

"You, boy, are still a child. The magic for this type of shifting is easier to access than what you need for the warrior form. You have to be able to automatically pull the energy to you without thinking about it to shift to your wolf form. This will help you make the shift to warrior. You're really far behind other boys your age. Usually, by now, boys have been shifting to their wolf form for years, and it's a natural reflex. I'm worried since you haven't had those years of practice, your body and mind aren't strong enough yet to hold the more powerful magic of your warrior form."

"But isn't shifting a natural part of us? Isn't it our gift, like the girl's Talents?"

"Your friend, Chariel, is a Gray, right?"

Blazel nodded.

"Hasn't she had to learn to channel and use her Talent properly?"

"Yeah. The first time she had a prophecy, it scared the snot out of us. She got stuck in the trance, and the Supreme had to help her get out of it."

"This is the same thing. If you're not strong enough, or focused enough, you'll get stuck between forms. It isn't a pretty sight, nor is it fun. It hurts worse than monster ichor landing on your skin."

Blazel pondered this silently for a moment. "I'll go back to practicing now."

Afterward, Blazel threw himself into his training, working harder and longer than Histrun expected. Soon, Histrun added the fighting forms designed to create the reflexes warriors needed to fight the Malvers' monsters to prevent injury. *I wish there were more fighters and young boys available to train with Blazel. I can't teach him how to fight within a pack without them.* Histrun improvised and created a fighting style Blazel could use alone. He couldn't take on a nest by himself, but he could, at least, defend himself until help arrived.

Histrun leaned forward, propping his chin on his fist, watching Blazel. *The boy has promise. He's quick and agile. Before I leave the Sanctuary, I'll talk to the Supreme about Blazel coming back to Strunland Keep with me. The boy needs to be around other males, other Posairs, besides just the White Priestesses. He needs a normal life.*

After Blazel continued his training without complaint for two more chedans, Histrun decided to reward the boy's hard work. Over the years of coming to the Sanctuary for the Alpha Competitions, Histrun had discovered several places within a day or two's ride suitable for camping and hunting. Blazel needed to learn how to hunt, both as a man and as a wolf. Whenever the fighting-packs were away from the keeps, they supplemented their diets with fresh game. Living off the staples of rice and beans found in the safe-houses could be tiring. Blazel wouldn't always live in the luxurious Sanctuary. If he joined Histrun in returning to Strunland Keep, he'd need to know how to hunt. Otherwise, the other boys would ridicule him for not knowing this basic, and necessary, skill of a Posair male.

With Rokdar, the second lunadar of autumn, nearly half over, they needed to go on their first outing before the snows fell and made hunting more difficult. Once Blazel had the basics down, Histrun would take him out in the winter to learn how to hunt in the snow. Histrun made arrangements with the quartermaster for supplies and cleared the trip with Blenora.

"Tomorrow, we'll be training somewhere else," Histrun informed Blazel on their walk back to the village.

"Where? Will Chariel be able to watch? She keeps bugging me about when she can come and train with me."

"But, she can't!" Histrun blurted, scandalized by the idea. If the girl had had a hint of Red Talent or even any other Talent besides White and Gray, Histrun would have allowed her to participate.

Blazel frowned at him. "Why not? The other girls learn how to fight."

"She's a White Priestess. It would be sacrilege if she fought."

Blazel's brows drew together and his lips tightened. "That sounds discriminatory. Are you so old you don't remember your history lessons?"

Histrun scowled at Blazel. "What are you talking about?"

"Shandir. She's the one who ended the Great War."

"And?"

"She was a White Priestess. The mural of the Goddess as a warrior shows her with white eyes. So why can't Chariel learn to fight with me? At least let her do the fighting forms with me. The ones requiring a partner would be much easier to do with someone besides just you. Who will I practice with when you're gone?"

Histrun paused. Blazel's points were valid. Traditionally, White Priestesses didn't fight now the Posairs didn't need them to defeat the enemies they'd fought during the Great War. The Malvers' monsters were the Posair's only enemy, and Histrun shuddered at the thought of a White Priestess fighting those beasts. But what would it hurt if he taught the girl the fighting forms?

"Oh, all right," Histrun relented. "When we return from our excursion, she can start learning the forms with you."

"Yippee!" Blazel threw his fist in the air and jumped around.

Histrun watched him, a smile playing at the corners of his mouth. It took Blazel several milcrons before he stopped his antics and stared at Histrun.

"Wait. Did you say excursion? Are we going somewhere?"

"We're going on a hunting trip. Do you know how to ride a horse?" He scowled at not thinking of that before now.

"Of course I do," Blazel sounded affronted. "Well, a little. Chariel and I have ridden to the Seven Falls before with Mother and Grandmother."

"Good. Pack a bag with three changes of clothes. The nights are becoming cold, so bring a warm cloak. Bring your helstrablade, too. You do have one, don't you?"

Blazel nodded. "You gave it to me when I was little."

Histrun raised his eyebrows. He didn't remember doing so. But it wouldn't have meant much to him, whereas for a little boy, it would have been a momentous event. He certainly remembered when he received his first helstrablade over eighty-five years ago.

"Meet me at the stables in the morning."

"Yes, sir!" Blazel saluted with a face-splitting grin, then ran across the grounds toward the cloister.

Histrun turned into his yard and winced as his knee buckled. He envied Blazel's youth. He bent over, and as he massaged his knee, he glanced up. Not a cloud marred the clear blue expanse. He turned around and ambled to the common room in search of a Blue, who worked with the weather. He found her in a small cottage similar to his. At his request, she wandered outside and gazed for a long time at the sky.

"The first storm's coming," she told him, rubbing her arms. "But it won't arrive for another chedan, perhaps ten days. It feels like we'll receive rain at this elevation, but if you go much higher, there will be snow flurries."

Histrun thanked her before returning to the quartermaster's office to requisition rain gear. He planned on staying in a cave he'd discovered, so he didn't bother with a tent. The cave would be warmer—and drier—if the rain arrived sooner than expected, and they were caught in the storm.

The next morning, the horse-master brought out Telen and a dark-chestnut gelding, already saddled. Four white socks covered the gelding's ankles. He had a white blaze on his nose, and a lighter brown mane and tail. He looked small next to the big, black stallion. The lack of stripes indicated the horse wasn't plains-bred.

"Who is this fine boy?" Histrun rubbed the gelding's nose.

"Bosetel," the horse-master said. "He's a gentle soul and will take good care of young Blazel."

The door from the cloister slammed open, and Blazel ran through it, his bulging saddlebags thumping against his back. He skidded to a halt in front of Histrun. His eyes widened at the sight of Telen, who at 17.2 hands was nearly as tall as Histrun at his withers.

"That's a big horse." Awe filled Blazel's voice.

"Telen's mine." Histrun pointed to the much smaller gelding. "That one is yours."

Blazel sighed heavily, then gave him a sheepish grin. "Oh. I know Bosetel. I've ridden him before."

Histrun affixed his saddlebags to the back of his saddle, then mounted. Crossing his hands over the pommel, he swished

Telen's reins through his hands, waiting for Blazel to mount his horse. The horse-master took time to show Blazel how to buckle on the saddlebags, check the girth strap, and adjust the stirrups. Finally, Blazel clambered into the saddle, fidgeting in his seat. The gelding didn't sidle or jump at his rider's antics. Histrun glanced at the horse-master.

"He's voice trained," she explained.

"Ah, good choice."

"Good luck." The horse-master waved at them.

Histrun urged Telen forward while telling Bosetel, "Walk." The gelding plodded along beside Telen, giving Blazel time to sit deeper into his saddle. Histrun sighed, adding riding lessons to his training agenda. As they rode from the courtyard, Blenora stood in the doorway to the cloister, with her arm over Chariel's shoulder. Blenora waved a cheery farewell. When Blazel didn't notice Chariel, her shoulders fell, and her head drooped. Histrun didn't recall seeing her with any other children. A tendril of guilt threaded its way through him, and he resolved to take her under his wing as well.

Chapter 16

Histrun led his charge out the gate and kept to the firmly packed sheadash road. After an octar of riding, Blazel finally settled into the rhythm of his horse's gait. Histrun gratefully increased their speed from a plodding walk. Soon afterward, they passed the Sanctuary's walls, and he turned Telen off the road to cross the wide valley. They trotted through the meadows where multas and sheep grazed and climbed above the Sanctuary grounds. Within a measure, the trees thickened, and the forest closed around them.

The trail meandered through the trees. Histrun shivered in the coolness where the sun didn't reach through the foliage. The sound of rushing water came from ahead of them, and after another half-octar of riding, they reached the Storengher River. He rode in a parallel course for a few measures before veering away.

"Can we stop soon?" Blazel asked, a whine in his voice. "My rear-end is numb, and I'm hungry."

"I'd rather continue until we reach the cave. We only have a few more measures of riding to reach it."

Blazel's grimace of pain reminded him the boy didn't have experience staying in the saddle for long periods. Taking pity on him, Histrun reined his horse to a stop and dismounted. Telen immediately dropped his head to graze on the tall meadow grass. Blazel remained sitting on his horse.

"Well, aren't you getting off?" Histrun asked.

"I'm trying, but I can't move." Blazel groaned.

Histrun strode to the horse and lifted Blazel down. Tears sprung to the boy's eyes as his feet touched the ground, and he slumped into Histrun's arms with a whimper. Histrun growled at himself for forgetting the toll riding a horse took on a novice.

After a few milcrons, Blazel pushed upright. "I can finally feel my legs again." He bit his lip as he walked away, keeping his legs wide apart.

Histrun had also forgotten about saddle sores. "Walk around a bit before sitting."

While Blazel tottered around the small clearing, Histrun searched through his packs, found the ceramic jar of healing salve, and handed it to Blazel. "Here, put some of this on your sore thighs."

Histrun raised an eyebrow when Blazel disappeared behind a tree, presumably to drop his trousers to apply the salve. Most Posairs didn't have any issues with nudity as they bathed together and the safe-houses offered little privacy. As he thought about it, Histrun didn't recall ever seeing Blazel in the community bathing room in the staff's village. He had a hunch Blazel didn't bathe with the White Priestesses either. Histrun shrugged. He'd give the boy his privacy and not force the issue. But if Blazel returned to Strunland Keep, he'd have to get used to being around others unclothed.

Histrun pulled open the pack of food and took out a travel bar and apple for each of them. He'd finished his travel bar and was munching on his apple when Blazel finally emerged from the trees. Pain still tightened the corners of his mouth, but he moved easier. Histrun tossed him his food.

Blazel gingerly sat on a rock. "I never knew it would hurt so much to ride a horse." He glared at Bosetel. "I don't want to get back on him for a while—maybe never."

"Well, you can't walk everywhere. It does get better after a while."

Blazel massaged his legs as he ate. Riding now would only break open the sores again and wouldn't allow the healing salve to work. Histrun rubbed the back of his neck as he decided what to do. Blazel's wolf form shouldn't cause him any more pain. It might even hasten the healing with the magic flowing through him to keep in the form. Histrun considered the distance to the cave and decided it shouldn't be too far for Blazel to run in his wolf form. Besides, it would be good training.

"In our practice," Histrun said, "you've only stayed in your wolf form for short periods of time. There may be instances when you need to stay in it for a long time. Such as, when you're tracking a group of escaped monsters, or when you're hunting for your fighting-pack."

A look of longing crossed Blazel's face, making Histrun more determined to talk to the Supreme about taking the boy back with him.

"This isn't a pleasure trip." Histrun stood and strode to Telen, giving him the other half of his apple. The horse crunched on it. "We're out here to train. Your training exercise will be to follow me to the cave in your wolf form. Try to keep up. If you fall behind, use your nose and your other wolf senses, like we've practiced, to find my trail." He bent over, using the grass to wipe away the horse drool from his hand.

Blazel nodded as he finished his midday meal. He groaned as he stood. After taking a couple of careful steps, he grinned. "My legs don't hurt as much!" He followed Histrun's example and gave his apple core to his horse.

While the horse happily chomped on the treat, Histrun walked to where Telen had wandered in his grazing. He caught up the reins and prepared to mount.

"Is he going to be afraid of me?" Blazel asked, stroking Bosetel's nose.

Histrun started to shake his head, but paused and dropped back to the ground. "Our horses are used to being around us in all our forms. But Bosetel is a Sanctuary horse, so he might not have been around anyone in their other forms. Give me his reins before you shift." Histrun held out his hand.

Blazel led the horse to Histrun and gave him the reins. Histrun took a firm grip on Bosetel's bridle, where he could control the horse if he spooked. He nodded to Blazel. "I have him. You can shift."

The boy took a few steps back, then blurred as he shifted. A red-brown wolf with a gray streak along its back and nose stood where Blazel had been. The horse snorted and tried to shy away, but Histrun's firm grip didn't allow him to move. After a moment, he chuffed and calmed down. Satisfied the horse wouldn't bolt, Histrun mounted Telen and urged him forward.

He kept the pace slow during the first couple of measures, making sure Blazel could keep up with the horses. When it appeared Blazel ran comfortably in his wolf form, Histrun increased the pace, widening the distance between them but keeping Blazel in sight. When Histrun crossed a stream, he kicked Telen into a canter, leaving Blazel behind. They were close enough to the cave if Blazel became lost, Histrun could easily find him.

Histrun had pulled off Telen's tack and almost finished currying him when Blazel trotted into the clearing in front of the cave, his tail held high. He saw Histrun and yipped a 'found-you,' before shifting to his normal form. Sweat beaded his forehead, and he panted a little, but otherwise he didn't appear like the experience had taxed him too much.

Histrun patted Blazel's shoulder in approval. "Unsaddle your horse, tie him up where he can graze, and bring your tack inside."

Histrun lugged his own tack and packs into the cave, setting them to the side. A blackened ring of stones marked a fire pit. Nearby lay a small stack of wood left by the last people who had used the cave for shelter. After Blazel carried in his own gear, Histrun sent him for more firewood, while Histrun lit a fire to ward against the coming night's chill.

He pulled out the camping gear, which included a frying pan, a spit, and a kettle. As soon as he had the fire going, he filled the pot with water from the nearby stream and put it on to heat. He wrinkled his nose at the pile of travel bars inside the food pack. *No need to eat these when fresh game is nearby.* He considered taking Blazel with him to hunt, but he wanted to eat sometime tonight. Tomorrow would be soon enough for a hunting lesson.

Blazel soon returned to the cave with an armful of wood.

"Wait here," Histrun grumbled. "Keep the fire going and brew some taevo. I shouldn't be gone long."

Outside, Histrun shifted into his wolf form, trotting from the clearing and deeper into the forest. After a few milcrons, his sharp nose caught the scent of a rabbit, and he changed course to follow it. The rabbit bolted in front of him, and he gave chase. He hadn't had to hunt in a long time, and he almost lost the rabbit. Before it dove into a hole, Histrun put on a burst of speed and snatched it behind the head. A quick jerk snapped the rabbit's neck. He ruefully admitted he could also use more practice in hunting in his wolf form. The joy of running as a wolf coursed through him. It struck him he hadn't been in this form since before leaving Strunland Keep on the dreadful journey to Dehanlair. Rather than shifting back to his natural form, he picked up the rabbit in his teeth. He trotted back to the cave with his tail waving behind him.

At the cave, he dropped the rabbit at Blazel's feet and shifted back into his natural form.

"Do you know how to gut and skin it?" he asked, shaking off the last tingles from his change.

Blazel eyed the carcass and shook his head. Histrun showed Blazel how to gut and skin the rabbit. All the while, wishing he'd caught two rabbits, so there'd be enough meat left after Blazel finished his butchering job. Histrun placed the meat into the frying pan, added a healthy portion of tubers and some herbs, then covered it with water.

While dinner cooked, Histrun grabbed a piece of wood and started carving. Blazel sat watching him for a moment before digging into his own packs and pulling out a book. Histrun sighed. Although every Posair knew how to read, most fighters didn't take books with them into the wilderness.

"Boy, do you know how to play keshe?"

Blazel glanced up and nodded. "I play it with my mother and grandmother all the time."

"Good. I brought a board with me. It's a good game to learn strategy. How about jelehan?"

Blazel's eyebrows scrunched together. "I don't know what that is."

"It's a throwing game fighters play to help them build the hand-eye coordination necessary for fighting the Malvers' monsters."

"No, there's nothing like that in the Sanctuary." Blazel shrugged and returned his attention to his book.

Histrun glanced down at the piece of wood in his hands and changed his mind about what to carve. Instead of a wolf, the wood would become a jelehan stick.

After eating, they brought the horses into the rear of the cave for the night.

"Ugh, that's awful." Blazel waved his hand in front of his face when Bosetel dropped a pile of manure on the ground.

"We can either endure the stench," Histrun said, tying Telen's lead rope to a picket line, "or walk the fifteen or so measures back to the Sanctuary. Although there aren't any Malvers' monsters or narhili beasts in the mountains, there are other predators that love horseflesh here, like highland wolves or cougars."

"I'll deal with the smell." Blazel plugged his nose with his fingers.

"You'll get used to it in a little while. The horses will also add their body heat to keep the cave warm. Later tonight, when the temperatures drop, you'll be glad they're in here with us."

Blazel looked at him like he was crazy before picking up his book. Histrun wasn't sure how he could read in the fire's dim light. After just a few milcrons, Blazel sighed and put the book back in his pack. He pulled the bedroll close around him.

"Good night, Histrun," Blazel mumbled. "Thanks for doing this for me. Nobody's done anything like this for me before."

Histrun smiled, pleased. He continued to whittle by the dying flames of the fire until it became too dark to see, then he climbed into his own bedroll. For the first time since Zehala had died, he didn't have trouble going to sleep.

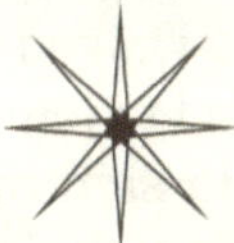

The next morning, Histrun and Blazel awoke to frost on the ground. While Blazel mucked out the horses' droppings using a sturdy forked branch, Histrun built up their fire and boiled porridge to break their fast. He added the leftover rabbit bits and tubers to the pot.

Blazel looked askance at the additions. "Shouldn't you add berries or other fruit to our porridge, not meat?"

"No. You'll need the additional nourishment for your training today." Histrun allowed a corner of his mouth to twitch up. "It takes a lot of energy to shift into your warrior form, especially the first few times."

Blazel's spoon clattered into his bowl, and his jaw dropped open. "Really? I get to shift into my warrior form?"

Histrun nodded.

"Oh, thank you, Warrior!" Blazel did a little dance in his seat.

"Eat up. You'll need your strength."

Blazel gulped down his porridge and taevo. Within milcrons, he'd emptied his bowl. "I'm ready! Let's go." He jumped to his feet.

Histrun sighed at the exuberance of youth. "You have chores to do first. Take care of your dishes, straighten up your bedroll and packs, and lead the horses to the stream to water them."

"Yes, sir!" Blazel hurriedly rolled up his bedroll, splashed water on his dishes, and ran outside.

Histrun finished his porridge, cleaned his dishes, and straightened his own bedding. He stood at the cave's mouth, sipping his taevo while watching Blazel finish his chores. He smiled, pleased. Even in Blazel's excitement, he didn't skimp on the horses' care.

"I've done everything you asked." Blazel skidded to a stop in front of Histrun, panting slightly. His eyes were alight, and he wore a huge grin.

"Take a deep breath and relax." Histrun took a deep breath himself, then another, encouraging Blazel to follow his lead. He put down his mug and walked to the center of the small clearing, gesturing for Blazel to join him.

"Accessing the magic to shift into your warrior form isn't much different from what you do for your wolf form," Histrun explained. "The difference is how you direct it. Use your will to visualize yourself as a warrior. You'll feel your arms and legs lengthen, your muscles bulk, and your face and jaw change shape. The first few times you do this, it will hurt. But with practice, it will only take a few moments, usually, the space of three breaths or less."

Histrun reached for the magic and let it wash over him. The change always left him feeling tingly, and he shook his fur to rid himself of it. He now stood over six-feet tall and weighed nearly a hundred pounds more. Long claws tipped his hands and feet, and as he flexed his front claws, he released a small amount of venom from the sacks under his pads. In this form, he could fight the Malvers' monsters, and his fur protected him from their acidic ichor. Blazel had taken a step back when Histrun changed. He cocked his head, examining the boy. *Oh, he hasn't seen many men in their warrior form, except during the Alpha Competitions. Even then, he probably didn't get close to them.*

"Can look," he growled, his jaws mangling the words.

Blazel gulped and took a deep breath before stepping closer. He slowly walked around Histrun and stopped in front of him.

Histrun released the magic, returning to his natural form.

"Now it's your turn," he said. "Reach for the magic within you, and listen to my voice. I'll guide you in shifting each part of your body. The first times will take quite a while to finish the change. Keep going. If you feel like you're becoming stuck, take a deep breath, relax, and allow the magic to flow. I'll be monitoring you and will guide you through any tight spots." Histrun allowed his voice to harden, and he narrowed his eyes. "Until you can shift easily, always—and I mean always—shift while you're with me. If you don't, you can become stuck in between forms, and it's the Crone's own fires to get you out of that state."

Blazel looked sufficiently scared. Histrun doubted he'd try it on his own. Out here, by themselves, he should be safe. He wouldn't have other boys egging each other on to shift without supervision. Over the years, Histrun had helped more than a few boys get unstuck. It was never fun or easy, for the boy, or for him.

"Are you ready?"

Blazel nodded, taking a deep breath.

"Good. Now listen to my voice." Histrun accessed his own magic but didn't shift. In this state, he could "see" Blazel's magic and monitor his progress. He guided Blazel through the change, going slowly, letting each body part shift and acclimate to the new form before moving on to the next. Blazel listened well and didn't rush, unlike other boys Histrun had taught. The process went smoothly. An octar later, a young warrior stood in front of him, panting heavily, with joy lighting his face and eyes.

"Did it!" Blazel managed to get through his jaws, and pumped a fist into the air. He yipped as the claw tips punctured the pad of his paw. He'd soon learn what he could and couldn't do in his new form.

"Okay, the process to return to your natural form is much easier," Histrun told him. "Your body wants to be in it. Think about your natural form and being a boy. Release the magic, and let it flow back into your inner well."

A handful of heartbeats later, Blazel stood in front of him, beaming. "Let's do it again!"

"Not so soon. A lot of magic flowed through your body. It will take time for it to recover. Walk around the clearing, go get a drink of water, and eat half of a travel bar."

Over the next few days, Histrun worked with Blazel to shift to his warrior form. Blazel picked it up quickly, changing faster and easier each time he tried. They practiced moving and fighting in this form. In-between sessions, they shifted to their wolf form, and Histrun taught Blazel how to use his wolf senses to hunt.

In the evenings, they played keshe, and Histrun continued carving the jelehan sticks. He didn't have anything with him to smooth the wood. By the time they returned to the Sanctuary, he would have enough various sized sticks to start teaching Blazel to play.

Blazel progressed rapidly over the next chedan. As they walked back to the cave from a hunting expedition, he smiled as the boy happily recounted how he'd caught the two pheasants he carried. Histrun had only managed to catch a single rabbit, and only then, through sheer luck. He'd been too busy watching Blazel stalk the pheasants to hunt himself.

The breeze shifted, and Histrun caught a musky scent. Holding up a hand to silence Blazel, Histrun lifted his head and sniffed. Highland wolves! The whinny of a terrified horse reached them.

"Hurry, Blazel. We have trouble! Stay close behind me. When we reach the clearing, if you can, catch the horses and take them into the cave. But only if you can do so safely." Histrun took off at a run, trusting Blazel would keep up.

Another horse screamed, this time in anger, ripped through the still afternoon, followed by a deep howl. When Histrun reached the clearing, Telen was bucking and whirling, keeping three wolves at bay. A sharp kick caught a wolf in the chest. It flew across the clearing. It regained its feet and curled its lips into a snarl. Two wolves circled Bosetel. He wasn't a trained war horse, and wasn't having as much success in keeping the wolves off him. Several long gashes marred his haunches.

The wolves were much larger than their cousins found below the White Mountains and were an even match for a man in his wolf form. If there were only one or two wolves, Histrun could take them in that form. But with five wolves, Histrun's only chance was to fight them in his warrior form. He tossed the rabbit to the ground and reached for his magic. With a howl of his own, he entered the fray, first attacking the wolves menacing Bosetel.

He caught one wolf mid leap by the throat, his claws digging into the thick fur, trying to reach the jugular vein. Warm blood trickled onto his paw. With a roar, he gripped both hands on either side of the wolf's head, holding the snapping jaws away from him, and twisted, breaking the wolf's neck. He dropped the body.

Histrun whirled toward the second wolf. His claws ripped a long gash into its flank. It yipped and turned away from the horse, snarling at this new foe. It leaped for Histrun's throat. He spun out of the way and, using the greater reach of his arms, swiped it again as it flew past him. Bright red blood gushed onto the ground. Histrun jumped on the wolf, clamping his bigger, stronger jaws around its throat and biting down until the body sagged in his jaws. He spit it out.

Bosetel wasn't in sight, and Histrun hoped it meant Blazel had captured him and taken him into the cave. He didn't want to go chasing a frightened horse after finishing with this mess. He ran toward Telen, who kicked another wolf in the chest. Histrun let the wolf sail past him, then pounced when it landed, stunned. He broke its neck with a quick jerk. Only two more wolves.

A blur of red-brown fur raced toward them. It stopped in front of Telen just as a wolf leaped toward the horse's neck. Blazel, in his warrior form, howled as he swung, his fist connecting with the wolf's jaw, knocking him down. The wolf shook its head and snarled. The second wolf paced behind Blazel, its hackles raised, its lips pulled back.

A moment of déjà vu assailed Histrun. He saw Zehala again in the janack's grip. Shaking his head, he snapped himself out of his momentary lapse. He couldn't allow someone else he cared about to get hurt—or killed—because he was too old, too slow. Roaring, he raced the last few feet and leaped, landing on the back of the wolf ready to tear into Blazel from behind. His greater weight crushed it beneath him. He drove his claws into its throat and ripped it out. He jumped to his feet, searching for the last wolf, terrified he'd see Blazel's still form. Instead, Blazel stood over the wolf, blood dripping from his claws and teeth.

Histrun ran toward him. He stopped when Blazel turned and snarled at him. As soon as Blazel realized it was Histrun, he dropped his head and whined. Histrun surveyed the battlefield. Satisfied all the wolves were dead, he shifted back into his natural form, wincing at the gash along his forearm. He didn't remember when he'd received it.

He reached out and grabbed Telen's lead rope, frayed where he'd pulled it from the picket line in his frenzy. The stallion pawed at the ground, then shook his hide. His eyes shone white, and he trembled.

"Easy, boy. It's all right. The fight is over." Histrun said in a calm, soothing voice. He ran a hand over the horse's neck and shoulder. Once the horse settled, Histrun turned his attention to the frightened boy.

"Blazel," Histrun said, in the same tone he'd used on Telen, "it's over. You can shift back now."

"Can't," Blazel whimpered. "Trying."

Histrun slowly approached him. "Take a deep breath. Relax. I know it's hard with all the adrenaline rushing through you, but you can't shift until you relax. Let go of your fear."

"Not afraid."

"Let go of your anger. It isn't helping you now."

Blazel's shoulders and chest rose and fell as he took several deep breaths. A shudder went through him as he released the magic. Blazel gazed at his bloody hands, then at the dead wolf laying at his feet.

"He was going to hurt Telen. I couldn't let him."

Histrun pulled Blazel into his chest, patting his back. "It's okay. You did well, boy. It's our job as warriors to protect those who can't protect themselves, which includes our horses." He held Blazel as he shuddered, a sob escaping him.

Histrun continued to hold him, muttering soothing words. This was Blazel's first exposure to the violence of a fight to the death. He'd lived a sheltered life in the Sanctuary and hadn't experienced this daily, the way most Posairs had.

After a few milcrons, Blazel pushed away from Histrun's chest. "I'm okay now." He wiped at his face, then reached for Telen's rope. "Come on, Telen, let's get you taken care of."

"Where's Bosetel?" Histrun fell into step next to Blazel as he led the horse to the cave.

"In the cave. He's bleeding."

"I'll look at him to see how bad he is. Are you hurt?"

Blazel shook his head and winced, rubbing his shoulder. "Not bad."

Histrun washed the blood from Bosetel's injuries. "They aren't too deep." He breathed out a relieved breath. "He'll need a few days to heal before you can ride him again." An examination of Telen revealed he'd received only a few minor cuts and scrapes, mostly on his legs from the wolves nipping at them.

Histrun wished they had a Red with them to burn the wolf carcasses so they wouldn't have to worry about scavengers. Instead, they dragged the carcasses well away from the clearing.

That night, the predicted storm hit. The rain lashed in angry streaks, lightning lit the sky, and thunder echoed off the cave walls.

"Good," Histrun said, watching the rain from the cave's mouth. "It'll wash the blood away. We shouldn't have to worry about scavengers now."

Histrun and Blazel huddled in the cave around the fire, playing keshe while they waited for the storm to pass. Histrun continued to sit by the fire long after Blazel crawled into his bedroll. In the flames of the fire, he relived the wolf leaping at the boy and his terror of how close he'd come to losing Blazel. This time, he hadn't been too slow, and had snatched a loved one from the jaws of death. Maybe he wasn't as worn-out and useless as he'd been thinking ever since Zehala's death. He looked over at the sleeping boy. Maybe he did have something left to offer the world.

Chapter 17

It rained steadily for two days. The third morning after the wolf attack, Histrun and Blazel awoke to the ground covered in a light dusting of snow. Histrun examined Bosetel's injuries.

"He's fit enough for you to ride, Blazel. However, it would be good practice for you to run part of the way in your wolf form."

Blazel grinned. "I'm much better at it now. I'll be able to keep up this time."

They packed their belongings, cleaned the cave, and restocked the firewood for the next traveler.

As they rode away, Blazel sat in his saddle much more secure than he had earlier. His whole demeanor had changed during the time they'd been away from the Sanctuary. The boy had become a confident young man. Histrun would proudly take him back to Strunland Keep with him and introduce him to the fighting-packs there.

The snow melted by midmorning, but the air held onto the chill of the coming winter. Dark clouds billowed behind the mountain peaks, and Histrun pushed them into a faster pace. He didn't want to be caught away from shelter when the next storm barreled down the mountains. An octar after stopping for their midday meal break, they crested a hill overlooking the Sanctuary's valley. Multas and sheep no longer dotted the hillside, and the grass had turned brown while they'd been gone. Only a few trees still had colorful leaves clinging to their branches.

A cold wind blasted them from the north. Histrun shivered in his cloak and blew on his hands, wishing he'd brought fur-lined gloves and boots to keep his hands and feet warm. He urged Telen into a canter down the hillside and across the empty meadow. The horse's hooves clattered onto the sheadash stone road, an unwelcome change to their softly muted footsteps in the forest. The guards at the gate waved them through, then hurried back into their shack.

Histrun led them directly into the stables, grateful to get out of the cold wind.

"What in the Crone's fires happened?" the horse-master asked when she saw the healing gashes on the horses.

Histrun pulled his bags from Telen's back. "Highland wolves attacked us. They almost had Bosetel for lunch, but we stopped them." He thumped Blazel on the shoulder. "He did well, killing one by himself."

"Very good, Blazel," the horse-master beamed at Blazel, who threw his shoulders back and stood taller at her regard. Worry creased her forehead when she turned back to Histrun. "How far away were you? Do we need to send a hunting party out to kill the pack?"

Histrun shook his head. "We killed the five attacking us. It happened just before the storm hit. I think they were traveling through ahead of the storm, and the horses appeared to be an easy meal."

"I'll let the others know to be watchful when they go out. It's early for wolves to be lurking around here."

"If there's more trouble, I'll be happy to join in a hunt."

"Thank you. It will be good to have an experienced warrior, such as yourself, with us. I'll put these boys in a warm stall and check their wounds to make sure they're healing well." She nodded to Histrun and Blazel, then gathered the horse's reins and led them farther into the stable.

"That's our cue to head to our rooms." Histrun clapped Blazel on the shoulder. They hurried across the courtyard. When Blazel opened the door to the cloister, Histrun stopped him. "Go warm up and get some rest. We'll start training again in the morning."

Blazel didn't quite hold back a moan. "More training?" he grumbled under his breath.

"Yes, more. You have a long way to go to reach the level most boys your age are at." Histrun adjusted his pack and remembered his promise. "Bring Chariel with you. She can learn the fighting-forms."

Blazel brightened and gave Histrun a salute before scurrying through the door, letting it bang behind him.

Histrun shouldered open the door leading to the staff village, the wind making it difficult to open. He jogged to his cottage and slipped inside. Someone had already lit the fire for him. The horse-master must have sent word of his arrival ahead to Naedera. He held out his hands, sighing at the warmth, and noticed a pot of stew hanging over the fire. The door rattled as the wind shook it, and he silently thanked Naedera for her thoughtfulness. He wouldn't have to go out in the storm to get dinner. He lifted the pot's lid and breathed in the scent of roasted mutton and tuber soup.

The next morning dawned bright with the light reflecting off several inches of snow. Histrun stood in his doorway, rubbing his arms. *We can't continue to train in Blazel's spot by the river. It's too cold. But where else can we go that is private?* He scratched his beard and palmed his forehead. The guest quarters held the perfect place. When Blazel and Chariel knocked on his door, he led them to the practice arenas used during the Alpha Competitions.

Chariel unexpectedly picked up the forms quickly. Her priestess duties and training prevented her from joining them every day. She practiced with Blazel often enough for him to make faster progress.

The quick reflexes of the youngsters kept Histrun on his toes when they played jelehan. Chariel gave him a mischievous wink before tossing two of the sticks to him in quick succession, while throwing one to Blazel. Histrun caught the first two, and tossed them awkwardly toward Blazel. His attention on his throws, Histrun jerked back in surprise at a third stick from Chariel speeding toward his face. He fumbled the catch, dropping the stick. Laughing, he picked it up and bowed, leaving their small circle.

"Nice work, Chariel. Blazel, you're getting faster. You'll have so much more fun when you play with a full circle of ten or twelve." It had been a good choice to add Chariel into the jelehan circle. She made the game more challenging—and fun.

The days grew shorter and colder as winter settled in. Histrun continued his sessions with Blenora, although now they mostly talked while playing keshe. Sometimes, when the weather prevented them from going to the practice arena, Blazel and Chariel would join them. Over the chedans, the pain in Histrun's heart eased, and if he wasn't happy, he was at least content. He couldn't pinpoint the exact moment when the change happened. Perhaps it had been when he saved Blazel from the highland wolf.

One day while the wind howled outside, Histrun sat with Blenora, playing keshe. He frowned at the number of pieces she had on the board, and his lack of pieces.

"Where did you meet Zehala?" Blenora asked, capturing another of Histrun's pieces.

"Here, actually." Histrun sat back, contemplating the board. He didn't have many moves left before he'd have to concede she won this game. "It was at an Alpha Competition. My lover at the time, Sujeen, was competing for the position of Strunlair's Clan Alpha. She thought she had it, since I was the clan alpha, and my term wasn't up for challenge.

"This beautiful woman with thick, wavy, dark-auburn hair with gold highlights strode into the arena. She held her head high and oozed confidence. She caught everyone's attention because she was so young."

"Zehala?" Blenora took his last piece. "Wasn't she the youngest to become a Clan Alpha?"

Histrun nodded, gathering the pieces to put to put the game away. "She was only forty-five. Sujeen claimed she couldn't challenge for the position because she wasn't sixty or older. But Zehala had done her research, and she said the age brackets for the various alpha positions were simply guidelines and tradition.

"Sujeen took the issue to the Supreme and lost. Zehala was correct. Anyone can take the challenges for the Clan Alpha position. They are designed to find the best person as alpha, not the oldest. Zehala won—far, far ahead of Sujeen." Histrun smiled at the memory, watching Zehala in his mind's eye outsmart and outmaneuver all her competition with style and grace.

"She became my co-alpha. Her audacity intrigued me, and it didn't take long for a relationship to kindle between us. Her sharp intelligence initially attracted me, but after getting to know her, I fell in love with her because of her passion and caring. She hadn't become the Clan Alpha for the power it offered, like Sujeen, but because she wanted to help and serve her people. Being the Clan Alpha provided her the best way to do so. We became bond-mates within a year of meeting."

"You realize this is the first time you've talked about her," Blenora said, twirling a keshe piece.

"Huh." Histrun gazed at the ceiling and examined how he felt.

"You're making good progress in your healing."

"I like being able to remember and talk about the good times Zehala and I had together. It's much better than only remembering how she died."

After that, Histrun would tell stories about his and Zehala's life, how they developed the Zehis method, and their time as Clan Alphas to anyone who would listen.

Watching Blazel and Chariel train, he finally knew how he could still contribute to the keep. He liked teaching the boy and molding him into a fine young warrior. By the time the spring thaw hit and the flowers pushed through the snow, he was antsy and ready to go back home.

Four chedans into Ahdar, the first lunadar of spring, word finally reached the Sanctuary that the mountain pass to Strunhelos was clear of snow. Histrun immediately made an appointment to meet with the Supreme. Blenora walked with him to the audience chamber. The windows were open, and a warm breeze fluttered the white drapes. The Supreme's crystal throne glittered and sparkled in the sunlight. It fit his mood.

"Blenora tells me your heart has healed," the Supreme said after motioning him to stand. "I can tell by your aura it's true. Have you enjoyed your stay with us?"

"Yes, your grace. Very much so. I especially liked training young Blazel."

"I hear you have also included Chariel in your training."

"Yes, your grace."

The Supreme leaned her chin on her fist. "At first, I didn't think it was a good idea to train one of my White Priestesses to fight. Blazel reminded me Shandir had been a White Priestess."

"He did the same for me." Histrun smiled at the memory.

"It does not bode well that our strongest oracle in generations has learned to fight. The Goddess is sending me disturbing visions. In the not too distant future, we will battle a great evil. Our survival hangs by a thread. It is for this reason I have allowed Chariel to work with you and Blazel."

Histrun's stomach clenched at her words. His people had been fighting for survival since the Great War. He and Zehala had hoped their method would help their people finally do more than just survive. But if the Supreme's visions were true—and he had no doubt they were—they would need all the good fighters they could get. Like Blazel.

"Speaking of Blazel." He paused as her drumming fingers stilled. Licking his lips, he forged ahead. "Blazel is a gifted fighter. He's wasted staying here. I want to take him back with me."

The Supreme's eyes narrowed, and her mouth tightened. The rings on her fingers dinged as she resumed tapping a staccato on the arm of her throne. "I was afraid you'd ask. The answer is no. He must remain here."

"But why?" Histrun risked breaking protocol to question the Supreme's ruling. The boy deserved more than to be locked away with only women for company. "Do you want him to be labeled a rogue? That's what will happen if he doesn't join a pack soon. Our society tolerates a child without a pack, but not a man. And Blazel is no longer a child."

"He is to me. Let him stay a gentle child a while longer. If he goes out into the world with you, he'll lose his special sweetness."

"Will you keep him tied to you all of his life? When will you allow him to become what he is—a Posair warrior?"

"Only for a while longer. Once he turns eighteen, he can no longer stay here."

Histrun frowned. What difference would six years make? He gazed into the Supreme's white eyes, ringed with black. She was the Goddess's representative. Who was he to question the ways of the Goddess?

"I'll be back on his eighteenth birthday," Histrun promised.

The Supreme inclined her head. "You will be welcomed, and I will release Blazel into your care."

"Can I return to continue his training?"

"You may, but no more than twice a year."

"Thank you, your grace."

The Supreme turned to gaze out the window, resting her chin on her fist.

"Is the audience over?" Histrun whispered to Blenora. She shook her head. He clasped his hands behind his back and prepared to wait until the Supreme dismissed him. She finally sighed deeply and turned her attention back to him.

"I'm unsure of the wisdom of telling you this," the Supreme said, rubbing her temples. "Take care of your daughter, Rizelya. Make sure you teach her to be a leader. She will have a pivotal role to play in the coming fight. As will Blazel. You may think it unfair of me to keep him here. But it is necessary for how his and Rizelya's destiny will unfold. Even for Chariel. Speak nothing of this to the children. Nor you, Blenora. They must come to their destinies on their own."

Histrun placed a hand over his heart, pressing hard to keep it from leaping from his chest. What would the Goddess want of Rizelya—a Red?

"Travel safe, Histrun. May the Goddess's blessing be on you." The Supreme blessed him. Her magic tingled as it sank into him.

Blenora's face was pale as they left the audience chamber. A frightened look haunted her eyes. Outside the temple, he took her hand in his.

"It will be all right," he assured her—and himself. "The Goddess won't ask more of them than they can handle. Our children will be fine."

"I've always wondered why she allowed Blazel to stay after he turned five, and why she's taken an interest in him." Blenora stared at the temple. Her fingers twisted together. "Did you know she personally works with his Talent? He can do things no other male can do. I fear for my son. What destiny awaits him that he must be alone?"

"He won't be alone." Histrun pulled her into a hug. "He has you and me. I'll come whenever I can. Rest easy that when the time comes, I will be here to take him to Strunland Keep."

She wiped her eyes. "Thank you. You've been very good with him. He adores you."

"And I him."

Later that day, Histrun laid out his things to pack, surprised at how much he'd accumulated in the four and a half lunadars he'd been in the Sanctuary. He set aside the gryphon carving. He'd worked for chedans to carve it and to rub oil into it to make it gleam.

Blazel knocked on the door and poked his head inside. "Are you coming, Histrun?"

"Come in, boy, come in."

Blazel frowned at the mess. "What are you doing? Are we going on another hunting trip?"

"Packing." Histrun sat on his favorite rocking chair and pointed to the other one. "Sit down."

Blazel lacked his usual grace as he made his way through the cottage. He sat stiffly on the chair.

"My time here is done, and it's time for me to go back home. I'm leaving in the morning."

"But you can't go!" Blazel surged to his feet. "Who will I train with? There's so much more I need to learn to be a Posair male. If you leave, there won't be anyone to teach me. I know." He snapped his fingers. "I'll come with you. I'm sure Mother will let me. She speaks highly of you."

"Blazel, son. You can't go."

Blazel's shoulders drooped. "Don't you want me?"

"Oh, I want you. The Supreme won't allow you to leave. You have to stay here and continue your training with her. But I'll be back often to work with you."

"I'll go talk to her! She has to let me go." He spun around for the door.

Histrun stood quickly and stopped him. "No. Her word is final. I tried. I really did. You're turning into a fine young man, and it makes me proud to see how you've grown." Histrun reached for the carving. He held it out awkwardly. "Here, I made this for you."

Blazel took it and examined it closely. "This is a beautiful gryphon. It looks like it could take off in flight at any moment. Thank you." Blazel threw his arms around Histrun.

Histrun held the boy, blinking back the moisture in his eyes. He'd come to love him over the lunadars and would miss him. "I'll be back."

The next morning, when Histrun rode out through the Sanctuary gates, he felt he was leaving a part of himself behind. He turned in his saddle. Blazel stood forlornly at the gate, waving at him. Histrun waved farewell, then set his heels to Telen's side and cantered away, ignoring his blurry eyes.

He had arrived at the Sanctuary as a broken, grief-stricken man. He was leaving it a much better person. Histrun touched his bond-mate torque at his throat. A part of Zehala would always be with him and in his heart. She'd approve of the man he'd become during his time mentoring Blazel.

A warm breeze caressed his cheek. He smiled. Yes, she was always with him.

Epilogue

The Supreme stood at the window, watching the red-headed boy and the girl with dark charcoal hair run from the library to the cloister gate. Soon, it would be time to move Blazel from his mother's cottage in the cloister and into the staff village. He was getting too old to live with the girls. She also didn't want the friendship between Blazel and Chariel to deepen into something more. Now, as children, they were simply best friends. They'd naturally gravitated toward each other as outcasts within the Sanctuary community. The Supreme encouraged the friendship. They needed each other. But she couldn't allow them to fall in love. Another was destined for Blazel.

She'd almost said yes to Histrun when he'd asked to take Blazel back with him. It almost broke her heart to deny the boy the chance of becoming a normal child. But that didn't serve his destiny. He needed the strength and self-reliance he was learning from living in the Sanctuary as the only boy.

Turning away from the window, she returned to her desk and sat, leaning her head against the soft cushion of her chair. Her eyes drifted closed, and again she saw the fire streaking through the sky and the blood soaking the ground from the thousands of dead. Central to the fighting stood a tall warrior with a gray-streak in his hair. Next to him fought a young woman with dark auburn hair and dark brown eyes. She had strength and courage, as well as compassion. Together, Blazel and Rizelya would lead their people to victory. Behind them a Gryphon flared. She didn't know how the Posairs' ancient allies rejoined their forces, but she did know Blazel and Rizelya played a large part in making it happen.

Her vision usually stopped at this point, but this time, it kept going. On the battlefield walked two priestesses. From the hair color of one, she recognized Chariel. But the other's face was blurry, as always. The Goddess promised her a successor, but never showed her the girl's face. She hoped she'd recognize the child when she arrived so she could begin her special training.

The Supreme rubbed her face as the vision faded, then poured herself a cup of taevo. Sipping it, she examined this new aspect of her vision, particularly the White Priestess. The woman appeared to be about Rizelya's age. If so, the child may have already arrived at the Sanctuary. She'd have to examine the young ones more closely.

In times past, the child destined to become the new Supreme was born, while the old one was still young enough to train her successor. When the Supreme turned fifty, then seventy-five, then ninety without a white-eyed, white-haired girl-child being born, she'd begun to worry. Now, decades over her century mark, she was terrified of dying and not having her replacement trained. A gentle presence touched her mind and heart, and the fear eased. She'd have time. Her successor wasn't coming in the normal way. *Who is she?*

Danger was coming to her world, but they had time to prepare. In her vision, Rizelya was a grown woman. She was now a child of five or so. The Supreme vowed she'd do everything in her power to make her people strong enough to survive the coming war.

The first thing to do was ensure the swamp's malignant magic didn't poison anymore people, like Mendehan. She shuddered at the atrocities Histrun and Lorstriel had witnessed Mendehan commit. They reminded the Supreme of what their ancient enemies had done before and during the Great War. She couldn't allow the foul magic to revive.

The Supreme finished her taevo and put the empty cup aside. She moved from her desk to a comfortable chaise. The work she had to do would tax her strength, especially in her advanced years. She didn't want to fall off her chair while working.

She closed her eyes and reached out with her mind, sending it far to the eastern ocean and the island located there. The magical barrier around it still held. As she scrutinized the barrier, she noticed several holes, more than she'd ever sensed before. A particularly large one caught her attention. It allowed the influence of the evil behind the barrier to seep out and cause Mendehan's malaise. Using the methods taught to her by her predecessor so many, many years ago, she patched the holes in the barrier.

It would hold back the evil. But for how much longer?

What to Read Next

The Legends of Lairheim starts with *Ancient Enemies*, where you'll meet Rizelya all grown up. The next episode, *Ancient Allies,* starts with Blazel's journey. If you've read these stories, the next exciting episode in the completed Legends of Lairheim series is *The Scourge Incursion.*

You can purchase this, and all my books, directly from me at *Shop.ToraMoon.com* or at your favorite retailer.

Ancient Enemies, Book 1

A dark secret exposed...
A reluctant leader's courage...
A battle to save her people...

A centuries-old battle for survival rages in the mystical realm of Lairheim. The Goddess's magic flows through the veins of her people, giving them the Talents to fight the monsters plaguing their land.

When a new and insidious threat appears, Rizelya, a Red with fire Talent, finds herself thrust into a role she never sought: a leader. In a daring act of rebellion against tradition, Rizelya gathers a diverse team of women, each wielding a different magical Talent. Together, they uncover the startling revelation that their magic is as potent as a Red's fire to destroy the monsters.

With the fate of her people hanging in the balance, Rizelya embarks on a dangerous journey of discovery. Amidst the chaos and uncertainty, haunting visions beleaguer Rizelya of a mysterious woman whose hatred threatens the very fabric of her society. Who is this enigmatic figure, and what dark secrets lie buried in the past?

As Rizelya delves deeper into this mystery, she unearths the shocking truth behind the monsters and her world's forgotten history.

With its gripping narrative, richly drawn characters, and breathtaking world-building, "Ancient Enemies" will captivate fans of epic science-fantasy. Prepare to be transported to a realm with innovative magic, unique monsters, and powerful shapeshifters.

Ancient Enemies is the first book in the spellbinding epic science-fantasy series, Legends of Lairheim, where destiny awaits, and the true test of heroism begins.

Experience the magic of Lairheim today!

ANCIENT ALLIES, BOOK 2

A prophecy revealed...
A reluctant leader's quest...
An alliance to save the world...

Prophecy thrusts Rizelya, a Red with fire Talent, into a perilous journey north to the Deep Mountains to seek the mythical Gryphons. Struggling with newfound leadership, she strives to unite her diverse group into a cohesive force. Blazel, a lone wolf in every sense, returns to Posair society after years of isolation, facing the daunting task of reintegrating with his people and forging pack bonds.

Joined by an eclectic team—a centaur, a warrior, a White Priestess, and the Gray Oracle—Rizelya and Blazel venture into uncharted territories. Their mission: to rekindle the ancient alliance between the Posairs and the Gryphons, whose help is essential to combat an emerging threat. As the questers struggle to survive, deep bonds of friendship and unexpected love blossom.

Old wounds and mistrust surface, threatening to derail their quest. A new threat emerges from the sky, bringing a powerful enemy that could destroy them all. Can Rizelya and Blazel convince the mythical Gryphons to unite with the Posairs to save Lairheim from annihilation?

Ancient Allies is the second book in the epic science-fantasy series, Legends of Lairheim, where epic battles and mythical creatures intertwine with the enduring power of unity.

Discover the thrilling world of Lairheim today!

THE SCOURGE INCURSION, BOOK 3

An alien invasion...
A desperate battle begins...
A quest for survival unfolds...

Rizelya, now a seasoned leader, commands a battalion against the alien invaders, the Scourge, who seek the nucla mineral—and slaves. But when the Scourge captures her heart-sister Kaieli, Rizelya's resolve is tested while navigating the perils of leadership and love in a world under siege.

Blazel returns to the treacherous swamps, searching for herbs to concoct a potent poison to cripple the Scourge. In his new role as the Battle Commander's second, Blazel grapples with being a leader as he and his Gryphon friend lead the charge against the alien menace.

Meanwhile, Kaieli, a gentle healer, discovers a method to purge the nucla poison from the enslaved Posair men. Teaming up with Rolstrun, a fighter who learns the true meaning of courage and love, Kaieli sparks a rebellion within the camp. Amidst the horrors of slavery, a tender love blossoms between them.

The Posairs and their Gryphon allies refuse to yield to the Scourge's subjugation and terror, valiantly fighting for freedom against the technologically superior Scourge.

Can Rizelya and Blazel lead their people to victory? Will Kaieli and Rolstrun's newfound courage be enough to turn the tide?

Rizelya and Blazel fight to save their world on the brink of annihilation. Be prepared to be captivated by this thrilling tale of bravery, cooperation, and the battle for freedom.

The Scourge Incursion is the third book in the epic science-fantasy series, Legends of Lairheim, where amidst the darkness and despair of war, hope shines and the enduring power of love and friendship triumphs.

Explore the exciting world of Lairheim today!

Appendix

The Cast

(In order of appearance)

Histrun - (His-strun) Former Strunlair Clan Alpha; Strunland Keep, Rizelya's father. bond mate with Zehala

Zehala - (Zay-hal-ah) Red with Brown; Naila and Rizelya's mother; former Strunlair Clan Alpha; Strunland Keep, bond mate with Histrun

Naila - (Neigh-la) Red and Yellow; Strunland Keep; Rizelya's sister

Rizelya - (Rha-zeel-yha) Red with Brown; Strunland Keep

Wisah - (Wee-sah) White and Grey with some Blue; Strunland Keep; Naila's daughter, Rizelya's niece

Koriana - (Core-ee-ana) Red with Yellow; Strunland Keep Alpha

Kolstrun - (Kol-strun) Strunland Keep Alpha

Maheli - (Ma-he-lee) Red with Green; Strunland Keep

Andriel - (An-dree-el) Red with Brown; Strunland Keep

Lorstriel - (Lor-stree-el) Red with Green; Strunland Keep

Kehali - (Ke-hal-lee) Red with Yellow; Strunland Keep

Lestrun - (Le-strun) Strunland Keep

Eidelstrun - (Eye-del-strun) Strunland Keep

Dorstrun - (Door-strun) Strunland Keep

Alixstrun - (Alix-strun) Strunland Keep

Chestrun - (Che-strun) Strunland Keep

Belhaas - (Bell-haas) Haasper Keep Alpha

Maehaas - (May-haas) Haasneh Keep Alpha

Armelya - (Ar-mel-yah) Red with Brown; Haasneh Keep Alpha

Raelhaas - (Rail-haas) Haasneh Keep; Centaur

Vyolah - (Vi-oh-lah) Red with Green; Haasneh Keep

Jaehaas - (Jay-haas) Haasneh Keep

Daelena - (Day-lee-na) Blue with Yellow; Haasnelyn Keep; Captain of the Dawn Star barge

Gaehaas - (Gay-haas) Sailor on the Dawn Star

Dorhaas - (Door-haas) Sailor on the Dawn Star

Rodehan - (Roh-deh-han) Dehanrolos Keep Alpha

Freynara - (Fray-nar-ah) Red with Green; Dehanrolos Keep Alpha

Norvela - (Nor-vel-lah) Red and Yellow; Dehanrolos Keep

Tedehan - (Te-deh-han) Dehanrolos Keep

Betsia - (Bet-see-ah) Brown; Dehanlair Keep

Mendehan - (Men-deh-han) Dehanlair Clan Alpha

Salloreen - (Sal-lo-reen) Red with Brown; Dehanlair Clan Alpha

Lodehan - (Lo-deh-han) Dehanlair Keep

Wylara - (Wy-lar-ah) Head White Priestess of Dehanlair Keep

Deldehan - (Del-deh-han) Dehanlair Keep

Gordehan - (Gor-deh-han) Dehanlair Keep

Helvia - (Hel-vee-ah) Green with Brown; Dehanlair Keep

Meldehan - (Mel-deh-han) Dehanlair Keep

Nevdehan - (Nev-deh-han) Dehanlair Keep

Salordehan - (Sal-or-deh-han) Dehanlair Keep; Salloreen's son

Podehan - (Po-deh-han) Dehanlair Keep

Verdara - (Ver-dar-ah) Red with Yellow; Dehanlair Keep

Flothera - (Flo-ther-ah) Brown; healer; Dehanlair Keep

Argodehan - (Argo-deh-han) Dehanlair Keep

Marlora - (Mar-lor-ah) Red with Brown; Dehanreen Keep Alpha

Aistrun - (Aye-strun) Strunland Keep

Maehalya - (May-hal-yah) Brown with Red; metalsmith, Strunland Keep

Andreyan - (An-drey-an) Brown with Green; healer; Strunland Keep

Polvera - (Pol-ver-ah) White Priestess; Sanctuary

Jaekara - (Jay-kar-ah) White Priestess; Sanctuary

Felstrun - (Fell- strun) Strunlair Clan Alpha

Tylira - (Ty-leer-ah) Red with Yellow; Strunlair Clan Alpha

Raemy - (Ray-me) Brown; Sanctuary

Naedera - (Nay-deer-ah) Brown with Yellow/Green; Sanctuary

The Supreme - The head White Priestess; Spiritual leader; Sanctuary

Blenora - (Blen-nor-ah) White with Gray; Sanctuary; Blazel's mother

Blazel - (Blay-zel) Sanctuary

Chariel - (Char-ee-el) Gray; Sanctuary

THE HORSES

Telen - (Tel-en) Histrun's black stallion

Kylara - (Ky-lar-ah) Zehala's blue roan mare

Jaelen - (Jay-len) wild white stallion with black stripes

Bosetel - (Bose-tel) Blazel's chestnut gelding

THE WORLD

The main continent is called Lairheim. The Barrens is an area of desolation, with only petrified wood and sand-glass in it. It covers a hundred-mile radius from Shandir's Crater, which is in the center of the isthmus between the main continent and the sub-continent. After the Great War, travel south of the Barrens became taboo, and so no one knows what the area is like. The sub-continent is believed to be covered by one huge swamp and is located south of the Barrens.

No one sails the oceans anymore because of the sea monsters created during the Great War. There is limited travel along the coasts.

The Provinces

There are eight provinces, each divided into eight territories. Each clan takes the name of the Province.

Strunlair

Ledonlair

Andranlair

Posanlair

Haaslair

Dehanlair

Ronanlair

Keistanlair

Days and Time

Milcron - equivalent to a minute.

Octar - roughly equals an hour. There are 16 octars in a day.

Chedan - roughly a week, consisting of eight days.

Lunadar - a month consists of eight chedans, or 64 days.

A year is eight chedans, or 512 days.

Measure - term for distance, a little less than a mile (5,000 feet)

The Months

Ahdar - Month one; Spring

Neydar - Month two; Spring

Sandar - Month three; Summer

Drudar - Month four; Summer

Godar - Month five; Autumn

Rokdar - Month six; Autumn

Eyedar - Month seven; Winter

Hondar - Month eight; Winter

The Moons

Kelar - the largest moon takes 64 days for a full cycle, measurement of a month.

Zelar - the middle-sized moon takes 32 days for a full cycle.

Chelar - the smallest moon's cycle takes 8 days, measurement for chedan, or eight-days.

Magical Abilities of the Women

There are eight types of magic, called Talents, worked by the women. Men exchanged the ability to do magic (except very basic skills) for the gift of shapeshifting into their warrior form when the Malvers' monsters appeared after the Great War. Hair and eye color indicate of the type of magic the person uses. Hair color indicates the person's major Talent and the eye color their secondary Talent. The darker the hair or eye color, the more powerful in that Talent the person is. A woman with fire magic is called a Red, one with water is called a Blue, and so on. Hair color pales with age.

The Powers

Whites - have shades of white hair. Priestesses — mind and soul workers, spiritual leaders. (Unseen in men.)

Grays - have shades of gray hair. Priestesses — also mind and soul workers but they work more with the transitions of the soul. This is a rare Talent. (Unseen in men.)

Reds - have shades of red hair — the fire workers and warriors.

Yellows - have shades of blond hair — the air workers.

Blues - have shades of blue hair — the water workers.

Greens - have shades of green hair — earth workers, plants, and are healers.

Browns - shades of brown hair — earth workers, animals and minerals/metals, and are healers.

Blacks - shades of black hair (extinct) — can work all types of magic.

GLOSSARY

billocks - (bill-ox) a wild, large herd beast and resists domestication

brecha - (bray-cha) one of the symbiotic pair of monsters collectively called the Malvers' monsters

ducorn - (dew-corn) a type of antelope with two twisty horns

helbraught - (hell-brac-kt) the magical halberd type blades the women use to fight the monsters; the wooden staff is the height of the woman with a 16"-24" inch blade made from helstrim attached to the end

helstrablade - (hell-stra-blade) knives made from helstrim but not keyed to any type of magic

helstramiester - (hell-sta-my-ster) masters of the helstrim alloy

helstrim - (hell-strim) a special alloy that accepts and holds magic used to make helstrablades and helbraught blades

janack - (jan-ack) one of the symbiotic pair of monsters collectively called the Malvers' monsters

jelehan - (jay-lay-han) a throwing game using sticks of varying lengths with colored bands

kehani - (kay-han-ee) the flowers of the kehani tree are sacred to The Goddess and are used by the priestesses in the temples as perfume and incense

keshe - (kay-she) a strategy board game. It can be played with as few as two players or up to ten players; the more players added, the more complicated the game becomes

mookti - (mook-tee) an early ripening spring berry that is sweet, dark purple, and grows in small clusters

multa - (mul-ta) a pack animal with cloven, platter-like feet able to carry heavy loads

narhili - (nar-hee-lee) also called narhili beasts, predators that live in the swamps during the day and hunt the surrounding area at night

paether - (pae-ther) a canid-like predator found in the northern part of Lairheim

sheadash - (shea-dash) a type of white stone that repels and negates any malignant magic. The Malvers' monsters can't cross it and so it is used for buildings and roads

taevo - (tay-vo) a stimulating drink made from the leaves and berries of the taeve bush

STAY IN TOUCH!

Sign up for Tora's newsletter to keep in touch with what's happening in the world of Tora. Receive exclusive extras, news, and discounts on my books, products, and art. I have lots of ideas and always have a project—or three—in progress.

ToraMoon.com/subscribe

Also By Tora Moon

Legends of Lairheim (Epic Science-Fantasy)

Ancient Enemies (Book 1)
Ancient Allies (Book 2)
The Scourge Incursion (Book 3)
Exile's Vengeance (Book 4)
Redemption - A Novel

The Sentinel Witches (Urban Fantasy)

Crossroads to Destiny (Book 1)
Descent Into Darkness (Book 2)
Well of Sorrows (Book 3)

Indie Author Guides

Business & Accounting for Authors
Business Plans for Authors

To get an up-to-date listing of all my books or to purchase visit
ToraMoon.com

Thank You!

I hope you're enjoying discovering the world of Legends of Lairheim world and Rizelya and her team's story.

If you have a moment, please help others enjoy these books too by leaving a review on my shop or the retail site where you purchased this book, review it on a blog, share it on your social media, or even just tell your friends about it.

Reviews help other readers choose what to read and authors depend on reviews to get the word out on good books. Honest reviews and genuine word-of-mouth recommendations make all the difference.

I'm not asking for one of those awful book reports we did at school. Leaving a review will only take a minute: it doesn't have to be long or involved, just a sentence or two that tells people what you liked about the book. This will help other readers know why they might like it, too, and help me write more of what you love. But please, no spoilers!

The truth is, VERY few readers leave reviews. Please help me by being the exception.

About the Author

Tora Moon writes Goddess fantasy and science fiction, skillfully melding different sub-genres to create unique, memorable stories. Her completed series, The Legends of Lairheim, combines elements of epic, paranormal, and science fiction into a breathtaking tale of magic, courage, and the enduring power of unity.

Her series, The Sentinel Witches, blends her love of urban/magical realism, mythology, and portal fantasy—and skates close to the edge of thriller and horror. Throughout all her works, you will find Tora's love of Goddess mythology as she weaves aspects of these into her stories.

As Tora-Iresh'nai Moon, she writes about Goddess Spirituality and shares her nearly fifty years of experience of connecting with the Goddess and the Feminine Divine.

Tora is also an artist who explores drawing and watercolor painting. Her current passion is creating and coloring mandalas inspired by the Goddess. Tora also expresses her creativity through various handcrafts.

You can find out more about Tora, her books, and her art at: ToraMoon.com